# A Questionable Character

# A QUESTIONABLE CHARACTER

## Lorna Barrett

BERKLEY PRIME CRIME

New York

BERKLEY PRIME CRIME
Published by Berkley
An imprint of Penguin Random House LLC
penguinrandomhouse.com

Library of Congress Cataloging-in-Publication Data

Names: Barrett, Lorna, author.
Title: A questionable character / Lorna Barrett.
Description: New York: Berkley Prime Crime, [2023] | Series: A Booktown mystery
Identifiers: LCCN 2022060746 (print) | LCCN 2022060747 (ebook) |
ISBN 9780593549414 (hardcover) | ISBN 9780593549438 (ebook)
Subjects: LCSH: Miles, Tricia (Fictitious character)—Fiction. |
Murder—Investigation—Fiction. | Women booksellers—Fiction. |
LCGFT: Detective and mystery fiction. | Novels.
Classification: LCC PS3602.A83955 Q47 2023 (print) |
LCC PS3602.A83955 (ebook) | DDC 813/.6—dc23/eng/20230105
LC record available at https://lccn.loc.gov/2022060746
LC ebook record available at https://lccn.loc.gov/2022060747

Printed in the United States of America
1st Printing

Book design by Laura K. Corless

*In memory*
*of "the Sisti,"*
*Carolyn Thomas*

# ACKNOWLEDGMENTS

My thanks go to my agent, Jessica Faust, who went to bat for me when I was going through a tough time. She's the best! I'd also like to thank members of the Lorraine Train for their continued support (especially during a very short timeline). Thanks, Amy Connolley, Debbie Lyon, Pamela Fry Priest, and Rita Pierrottie. I'd also like to give a shout-out to my Facebook group (Lorraine's & Lorna's Perpetual Tea Party) members, who have become my social media family, cheering me and encouraging me (and each other) on a daily basis. You guys are the best!

# Cast of Characters

**Tricia Miles,** owner of Haven't Got a Clue vintage mystery bookstore

**Angelica Miles,** Tricia's older sister, owner of the Cookery, the Booked for Lunch café, and the Booked for Beauty day spa, and half owner of the Sheer Comfort Inn. Her alter ego is Nigela Ricita, the mysterious developer who has been pumping money and jobs into the village of Stoneham.

**Pixie Poe,** Tricia's assistant manager at Haven't Got a Clue

**Mr. Everett,** Tricia's employee at Haven't Got a Clue

**Antonio Barbero,** the public face of Nigela Ricita Associates, Angelica's son

**Ginny Wilson-Barbero,** Tricia's former assistant, wife of Antonio Barbero

**Grace Harris-Everett,** Mr. Everett's wife

**David Price,** a twenty-something grad student hired as a summer intern at the Stoneham Chamber of Commerce

**Ian McDonald,** chief of police, Stoneham Police Department

**Becca Dickson-Chandler,** former tennis star, ex-wife of Marshall Cambridge

# Cast of Characters

**Dan Reed,** owner of the Bookshelf Diner

**Jim Stark,** Angelica's contractor, owner of Stark Construction

**Toni Bennett,** Jim Stark's wife, owner of the Antiques Emporium

**Candace Mitchell,** server at Bar None bar and restaurant

**Elise McKenzie,** Stoneham resident who lives across the street from the Morrison Mansion

**Mike Foster,** carpenter, employed by Stark Construction

**Sanjay Arya,** Jim Stark's right-hand man, murder victim

**Marshall Cambridge,** murder victim, Tricia's ex-lover

# A Questionable Character

# ONE

**The sun** had been up for a little over an hour when Tricia Miles arrived on her sister's doorstep on that early Monday in June. It was to be a busy day, what with welcoming the Chamber of Commerce's summer intern, getting him settled, and attending to her vintage mystery bookstore, Haven't Got a Clue.

Tricia and her sister were co-presidents of the Stoneham, New Hampshire, Chamber—a job they'd held for nearly six months. It had been a rocky experience trying to revive the operation their predecessor had so diligently tried to destroy. Thanks to Angelica's previous tenure at the organization's helm, and Tricia's involvement as her woman Friday, they'd slowly been rebuilding the trust of their members. But welcoming the new intern was only one part of the day's plan.

Angelica Miles was a woman of many talents—and two personas. She was a successful businesswoman in her own right, owning the

Cookery book and kitchen gadget store; Booked for Lunch, a small retro café dedicated to the midday meal; the village's day spa, Booked for Beauty; and a half share of the village's most expensive bed-and-breakfast, the Sheer Comfort Inn. But it was her alter ego, the secretive Nigela Ricita, who commanded the utmost respect, and sometimes animosity, for transforming the somewhat sleepy village of used bookstores known as Booktown to a wildly successful tourist attraction. NR Associates owned the Brookview Inn, the local pub (the Dog-Eared Page), the Happy Domestic home/gift shop, a food truck, a real estate office, the other half interest in the Sheer Comfort Inn, and the most recent addition to the NR portfolio, the *Stoneham Weekly News*.

When Tricia thought about her sister's business acumen, she sometimes suffered from an inferiority complex—but not for long. Angelica actually spent little hands-on time with her companies since she'd built a team of top-notch and experienced individuals. She acted as the CEO of her empires, letting her son, Antonio Barbero, take on the day-to-day supervision. His wife, Ginny Wilson-Barbero, was the company's marketing director and mother to Angelica's grandbabies, little Sofia and baby Will.

On that morning, Tricia had agreed to accompany her sister to NR Associates' new world headquarters, a historic granite-clad building located off the village's main drag. The former mansion had been owned by Asa Morrison, another of the village's founders, who'd made his money producing whiskey, and his stately house had been built some 150 years before. During its life, it had been a home, a hospital, a school, and most recently office space. It was to be upgraded in the latter configuration with a new roof, HVAC, and plumbing before Angelica would personally choose the furniture and décor.

The workmen usually got started around seven, and Tricia and

Angelica had decided to set out to check on the progress of the renovations an hour before the construction crew arrived for the day.

Tricia texted her sister. *I'm here.*

*Be right down.*

Tricia would have been pleased to use the occasion to get in part of her morning three-mile constitutional but she knew her sister would insist on taking her car. The five-block walk was probably too far for her to ever walk, even though she'd given up her stilettos earlier that year.

Sure enough, when Angelica appeared she clutched her car keys in her right hand. She looked smart dressed in a peach cotton sleeveless blouse, black slacks, and sandals, sporting a black fanny pack that she'd never be caught wearing in a business setting, so she obviously didn't expect to be seen at that time of the day and especially at the construction site. Tricia's attire wasn't much different. She'd chosen a pink tee and jeans but would change into her usual sweater set and black slacks once the workday commenced. The weatherman had predicted an unseasonably warm day. It was already in the seventies. She'd be glad of the sweater once she cranked up the AC in her shop upon her return.

"Let's go," Angelica said brightly. "I need to make a list of things I want to be completed by the end of the week."

"Isn't that up to Jim Stark?" Tricia asked. Stark was the contractor Angelica had hired to complete the mansion's renovations. Tricia had worked with him, too, but these days the firm was booked solid months in advance. So much so that lately Stark's clients had been dealing with his right-hand man, Sanjay Arya, a personable man in his thirties with a ready smile and a reassuring presence.

"I hardly ever talk to Jim anymore," Angelica lamented as she started up the road toward the village's municipal parking lot, where the street's residents kept their vehicles. Angelica might not exercise as much as Tricia, but if she cared to, she could have excelled in competitive walking.

"When I do get to speak to the boss man, I always feel like him consulting his phone is more important than anything I have to say."

"He's a busy man."

Angelica glanced at her sister with disdain. "And I'm a busy woman."

She was indeed.

They arrived at the lot and headed for Angelica's car. Neither of them spoke until Angelica pulled the car onto Main Street and headed for the mansion.

"We should have done this yesterday," Tricia said, "especially if you don't want to run into the workmen."

"Are you kidding? Sunday is my busiest day of the week."

That was when Angelica hosted their weekly family dinner, although since baby Will had made his appearance two months before, they'd been gathering with the Barberos in their newly built home. Dragging the kiddies out took a lot of effort, but Angelica had adapted. She'd either have the meal catered or bring the ingredients for a delicious meal to the fabulous kitchen she'd designed for the family. In addition to Tricia and the Barberos, their "family" consisted of Tricia's friend and employee Mr. Everett and his wife, Grace. They'd been accepted as the children's honorary great-grandparents.

Angelica pulled up in front of the mansion, which at this point bore a rather ramshackle appearance. Landscaping was one of the last items on the list of things to be completed.

The sisters exited the car and stood before the building. Tricia studied Angelica's face. She could tell her sister was looking at the mansion with an eye to its future appearance.

"I love this place," Angelica muttered. "If only it was feasible to return it to its original use." She shook her head, looking wistful.

"You've got big bucks," Tricia commented.

"I do, but what would I do, one person living in so large a home? Besides, the older I get, the less I want or need."

Tricia was beginning to think that way herself. She looked at her watch: 6:10. If they wanted to be out before the workers showed up, they'd better start their inspection. She said so.

Angelica approached the lockbox hanging from the dull brass handle on the big oak door, punched in the code, and removed the key to the former palace, unlocking the door and letting them in. Antonio must have given her the combination to the electronic lock. Tricia hadn't visited the building since Angelica's initial walk-through almost a year before. Everything took so long. Permits, zoning, architectural plans. She'd been told that the future NR offices had actually been put on an accelerated schedule. Even so, the timeline for finishing the job was almost a month away.

Dust caked every surface. Where it had come from was anyone's guess. Random lumber and metal framing materials were piled in what had once been the home's grand foyer. It would be a shame if the beautiful marble floors were covered instead of being restored.

"I thought we should start on the second floor and work our way down," Angelica said, and headed for the grand staircase.

"They're not going to replace these magnificent stairs, are they?" Tricia asked, appalled at the idea.

"No. I was adamant about that," Angelica said as they made their way to the second floor. "But they'll be placing laminate on these floors," she said, indicating the scuffed wide-pine flooring beneath their feet.

"Why? It looks like it's in good shape."

"And I want to keep it that way."

Tricia studied her sister's expression. "What are you planning to do with this place in the future?" she asked with suspicion.

"Nothing. Nothing at all," Angelica said innocently.

Tricia didn't believe her. Perhaps Angelica *did* hope to restore the old building to its former glory after all—just not at this time.

They wandered through the upper rooms, admiring the cove moldings, the ceiling medallions, and other features before taking the back—or servants'—stairs to return to the main floor.

"What's your favorite part of the renovation?" Tricia asked.

"It'll be the communal kitchen. I had the most fun choosing the appliances and furniture."

"Is it located in the original kitchen?"

"Yes, but unfortunately, it'll be reworked on a smaller scale. Still, we're keeping some of the original features. Want to see the work in progress?"

"Why not?"

Angelica might not have visited the site much in person, but she seemed to have memorized the layout, for she led Tricia through corridors until they came to a door that was ajar. Angelica pushed through it.

The room was large and two of the walls had been stripped back to the brick. Like the foyer, boxes of building supplies littered its floor. Vintage subway tile covered two of the walls near where an old porcelain sink marred by rust stains sat and where an old range must have stood.

Tricia nodded toward a large dark door to the left. "Butler's pantry?" she guessed.

"Yes, and it's magnificent. We were going to use it as a supply cabinet, but that was before we decided to lease some of the space to other businesses." She sighed, once again wistful. "I can just imagine all the crystal, silver serving dishes, and cutlery that were once stored in it." She strode across the room, threw open the heavy door, and gasped. "Good grief!"

"What's wrong?" Tricia asked, coming up behind her sister. She came to an abrupt halt as her gaze raked across the cracked tile floor. Huddled in the corner was the body of a man with a head of dark hair matted with blood that had pooled around it.

Tricia groaned. "Why does this always happen to us?"

**When Stoneham's** top cop, Chief of Police Ian McDonald, arrived at the crime scene, Tricia expected him to be angry; at least that had been her experience in the past with other law enforcement officers—including McDonald. But his demeanor on that morning was almost solicitous.

She hadn't seen the man since the week before, when he'd crashed the Barberos' housewarming party with some cockamamie story about petty crime on Main Street and wanting opinions of the Chamber's co-presidents. He'd looked so serious. Always gracious, Ginny had welcomed him to the party. Within minutes he had a craft beer in his hand and schmoozed with the other guests, leaving Tricia feeling thoroughly puzzled.

"I'm so sorry you're going through this," he said.

She would bet he'd deliberately omitted the word *again*.

"Do you know the victim's identity?" he asked.

Tricia glanced in Angelica's direction.

"Sanjay Arya. He's the project manager for the mansion's renovations."

McDonald frowned. "Pardon my confusion," he said, his Irish accent surfacing. "But just what are you ladies doing here? I thought this property was owned by NR Associates."

"It is," Angelica agreed. "I'm their partner in the Sheer Comfort Inn."

"That doesn't answer my question."

"Uh, I've consulted with them on several projects. For example," Angelica went on, "I recently decorated the NR Realty offices for them."

"And you're here under whose authority?" McDonald pressed.

"Antonio Barbero."

"Ah, yes," McDonald said. "And he can corroborate that?"

"In a heartbeat," Tricia volunteered, her tone lighter than the situation warranted.

McDonald nodded and looked toward the body and then back to the sisters, studying their features. He'd obviously noted Tricia's tone. "Excuse me, ladies, but it seems to me that you aren't all that traumatized by discovering a dead man."

Angelica rolled her eyes and scowled. "It happens so often around here that, sadly, we're kind of inured to it."

McDonald's gaze narrowed. "How well did you know the deceased?"

"Not at all," Tricia answered.

"I'd spoken with him a couple of times," Angelica said. "Antonio Barbero is the point man on the renovation. He's the one who gave me the combination to the lockbox. I'd be glad to give you his contact information."

McDonald removed a small notebook from his back pocket and took down the numbers. He looked at Angelica once again. "What do you know about Mr. Arya?"

Angelica's gaze wandered to the prone form still on the floor. The blood around his head had begun to oxidize. "He seemed a very personable man. Always sported a smile. Antonio dealt with him on a regular basis."

"And your relationship with Mr. Barbero is?" McDonald asked.

Angelica's eyes widened and she glanced askance at Tricia.

"Ms. Miles?" McDonald prompted.

"Friends," Angelica blurted. "Good friends."

Was he hoping to catch Angelica in a lie? Few people knew that Angelica and Nigela were the same person—and fewer still knew the true connection between Angelica and Antonio was closer than mere friendship.

A commotion sounded out in the hall beyond.

"Sir! I told you you can't just barge in there. This is a crime scene!" But the man in question barreled into the room anyway, pushing Tricia aside.

"Oh my God," he cried upon catching sight of the body. "Sanjay!"

It was at this point that McDonald's patience finally seemed to fray. "And *you* are?"

"Jim Stark. I own the construction company that's renovating this building." Stark's face was drawn, the color having drained from it. "I heard a body had been found on the site. I had no idea it was Sanjay." He raked a hand through his thick salt-and-pepper hair, his face white with agitation.

McDonald had his notebook at the ready once more. "How long had Mr. Arya worked for you?"

Stark looked dazed and it took long seconds for him to answer. "Uh . . . maybe five years."

"And what was your working relationship like?"

Stark blinked as though startled. "He was like a son to me. We'd grown close—especially these past couple of years." Suddenly, Stark seemed to notice the Miles sisters were also in attendance. "What are you doing here?" he asked. His voice had grown suddenly cold. "How did you get in here?"

"Antonio Barbero gave us the combination to the lockbox," Angelica said succinctly.

"You have no business being on *this* construction site without *my* permission."

"I beg to differ," Angelica said, nearly matching his tone.

"Now, now," McDonald said, his tone placating. "We'll get this straightened out."

"I really don't think these women should be here," Stark nearly shouted.

"Angelica found the body. Would you have preferred one of your men found him?" Tricia asked.

Stark looked like he wanted to say something but then seemed to think better of it. Perhaps he remembered that both sisters had hired him in the past—and might do so again.

"I'm sorry. I'm upset." He looked down at the body again, then turned and looked away. "This is going to screw up my life something fierce."

"In what way?" McDonald asked.

"We're drowning in work. Sanjay was in charge of the logistics for every job the company has going. I depended on him." He shook his head, looking anguished. "Why would anyone want to kill him?"

That was a good question.

How long would it take until there was an answer?

# TWO

 **Hours had** passed since the sisters had found Sanjay Arya's body and McDonald was finished speaking with them. By then, Angelica had a Zoom meeting to attend with her NR Associates team. It was Tricia's job to drive to Nashua to pick up the Chamber's summer intern. Although most of the interview process had been conducted via e-mail, Tricia had had a dental appointment and missed the final online interview where Angelica offered David Price the job and he accepted. Not knowing what the young man looked like, Tricia made a sign to hold up, like the signs she'd seen scores of times held by limo drivers at airports. She, however, was heading to the bus station.

After parking her car, Tricia grabbed her purse and the sign. The bus was late—as she should have anticipated—but only by fifteen minutes, which had given her an opportunity to buy a cup of vending machine coffee that she'd taken one sip of and quickly dispatched to the nearest trash can.

The bus finally arrived and the crush of passengers disembarked. Tricia stepped back and studied the faces, a mix of middle-aged and elderly men and women. The only young person was a teenage girl who whooped with delight and fell into the arms of an older woman with cries of "Grandma, Grandma!" Had Tricia's charge missed the bus?

She lowered the sign and was about to trudge back to her car when the bus belched another gust of air and a pair of booted feet tromped down the steps to the asphalt. They weren't just any boots but were perfectly polished and reached to the knees. Above them were black pants and a purple pullover sweater with the sleeves pushed up to the man's biceps. Pinned to his left shoulder was a large brooch of colored glass in the shape of a bumblebee. His hair was a mass of tight, shoulder-length curls that he'd captured in a ponytail, and he sported a toothy grin surrounded by a few days' worth of whiskers. "Ms. Miles?" he asked hopefully.

"Tricia," she insisted, catching sight of the manbag slung over his left shoulder and the laptop case he held in his right hand. He tucked the latter under his arm and offered his hand. "David Price. Glad to meet you."

His damp grip could hardly be called firm and when Tricia released his hand she fought the urge to wipe her own on the back of her slacks.

"Thanks for this opportunity. I'm looking forward to the greatest summer of my life," David gushed.

Tricia refrained from judging just how disappointing his existence must have been prior to his arrival in New Hampshire.

The driver pulled the last of the luggage from the bus's belly. Four large cases sat on the tarmac. The rest had been retrieved by the other passengers. It seemed that David didn't travel light, but then he'd be working for the Chamber for just under three months.

"How did you manage all this on your own?" Tricia asked.

"I didn't. My dad dropped me off at the station before he left for work. All I had to worry about was this stuff." He gestured to his bag and laptop. "How long will it take us to get to Stoneham?"

"About twenty minutes." Tricia reached for one of the suitcases, realizing she would have to haul two of them to her car if they hoped to get going anytime soon. They weren't light. What had this guy stuffed into them? Lead weights?

"I thought the other Ms. Miles would be meeting me," David said, attaching the laptop to one of the bags and grabbing the other by its handle.

"We'd originally planned to come together but something came up." There was no need to tell him that one of those somethings had been a corpse.

David followed Tricia to her Lexus. Perhaps it was just as well Angelica hadn't ridden shotgun because the trunk and back seat were needed to contain all the luggage.

They got in the car and Tricia started the engine and pulled out of the lot.

"Where will I be staying? The other Ms. Miles said I'd get an apartment."

"Uh, yes," Tricia agreed. She wasn't about to tell the young man that its two previous residents had been romantically involved with her and had died violently. She hadn't wanted to stick the kid in the apartment she knew all too well, but it had been deemed unrentable by its exasperated owner, who was only too happy to have it occupied for the summer and had offered the Chamber more than a 50 percent discount in hopes of breaking the curse that seemed to have been placed on the joint.

"Some of the other places I interviewed for were only offering a room. This should be great."

"I hope you'll enjoy your stay," Tricia said with forced cheer. She braked for a red light.

"Uh, I did my due diligence before I signed on for the job," David said.

Tricia's hands tightened around the steering wheel. "Oh?"

"A lot of people seem to die in your village—and not of natural causes," he amended.

"It's unfortunate," Tricia said succinctly.

"I saw your name mentioned a number of times in the news reports."

Tricia swallowed, feeling distinctly uncomfortable. "As you know, I run a vintage mystery bookstore. I'm quite familiar with all aspects of crime. I've consulted with law enforcement in the past." Whether they wanted her opinions or not.

"Uh-huh," David said, sounding unconvinced. "I didn't mention the village's reputation to my folks. My mom would have pitched a fit if she knew and never let me come."

"Then why did you accept the job?" Tricia asked, and risked a glance in his direction, seeing him shrug.

"It seemed like it might be fun. If there're antiques shops, thrift stores, and tag sales, I want to go to them on my time off."

"Then you'll love my assistant manager, Pixie Poe. She lives for estate sales and acts as a picker for a number of stores in the village."

"Is her name *really* Pixie?" he asked skeptically.

"It's on her birth certificate."

"Wow. I can't wait to meet her. I'd also like to visit the library and all the booksellers, too."

David was a library science grad student, after all.

"I've also pulled up the websites of all the businesses. The Dog-Eared Page looks charming. How's the grub? Is it authentic?"

"I was in Ireland last fall. It's on a par with what I had there."

"Too bad the Bashful Moose craft beer tasting room won't be open until after I go back to school."

"The pub serves several of their brews."

"Great. I'd like to give them all a try," he said enthusiastically.

"Do you have any other questions for me?" Tricia asked.

"How often will I be interacting with you? Will you be training me?"

"My sister, Angelica, and I will both show you what needs to be done. We don't expect you to start today. I'll get you settled and give you a tour of our offices and the rest of the village." And try not to talk about what they'd discovered earlier that morning. "I'd also like to take you to lunch. The village has several eateries."

"Would it be presumptuous of me to ask to go to the Brookview Inn? I'd figured I'd never be able to afford it."

He really had done his homework. Since the Chamber was paying for David's apartment, he would be receiving only a stipend. It *would* be out of his price range.

"I'd be happy to take you there."

"Thanks."

The conversation turned to the Chamber and its procedures, the hours, and the duties he would be asked to perform. He seemed amenable to the tasks.

They entered the village and David took in his surroundings with wide-eyed interest. "This place is friggin' charming. I love the urns with all the flowers. Did the Chamber pay for them?"

"They were donated by Nigela Ricita Associates."

"Ah, the village's elusive benefactor. What are the odds I'll get to meet her?"

"Pretty poor. You'd probably do better playing the lottery."

"Why's that?"

"She doesn't live locally," Tricia said, glad her nose wouldn't grow with each lie she told.

"Then what's her interest in Stoneham?"

"It's quaint."

"That's hardly an answer."

Tricia pulled up in front of the building where David would be staying, glad for the diversion. She really didn't like being grilled when it came to Nigela Ricita.

They got out of the car and David stared up at the brickwork, his gaze traveling from the first to the third floor. He scowled. "Am I right in assuming I'll be living on the top floor?"

Tricia grinned. "Think of the stairs as a way to keep fit."

The scowl remained.

"If it makes you feel better, I also trudge up three flights multiple times every day."

David turned to look across the street to her store. "Wow. Your store looks just like Sherlock Holmes's digs."

"That was the idea," Tricia said with pride.

"I'd love a tour."

"That's part of today's plan." She glanced back to her car. "I think it'll take us two trips to get everything up to the apartment. Shall we get started?"

They retrieved the suitcases from the back seat and Tricia led the way. She liked to think that her daily three-mile walks kept her fit, but she was puffing by the time she reached the third floor after hauling up one of David's heavy bags. She unlocked the door and pulled the suitcase inside, with David following. Tricia deposited the case in the middle of the small living room and watched as David took in the space.

"Wow—this place is nice. Much better than I expected."

Tricia hadn't visited the apartment much when her ex-husband,

Christopher, had lived there, but she'd gotten to know it quite well when her friend with benefits, Marshall, had occupied the space.

"There are staples in the kitchen cupboards and some perishables in the fridge. That should give you a start."

"Where's the nearest grocery store?"

"In Milford, the next town over, I'm afraid. But I'm sure someone can take you there. Otherwise, just about everything else you'll need is within walking distance."

He nodded. "Do you mind if I take a look around?"

"Not at all."

Tricia moved to stand by the window overlooking Main Street. She really didn't want to visit the bedroom again. There were too many memories there.

David was gone only a minute or so and finished his walk-through by checking out the fridge and kitchen cupboards. "Looks like you thought of everything. I really appreciate it."

"We want you to be happy during your stay," she said, meaning it.

"Let's get the rest of the bags. I'm eager to visit the rest of the village and see where I'll be working."

"Let's get to it," Tricia said brightly.

The two trundled down the stairs to fetch the rest of David's luggage. Tricia's first impression of the young man was that he was personable.

It struck her that Angelica had used that same expression. It bothered her but she couldn't really say why.

# THREE

**By the** time closing at Haven't Got a Clue rolled around, Tricia felt as if the day had expanded from twenty-four hours to twenty-four days. She could hardly believe it had been only ten hours since Angelica had discovered Sanjay Arya's body. She hadn't connected with her sister since that time, so she had a lot to tell her.

"What a day," Pixie said as she returned from placing the day's receipts in the safe in the store's basement office. It had been a good day thanks to a tour bus that had visited the village that afternoon.

Pixie studied Tricia's face. "Boy, you look tired."

"Thanks," Tricia said, not able to keep the sarcasm out of her voice.

"It's not surprising what with everything you've crammed into your day."

She had that right.

Pixie shrugged out of her sweater. Once she hit the pavement, she wasn't going to need it. She grabbed her purse from behind the show-case that served as a cash desk. "Since you've had such a rough day, I thought I might bring in some muffins for the three of us tomorrow."

"That's sweet of you. Once David is trained, I'll have more free time and can get back to baking. What did you think of him when I brought him by?"

"He seems like a nice kid," Pixie said thoughtfully, but then she looked away. Was she comparing this young man with the son she'd met and lost just two months before? Tricia didn't want to ask.

"I don't suppose we'll be seeing much of him here at the store," Pixie said.

"Probably not. But I hope you'll consider taking him on at least one of your thrifting runs. I'm afraid there isn't much for a young person to do around here—other than drink, and I wouldn't want him getting into that habit."

Oh, no? And what was she about to embark on? Happy hour with her sister. On that day, she felt she deserved it.

Pixie headed for the store's front door. "See you tomorrow." She waved and pulled the door closed. Tricia made sure everything in the shop was secure before she gave her cat, Miss Marple, a kitty snack, grabbed her keys, and headed for the Cookery.

June, the Cookery's manager, had already left for the day and Tricia let herself in, locked up behind herself, and headed up the stairs to Angelica's apartment.

"Hello," she called, not that she needed to, as Angelica's bichon frise, Sarge, had heard her open the door marked PRIVATE and immediately started barking.

The little dog met Tricia at the apartment's door, jumping up and down but not on her—he was too well trained for that—and followed her into the kitchen, where she grabbed a couple of dog biscuits, which she tossed his way. He grabbed them and retreated to his bed to enjoy them.

"How was your day?" Angelica said, stirring the concoction in a crystal pitcher.

"Let's just say I'm more than ready for my first martini," Tricia said, and parked on a stool at the kitchen island.

"Me, too," Angelica agreed. "What with finding Sanjay and then a day filled with nothing but meetings—it's been brutal."

With a plate of cheese and crackers and no aroma of food in the oven, Tricia guessed they'd be having something simple from Booked for Lunch that only needed reheating. She was fine with that. She didn't have the oomph to cook that night and was glad it had been Angelica's responsibility to provide the evening meal.

"Let's go into the living room," Angelica said, poured the drinks into the prepared glasses, and placed them and the plate of snacks onto a tray. Tricia grabbed it and carried it to the coffee table in front of the sectional before taking her seat. Angelica followed, sat down, and passed her sister a glass.

"To Sanjay—may he rest in peace," Angelica toasted, and they clinked glasses.

"Have you heard anything since we left the mansion this morning?"

Angelica shook her head. "The gossip machine hasn't really gotten in gear on this one yet."

"Or is it just that you were so busy today that you didn't hear anything?" Tricia asked, and sipped her drink.

"A distinct possibility," Angelica agreed. "Wasn't Chief McDonald considerate of us this morning? So unlike his predecessor."

"I thought so, too. It was a refreshing change. Still, I wouldn't be surprised if he reverts to type."

"It's a possibility," Angelica agreed. She nibbled on one of her olives.

"What did Antonio have to say about you finding Sanjay?"

"Truthfully, I think he was more upset than me."

"Why?"

"He thinks it's a bad omen."

"He doesn't want to work in the new offices?" Tricia asked.

"He didn't say *that*," Angelica said. "Just that he felt uncomfortable knowing that a man died in our new building. And don't forget, *he* was the one who interfaced with Sanjay the most. I can't say they were friends, but they had a working relationship that goes back several years."

Tricia nodded. She'd always dealt with Jim Stark himself. "What's Antonio's concern?"

"He worries about me and wonders if we'll ever feel safe in that building."

"Well, unless you come clean to the world at large that *you're* Nigela Ricita, you probably won't make an appearance at the building unless there's some kind of public reception or other."

Angelica frowned. "I hadn't really thought about it." But it looked like she wished she had. Angelica had already admitted she loved the building. She might own it, but she wasn't going to be a part of it in the physical sense. She'd spent so much time picking the floors, paint colors, and everything else that went into refurnishing the rooms within its walls for others, while her workdays were going to continue to be spent in her own apartment. It was a pleasant enough home, but Tricia suspected her sister was beginning to feel isolated and was starting to get cabin fever.

Angelica ate her second olive before speaking again. "So, what did you make of our new intern after spending the afternoon with him?"

"I like him." Tricia tried to suppress a grin. "He wore a woman's brooch on his shirt."

Angelica frowned. "Was there a sign attached that said it was for women only?"

"No, it's just that . . . well, I've never seen a man wear that kind of jewelry before."

"What did it look like?"

"A bumblebee."

"He'd be a hit over at the Bee's Knees." One of the non-book-related shops on Main Street that featured products derived from a hive. "Do you think he's gay?" Angelica asked.

"I wouldn't care if he is—but no. It just seemed a little odd. He also wore his hair in a ponytail and had on a pair of knee-high boots."

"You mean like riding boots?"

Tricia shook her head. "More like Robin Hood."

Angelica shrugged. "Imagine that. A man who bucks the outdated cliché of machismo. I'm looking forward to meeting him."

"You'll get the chance tomorrow, that is if you don't have another day filled with NR business."

"I do on most days—as well as looking after my own enterprises—and this week looks like it's going to be really packed. I hope you won't mind taking care of most of David's training."

"Unlike you, I only have the one business to oversee—and two fantastic employees I can depend on. I'll manage."

"What did David think of our little village?"

"He'd done his homework and said we had a reputation—one he wasn't willing to share with his family in case they wouldn't let him take the job."

"But he's in his midtwenties. Shouldn't he be making his own decisions?"

"If his parents are funding his degree, he might feel he has to abide by their rules."

Angelica shook her head. "Maybe it was good that Antonio didn't live with me when he was at university. It gave him a chance to spread his wings and try new things."

"I wonder if David's version of that is wearing brooches."

"You're not going to harp on that the whole time he's with us, are you?" Angelica asked.

"No. I guess I just consider it a little odd."

"Sounds more like he's his own man—seeking some semblance of independence and individuality."

"Was that what pushed him to the top of the list to fill our position?"

"Maybe." Angelica reached for a cracker and a sliver of cheese, but instead of eating, she merely stared at them.

"Anything wrong?" Tricia asked.

Angelica frowned. "I keep thinking about what Chief McDonald said about us not having much of a reaction to Sanjay's death. Does that mean that we've become hardened to murder? That the poor man's life was so trivial it barely registered with us?"

"I can see it registered for you."

"And you?" Angelica pressed.

"Finding a dead body is always unnerving, but . . . maybe he's right. Still, I've done everything I could today to distract myself from the knowledge that someone died in your new-to-you building. You were really excited about that kitchen. Now how do you feel about it?"

"Like someone tainted it. The one place in that house that I loved most—and now it's been spoiled for me." She shook her head. "I know that sounds selfish, but that's the way I feel."

Tricia could understand that sentiment. If she'd known the man she was sure she would have felt more invested. That said, the man had to have loved ones and friends who would miss him. There would be a huge hole in their lives where Sanjay Arya had been.

The thing was, a man was dead. That meant there was, once again, a killer on the loose. Logic told Tricia she should batten down the hatches and look over her shoulder when she stepped onto the sidewalk outside of Haven't Got a Clue. And yet, she hadn't done that. Was she so inured about yet another violent killing in the village that it had become commonplace and not worthy of her attention?

She hated to think so.

She preferred to think that she had so much on her traumatized mind that it was a self-survival tactic to avoid thinking about it.

"Penny for your thoughts," Angelica said, reaching for another cracker.

"Just wondering why the people in our village can't get along."

Angelica nodded. "We don't suffer a lot of petty crime, but when it comes to murder . . ." She let the sentence trail off, looking thoughtful. "Maybe the village needs an intervention."

"In what way?" Tricia asked. "A group session led by a shrink?"

Angelica frowned. "That's hardly the proper definition of a mental health professional."

"And how many of our residents are going to seek out help with their anger issues—especially if they don't have insurance?"

"Very few," Angelica admitted. "Still, I wonder if NR Associates could recruit someone."

"It's something to think about," Tricia agreed. She drained her glass and ate the second olive. "What's for dinner?"

"I had a hankering for some lo mein. I don't have the proper noodles, but I think I can substitute angel hair without dire consequences."

Tricia smiled. "There are at least three Chinese takeouts in Milford.

Do you think we could recruit one of those to move here, or just find another one to open?"

"It couldn't hurt to try either option," she said, and got up to get the pitcher to refill their glasses.

While she was gone, Tricia thought about Angelica's suggestion to bring in someone who could help the villagers with their emotional well-being. That would save those willing (or forced) to take the help from having to drive to Nashua or Concord. No wonder Angelica possessed two empires. She was always thinking about ways to improve the lives of Stoneham's citizens, whether it served her own needs or not. Tricia was pretty darn proud of her sister.

Angelica returned with the pitcher and more garnishes set on a small plate. She plopped them into the glasses and poured before taking her seat once again. "What should we drink to?"

"How about you?" Tricia suggested.

"Me?"

"I think you're pretty special," Tricia said sincerely.

"I think you must've had too much wine at lunch."

"I had one glass."

Angelica shrugged but they clinked glasses and sipped.

"What have you got on tap for tomorrow morning?" Tricia asked.

"Meetings until noon."

"I can give David instructions during that time. Pixie's used to handling things at my store. Would you be willing to devote the afternoon to him?"

"Can do."

"Great." Tricia's gaze drifted to the kitchen.

"What's the attraction?" Angelica asked.

"I'm eager for that lo mein. Can I help you make it?"

"If you want."

They got up from their seats, taking their drinks and the rest of the paraphernalia with them.

The day had held a few highs and a very deep low, but for some reason, Tricia felt encouraged.

How long would that feeling last?

# FOUR

The next morning, Tricia arrived at the Chamber's temporary office space half an hour early to set things up. She intended to train David on handling the mail, explain the filing system, and acquaint him with the computer system and software. After that, she'd give him the keys to the kingdom and cross her fingers that he'd work out. Somehow, she had a feeling Angelica had made the right call in hiring him.

David arrived ten minutes early for work, no doubt to make a good impression. His scraggly beard was a day longer and he was dressed in jeans, sneakers, and a red golf shirt. No brooch, and he'd twisted his hair into a man bun. Tricia wondered how that might go over with some of their more conservative members. He wore a pendant with the Superman S in burnished silver.

"Are you feeling particularly heroic today?" Tricia asked with a grin.

"Always," David replied. "What's on tap for this morning?"

"I've got coffee going."

"Oh," he said.

"Something wrong?"

"Uh, no. It's just that I prefer tea."

My, David Price was just full of surprises. "I'm sorry I don't have any tea bags here. I can bring some later."

"That's okay. I always travel with a few," he said, and pulled a wrapped one out of his back pocket. He glanced at the coffeemaker. "Is there another carafe for water?"

"Yes. I may as well show you where we store everything so you can make what you like."

And so she showed him the supply cabinet. While they waited for the water to heat, she walked him through how to use the copier and where the toner and developer were kept.

The phone rang several times, and Tricia hit the speaker button so that David could listen in on the conversations to get a feel for the typical questions Chamber members asked and inquiries from non-members. She'd developed a cheat sheet she'd used when she worked as a full-time volunteer for the Chamber during the months her store had undergone renovation after a fire and made sure he had a copy.

David was a quick study and picked up things fast. So fast, she let him take a call. Using the crib sheet, he answered the caller's inquiry with ease.

"Excellent," Tricia praised him.

"Thanks. Will I get to meet the other Ms. Miles today?" he asked.

"She'll be here this afternoon."

David nodded. "I take it this setup"—he gestured around the office—"is only temporary."

"Yes, there's a possibility we'll be moving to the old Morrison Mansion later this year. It's still up in the air."

"That's where Stoneham's latest murder victim was found yesterday," he stated.

"Um, you heard about that?" Tricia asked, just a little surprised.

"It was all anyone was talking about at the pub last night."

Of course.

"And once again, your name was attached to the story. You *and* the other Ms. Miles."

"Yes, well, it was unfortunate," Tricia said hurriedly, and got up from the chair beside David's desk.

It was a small office. Just one large room with three desks—one each for the co-presidents and the receptionist—a compact conference room that could accommodate up to six people, a washroom, and the area that served as a kitchen and supply room. Tricia retreated to her own desk and retrieved the membership list and the canned speech they used to call members to remind them to pay their dues. It was more efficient than sending out the paperwork. They'd streamlined the process so that members could pay online. She handed the paperwork to David and explained this part of the job. They rehearsed several times and then Tricia had David make several calls, which he aced.

"I'd almost swear you've done this job before," she said, pleased.

"I've done something similar," he confirmed. He scrutinized her face. "Can I ask a personal question?"

"You can ask. I can't guarantee I'll answer it."

He nodded. "How come you got all tensed up when I mentioned the latest murder here in the village?"

Tricia hesitated before answering. "When these things happen, they present a PR dilemma."

"I can see that. Who drafts a press release in these circumstances?"

"Usually me, but I'd be glad to offload that duty to you if you're up to it."

He laughed. "It sounds like you expect someone else to snuff it."

Tricia raised an eyebrow at that descriptor. "I meant press releases in general. We have a notebook of past notices you can look at to get a feel for what we've done before."

"Sure. I'd be willing to give it a stab."

Did he have to mention yet another method to kill?

"Another question."

Tricia wasn't sure she wanted to reply, but David barreled ahead. "How do you feel about being called the village jinx?"

"I *don't* like it," she said pointedly.

"I can understand that."

"What else have you heard?"

"That some call you the Black Widow."

"I've *never* been widowed," she told him.

"But three of your past lovers died violently, and the fourth is in jail."

Anger smoldered inside her. "I suggest you don't listen to idle gossip—and even more, don't spread it," Tricia said tersely.

"My lips are sealed," David said, and mimicked turning a key in front of his mouth. "But I thought it would be best to get all that crap out of the way so that we can start on level ground."

Before Tricia could reply, the phone rang. David answered the call and, consulting the notes she'd given him, was able to successfully answer the member's questions.

"Well done," she said, hoping he'd drop the line of their previous conversation.

He did. He withdrew a piece of paper from his pocket and unfolded it.

"I've got a list of questions I was hoping you could answer."

The first were about his lunch hour and closing the office, and they went through the rest of his concerns—all thoughtful.

The time passed quickly and suddenly it was noon.

"What are you doing for lunch?" Tricia asked.

"I thought I might try the Bookshelf Diner. I love diner food. I always freak out my friends when I order liver and onions," he said, and laughed.

Tricia grimaced. It was not a meal she would voluntarily eat. "I must warn you. They recently lost their short-order cook," she said, and that was because the woman was currently sitting in jail with a murder charge. She didn't mention that fact. "I haven't heard if the food has suffered."

"How about you?" he asked.

"I usually have lunch with my sister over at Booked for Lunch. We like to compare notes about our respective businesses and Chamber work."

He nodded. "Are the Chamber members used to the office being closed during the lunch hour?"

"My sister and I have been juggling keeping the office open for a couple of hours on weekdays. Having you here means we'll be open for eight hours every weekday. It's a vast improvement."

"And after I'm gone?" David asked.

"We hope to be able to hire someone full-time and have interns during winter and summer breaks to help out."

"Sounds reasonable," he said, nodding. "What do I do during the lulls in business?"

"Well, hopefully, you'll find things to do to help us operate more smoothly. I don't imagine that will happen until you have a few days under your belt. What were you thinking?"

"That I might like to read a mystery or two to get a feel for what you sell. I did an Internet search on vintage mystery authors and thought I might start with John D. MacDonald."

Tricia wrinkled her nose.

"You don't like that author?"

"There's nothing wrong with his prose, but as time goes by I find his work too misogynistic to enjoy—full of descriptions of beach bunnies, sex kittens, and the like."

"I guess you could say that about a lot of things that haven't aged well."

Tricia nodded.

"Who would you suggest I start with?"

"Dame Agatha Christie. Her Miss Marple and Hercule Poirot stories are classics."

"Okay. Maybe I'll check out your store in more detail during my lunchtime. Will you be there?"

"Yes. My employees usually go to lunch during the noon hour. I'll have to leave here a few minutes early so I can be there in time for them to leave."

"You've got two employees?"

"Yes, Pixie, who you've already met, and Mr. Everett."

"You call your employee mister?" David asked, his eyes going wide.

"Yes. And when you meet him, you'll understand why he deserves such respect."

David nodded. "I'll look forward to it. Is he—and Pixie—as knowledgeable about vintage mysteries as you are?"

"They are."

Again, he nodded.

The phone rang once again. Tricia retreated to her desk and listened as David answered and helped the caller. When he hung up, she sorted through the files on her desk, letting him putter at his own. After an hour or so, she felt more like she was babysitting their Chamber's new employee than training him. It was a relief to no longer have to face the ordinary tasks she'd been saddled with since she and Angelica had taken over the organization. Maybe she could even offload the Chamber's monthly newsletter on David. That would spare her for three months until he left. Already she was dreading the time when that came.

It was nearly noon when Tricia handed David a set of keys for the office and file cabinets.

"What time will I see the other Ms. Miles?"

"Probably after two. For at least this week, I'll put in a few hours every morning. Before you know it, you'll be handling most of the day-to-day tasks. Believe me, once the members know there's someone in the office eight hours a day, they'll keep you hopping."

"That's what I'm here for," David said cheerfully. He smiled at her. He had a nice smile. "I'll look forward to seeing you tomorrow—that is if I don't visit your shop this afternoon. You are open until six, right?"

"Yes."

He nodded. "Until later."

Tricia retrieved her purse from her desk drawer and headed for the door. She paused to wave and left the building feeling lighter than she had in months. It felt good. Now if she could just break the young man's tendency of asking awkward questions.


**Pixie and** Mr. Everett had been gone more than half an hour and David was a no-show—so far—but a customer had arrived to break the monotony, and Tricia had helped her find several volumes to fill out her Ngaio Marsh collection and suggested several contemporary authors she might try. Tricia was ringing up the sale when Haven't Got a Clue's front door burst open and Becca Dickson-Chandler barreled into the shop.

Becca and Tricia weren't friends, but they weren't enemies, either. Wary acquaintances seemed the best descriptor. Becca had once been married to Eugene Chandler, only Tricia had known him as

Marshall Cambridge—a man who'd been living under the government's Witness Protection Program before his untimely death some nine months before.

"Tricia! You've got to help me!" Becca implored, rushing up to the cash desk.

Tricia glanced over the shoulder of the woman she was serving. "Right this minute?"

Only then did Becca seem to notice Tricia was with a customer.

"As soon as possible."

"Am I in the way?" the woman asked, sounding just a little perturbed.

"Not at all," Tricia assured her, finished ringing up the sale, and sent the woman on her way with a couple of author bookmarks and a smile.

Becca didn't even wait for the door to close on the woman's back before she spoke. "You weren't at the town meeting last night." It sounded like an accusation.

"You're right. I wasn't."

"Then did you know the zoning board had the audacity to turn down the construction of my tennis club?"

"Oh, no! What happened?"

"It's that whole movement that's taking over the merchants; they're bound and determined not to welcome any business that doesn't pertain to books. Books schmooks! I have just as much right to open a business here as anyone else."

Did Becca realize she sounded like the epitome of privilege? That she hadn't also stamped her foot surprised Tricia.

Tricia had suggested Becca open a bookshop highlighting sports. Goodness only knew sporting celebrities were writing how-to guides and memoirs all the time. And she could sell tennis balls and rackets, baseballs, and hockey pucks. Instead, she'd decided to build the first of what she hoped would be a line of tennis clubs.

"You've bought up most of the available land outside the village, why can't you just build your club on one of those parcels?"

"Are you kidding? There'd have to be all kinds of hoops I'd have to jump through, not the least of which is an environmental concern. The property on Main Street came with none of that."

"And yet you still don't have the approval to build."

"No," Becca said bitterly.

"I don't suppose you'd be willing to sell the land so that it can be developed otherwise."

"Hell no. If anyone is going to develop it, it's going to be *me*."

Tricia nodded. "You could work with the Chamber of Commerce to determine your best option."

"But then I'd have to talk to the enemy."

"I'm *not* your enemy," Tricia said, aghast.

"No, but your sister is. She's one of the biggest developers in the village. And she would have bought that property if I hadn't snapped it up first."

There was no doubt of that.

"What am I going to do?" Becca implored.

"I already gave you my best advice."

"Thanks a lot," Becca groused. She frowned and Tricia could just imagine the gears in Becca's head whirling. "There's got to be a way to change their minds."

"Why the need to put your club in the middle of the village? It could only annoy your patrons. Just the parking alone during the summer would be a nightmare for them."

"Do you have to be so damned logical," Becca growled.

"I'm just pointing out the most glaring flaw in your original plan.

Besides, the taxes on such a large building would be brutal." There might not be sales tax in the Granite State, but real estate taxes were a killer. Tricia winced. Another reference to death. She had to stop letting stray thoughts wander back to poor Sanjay.

"You ought to start thinking of other development opportunities."

"You're right. I *should* have had a contingency plan because I should have known the hicks in this town—"

"Village," Tricia corrected.

"—don't seem to want to step into the twenty-first century."

That wasn't exactly true. It was just that they valued their historic roots and traditions more—that is until a storm takes out the Internet and then all hell breaks loose.

"I suppose when I develop the Main Street property I'll have to build some kind of replica of the types of buildings that have been here since aught-one."

"That's what Nigela Ricita had to do. The zoning board does have strict rules."

"How many hoops did *she* have to jump through to get it done?"

"If you give them what they want, it won't take as long."

Becca scowled. "Who do I talk to?"

Tricia told her who to contact on the Board of Selectmen.

Becca leaned against the counter, looking resigned. She heaved a sigh before speaking again. "So, I heard you found another stiff."

Again Tricia winced. "Don't say that. And besides, it wasn't *me* who found the man. It was my sister."

"But you were there."

It seemed everybody in the village knew her business. Again.

"Doesn't that get old?" Becca asked.

Tricia fought the urge to strangle the woman. "It appears to be my fate," she said instead.

"I heard the dead guy was an illegal alien."

Tricia's brow furrowed. "Who told you that?"

"The guy at the Bookshelf Diner."

Tricia just barely refrained from rolling her eyes. Dan Reed was full of conspiracy theories and a firm believer in alternative facts. Apparently, he saw everyone who wasn't born with blue eyes as a threat to his American way of life. That Sanjay had been of Asian descent probably rankled the guy no end—and Tricia was sure Dan wouldn't shed a tear or feel any sympathy or compassion for the man's death.

"Dan Reed is full of crap—and so are his opinions. Sanjay Arya came from a distinguished family of physicians and was American born—he was *not* an illegal alien."

Okay, Tricia wasn't exactly sure if that last sentence was 100 percent true, but who was going to argue with her about it? "Now, was there anything else you needed?"

Becca straightened, her eyes blazing. "Are you dismissing me?"

"Not at all." Tricia eyed the clock. "It's just that as soon as Pixie and Mr. Everett get back—any minute now—I'm eager to go to lunch. I'm starving." She wasn't, but Becca didn't have to know that.

"Speaking of which, we ought to go to lunch again—and soon," Becca declared. "I'd really like to pick your brain about how I should proceed."

They'd had that conversation at least three times and Becca hadn't listened to a word Tricia had to say. She faked a smile. "Real soon."

Becca glanced at her Cartier watch. "Oh, my, if I don't get going, I'll miss my appointment with my masseuse."

Tricia hadn't been aware anyone offered that amenity in Stoneham. Had the Booked for Beauty day spa expanded their services, was someone freelancing, or did Becca have to travel to Nashua for that luxury? Did she even care?

"Talk to you soon," Becca promised (or was that a threat?).

Tricia forced yet another smile and fingered a wave. The smile faded as the door banged shut.

# FIVE

**David didn't** make it to Haven't Got a Clue before it was time for Tricia to join Angelica at Booked for Lunch. She reluctantly admitted to herself that she was just a little disappointed. She loved to share her love of vintage mysteries with a new victim.

"Thank goodness you're here," her sister said. "I'm starving. I missed breakfast."

"Oh?" Tricia said, taking her seat across from Angelica in the booth.

"These early-morning—and back-to-back—meetings will be the death of me."

"Don't use that word," Tricia admonished.

"Death?"

Tricia nodded. "Speaking of which, have you heard anything concerning Sanjay's death?"

Angelica shook her head. "Just that I need to go to the police station to make a formal statement. How about you?"

Tricia realized she hadn't checked her phone in some time. Sure enough, Chief McDonald had texted her earlier in the day. "I guess I'll have to take a walk this afternoon, too." If McDonald was in a good mood, perhaps he'd update her on the Arya investigation. She may not have met Arya in life, but after contemplating McDonald's comment of the day before, she felt she should take more of an interest in him in death. Some might call it morbid curiosity, but because she'd been there when he'd been found, she now wanted to find out what happened to him—as well as why.

"Becca came to visit me just before I came here. Apparently, Dan Reed is up to his old tricks and spreading vicious gossip about Sanjay," she explained.

Molly the server arrived and poured coffee for the sisters before rattling off the specials. "What can I get you ladies today?"

"I'll have the taco special," Angelica said.

"Make that two," Tricia echoed.

"Good choice," Molly said, nodded, and left them.

Angelica reached for the creamer and doctored her coffee. "So, how did your training mission with David go?"

Tricia smiled. *Training mission.* "It went well. He's a quick study. When I left, he was answering phone calls as though he'd been representing the organization for months."

"Good. We've let a lot of our services go by the wayside. It'll be nice to offer them again, which can only attract past and new members."

"I hope so. Then perhaps we can pay someone a living wage to do the job in the fall."

"Now that you've spent more time with him, what do you think of David?"

Again, Tricia felt a grin brighten her features. "I like him. He asks the uncomfortable question now and then, but so far he seems perfect for the job. I suspect he's far more capable than the position demands. That said, if I could hand over the newsletter . . ."

"I hear you," Angelica agreed. She sipped her coffee. "So, what was the uncomfortable question David asked?"

Tricia sighed. "About my being a"—she lowered her voice—"jinx."

"Oh, my, that *is* awkward. I wouldn't say you're a jinx; you just have the unlucky ability to sniff out the dead."

"I hardly do that."

"Maybe it's karma," Angelica suggested. "I mean, we all have gifts. Mine happen to be a fantastic business sense—as well as a phenomenal success in every job I take on. *You* find the dead."

Tricia leaned forward and again lowered her voice. "May I remind you that it was *you* who found Sanjay Arya—not me!"

"Well, you were there, too," Angelica countered.

Tricia merely glared at her.

For the second time in less than an hour, Tricia fought the urge to strangle someone, and it was only Molly's arrival with their lunches that stopped her. Tommy, the short-order cook, had amazing culinary skills. Not only did he make the best cakes and pastries, but he could turn out all kinds of tasty entrées. The tacos could rival any premier Mexican restaurant in a bigger city.

While they ate their lunches, the sisters discussed Angelica's goals for their intern, which were pretty much the same as Tricia's: to unload as much of the mundane work as possible.

"David said he would come over to Haven't Got a Clue on his lunch hour to look at some books, but I guess he didn't have an opportunity."

"Why would a young man like him want to read vintage mysteries?" Angelica asked, dipping a corn chip into the last of the small bowl of salsa that had accompanied her entrée.

Tricia shrugged. "He said he wanted to get a feel for what I sold."

"Or was he just sucking up to you?" Angelica asked.

Tricia frowned. She didn't think so. The young man had seemed truly interested. "He is, after all, studying library science."

"I've studied cooking my entire life and I'm still not about to eat insects, no matter how much dark chocolate covers them," Angelica countered.

Tricia preferred to believe in David's sincere wish to better understand her.

The thought brought the ghost of a smile to her lips. She'd known the young man a scant twenty-four hours. Could there be a chance she was infatuated with him?

She gave herself a mental shake. David Price was twenty years younger than her. A mere baby. His choice of clothing and jewelry had intrigued her, nothing more.

Then why did the thought of him make her want to smile? Maybe it was as simple as wanting to converse with a different person. Someone with new ideas—not that he'd voiced any as of yet. Librarians knew a lot about the past. Did David fit that mold? And what about his choices of jewelry? Should she challenge him on that even though it wasn't pertinent to his work and abilities? Would *that* be an awkward question? Could it be considered intrusive or just plain nosy?

David had already been told Tricia was . . . inquisitive. Yes, that was a much better descriptor.

Angelica returned to the topic of feeling overworked, but Tricia hardly listened. Too many other ideas whirled through her brain.

The sisters finished their meals and it was time Tricia returned to Haven't Got a Clue. After all, she'd hardly made an appearance there and hadn't exchanged more than a few words with her employees.

"See you for cocktails and dinner tonight," Angelica said as they parted company outside of Tricia's shop.

"I wouldn't miss it."

Tricia looked down the road. Although she couldn't be sure, she thought she saw someone standing outside of the Chamber's temporary office just looking around, checking out Main Street on that pretty summer day.

It looked an awful lot like David Price, and he was looking in her direction.

**The afternoon** was growing short when Tricia realized she hadn't fulfilled her promise to visit Chief McDonald to give her witness statement. Thankful for Pixie's presence, Tricia left her shop and arrived at the Stoneham Police Department at 4:50. Polly Burgess sat at her desk, but instead of the perennial sneer that was usually plastered across her features, she wore a smile, and her eyes lit up at recognizing her visitor.

"Well, hello, Tricia. What can we do for you today?" the older woman asked.

Tricia blinked. Polly had been rude to her just about every time she'd entered the building. She'd taken a dislike to Tricia and nothing the latter could do seemed to melt the icy attitude that always greeted her. And yet, now Polly was not only grinning but being polite!

Tricia decided to pretend not to notice the woman's abrupt change in attitude.

"Hello. Is Chief McDonald in? He asked me to make an official statement in the Sanjay Arya case."

Polly nodded, apparently sadly. "Yet another unfortunate death in our fair village. I don't understand how this can keep happening. We're all such *nice* people."

Tricia's eyes widened in disbelief, but still, she said nothing.

"Let me buzz the chief and see if he's available to talk." She did so.

"Send her in," came McDonald's tinny voice through the little speaker.

Polly gestured toward the chief's door and smiled. It made Tricia's hackles rise and she found herself gingerly walking toward the door. She knocked softly twice before opening it and entering, shutting the door closed behind her.

She must have still looked shocked as she took a seat before McDonald's desk, and he looked her over before speaking. "Is something wrong?"

"Polly, she . . . she was actually polite to me. It's never happened before."

McDonald's smile looked smug. "Ms. Burgess and I had a little talk last week—about her attitude toward those who enter this establishment. You weren't the only one she's been rude to in the past."

"And just how did you perform that feat of magic?"

He shrugged. "I asked her if she'd like to keep her job."

The former chief of police could have done the same thing. That he hadn't meant he was just fine with an insolent subordinate. Another demerit for him.

"I came to make my official statement on Sanjay Arya's death," Tricia said.

McDonald was ready for her and handed Tricia a clipboard with a witness form already attached. He turned back to his paperwork as she filled in the form, taking her time to make sure her wording was precise. When it was as good as it was going to get, she cleared her throat to get McDonald's attention.

"All finished." She handed him the clipboard and he perused her statement before nodding.

"Pretty much what you told me yesterday."

"I called it as I saw it," she said. "Can you tell me anything about your investigation?"

"The cause of death was pretty much obvious," McDonald said. "Blunt force trauma."

"With?"

"A hammer. His *own* hammer, it turns out. And more than one blow."

Tricia winced. "And suspects?"

McDonald shrugged. "We're just getting started with our interviews."

Tricia nodded. "Anybody I know?"

McDonald grunted. "You probably know them all."

"Possibly. Would you care to name a few?"

"Not at this time," McDonald said, his voice level—almost serene . . . such a pleasant change from the office's former resident.

"Can you tell me anything about the crime?"

McDonald looked thoughtful. "Mr. Stark made the official identification of the body."

"And why was that?"

"No wallet. No ID. No keys. No cell phone."

"So, you think this was a case of robbery?"

"At this point, we can't rule anything out."

No, she supposed not. But how many people carried enough cash to make murder worthwhile? And why bludgeon someone for a few bills or credit cards?

Tricia gave the chief a wan smile.

McDonald smiled back.

"Has my sister been in to give her statement?"

"She has."

Knowing he wasn't going to say any more—give anything away—Tricia nodded and stood. "I guess I'd better get back to work."

McDonald stood. "And me, as well."

Tricia started for the door and his voice stopped her. "You aren't going to be nosing around on this one, are you?"

"Ian, in previous investigations, I've had a personal stake of some kind. I don't where Sanjay Arya is concerned. That is unless my sister is a suspect, and I don't think you believe that. Do you?"

"No."

Tricia nodded. "I guess I'll see you around."

"You will. Have a good rest of your day."

"And you."

Tricia closed the office door behind her.

"Have a nice evening," Polly called after her with a grin that once again unnerved Tricia. How had the woman managed to sound even halfway sincere? Or had her animosity of the past been just for show? Either way, Tricia wasn't sure she liked the new Polly Burgess. But one thing was for sure: Tricia was beginning to really appreciate Ian McDonald.

# SIX

Tricia wasted no time in returning to her store. Business had been brisk earlier in the day and she felt just a little guilty for having left her employees. But trade had wound down and Mr. Everett had already left for the day. Pixie was about to grab her purse and go home when David Price entered Haven't Got a Clue. "Shoot. It looks like it's closing time."

"It is, but I'd be glad to answer any questions you've got."

"Want me to stick around?" Pixie asked Tricia.

"I can handle David," she said.

He laughed. "Don't be so sure."

Tricia felt a blush rise up her neck to color her cheeks.

Pixie smirked. "See you tomorrow," she said with a wave, and exited the store.

Tricia turned to her sort of employee turned customer. "We talked about Agatha Christie."

"Yeah, can we look at some of her books?"

46

Tricia moved from behind the cash desk. "Right this way." She led him to a shelf that was stuffed with Christie's novels. "Now, you can read them in any order you please."

David pulled three different editions of *A Pocket Full of Rye* and compared them. "This looks the best."

"Are you judging the book by its cover?" Tricia asked.

"Why not?"

"But it's the same book no matter *what* the cover."

"Yeah, but this looks nicer. Which would you have chosen?"

"The oldest one." She nodded toward the copy with the yellowest pages.

David scrutinized the tome, riffled the pages, and one of them fell out. "And that's a good reason *not* to buy that edition." He handed her the two rejected books. She reshelved the intact one and held on to the other. She couldn't very well sell a defective copy. "Would you like to try another author as well?"

He shook his head. "I'll see if I like this book, then I may come back for more of the same or try something different. I like to give a read a decent chance before I reject it or an entire genre."

*Very commendable*, she thought wryly.

"Shall I ring this up for you?"

"Sure."

They walked over to the register. Was she being a hard-hearted businesswoman for not giving the book away or would giving it away prove she wasn't a good businesswoman?

She gave him a 25 percent discount.

"Thanks," he said.

"I often give discounts to new customers."

Well, sometimes.

David watched as she plopped the book into a small paper bag and added one of the bookmarks donated to the store by current mystery authors for advertising purposes. He leaned against the glass case, in no hurry to leave.

"People here in the village like to talk," he commented.

"I guess that depends on who you're speaking with," Tricia said.

"Oh, yeah?"

"The native New Englanders are pretty circumspect. It's the outsiders who are more forthcoming."

"Then I must have been talking to those from other states," David said.

"And the subject matter?" Tricia inquired.

"The latest murder here in Stoneham."

"Oh, David!"

"Everyone seems to have an opinion," he went on.

"On what?"

"A motive for it."

Tricia shook her head. "You really shouldn't listen to idle gossip."

"How else am I supposed to know what's going on in the village?"

"You could read the *Stoneham Weekly News.*"

"Do you?"

Tricia felt heat color her cheeks. "Well, not often enough," she admitted.

"Why not?" Another of David's impertinent questions.

"It's complicated."

His brow furrowed. "How can reading a newspaper be complicated?"

"It just is," Tricia grated. She counted to ten and forced a smile. "I'm sorry. It's just that—"

"You're tired of being associated with every death that occurs in the village?" he suggested.

"Well, yes."

"I don't blame you."

Tricia eyed the younger man, who looked preoccupied. Was he about to ask another inappropriate question?

"What are you going to do about it?" he said at last.

"About what?"

"Sanjay Arya's murder."

"Why do I have to do anything?"

David shrugged and held out his hands in submission. "Because that's what you do."

Tricia shook her head in denial. "No, I'm a bookseller."

"Oh, come on, Tricia. Everybody says you're a—"

"Nosy-body?" she challenged.

"Well, sort of."

Tricia frowned.

"I mean, *as* a vintage mystery bookseller, you're obviously well acquainted with the subject."

Naturally.

"So I don't understand why everyone would think it odd that you're interested in true crime, too."

"Not terribly," she said dully.

"But you've read it. Didn't your ex-boyfriend sell it?"

How much gossip had David been listening to—and who was spreading it? Or at least who was his source?

He'd eaten at the Bookshelf Diner and Dan Reed was not one of her—or Angelica's—fans. The man had probably been only too glad to disparage her to a stranger.

She didn't want to go there.

"What are you intimating?" she asked instead.

"I dunno. I just thought that you'd want to do *something* to find out what happened to the guy."

"That's the job of the Stoneham Police Department—not me."

"But you *have* consulted with the cops before," he insisted.

"Well, yes," she conceded. "But it wasn't always at their behest."

"How did you ever get into all that?" he asked with what sounded like sincerity.

"All what?"

"Solving crimes?"

"I do *not* solve crimes." Well, that wasn't exactly true. "I look for inconsistencies. When I find them, I report them."

"Like Miss Marple?" he asked, eyeing the paper bag that sat on the counter.

"As a good citizen," she corrected.

"How did you get started?" he persisted.

"You're not going to let this go, are you?" Tricia asked, growing perturbed.

"I'm curious. Can you blame me?"

Yes, she could. But as an inquisitive person herself, she could well appreciate his interest.

"If you must know, it was self-preservation. The sheriff thought I'd killed the Cookery's previous owner."

"Get out!"

"*And* that I stole a valuable cookbook. At the time, I could barely boil water."

"Oh, yeah. But that's changed, right? You were involved in a big-time bake-off last summer."

Tricia rubbed her forearm, which she'd broken that same week. It tended to give her trouble when it rained a lot. Who was feeding David so much information on her past?

"Angelica and I were in the running. We did very well, but we were too ambitious. It was a much simpler recipe that bested us." That was all she was willing to admit.

David nodded, looking thoughtful. "What would you say if *I* was to start looking into Sanjay Arya's background?"

"Why would you want to do that?" she asked, appalled.

"To be a good citizen, like you. I mean, you *are* going to pursue this . . . aren't you?"

"I hadn't planned on it," Tricia said truthfully.

"But you *always* look into these deaths," David insisted.

Did she? Well, yes, she supposed she did—but only if she had a personal connection. McDonald had indicated he didn't consider Angelica a suspect. She'd more likely be considered a trespasser if Antonio hadn't granted her permission to be on the premises. And it was entirely plausible that she'd be viewed as a consultant, thanks to her work decorating the Sheer Comfort Inn and NR Realty.

"You didn't answer my question," David persisted.

"What question?"

"What you'd say if *I* was interested in looking into the man's death," David repeated.

"I'd say let the Stoneham police handle it." Advice she'd ignored on far too many occasions. And why discourage him? Because he was young and inexperienced? If she looked at it logically, David was a quarter of a century old. Great things had been done by prodigies much younger. But then that was the point—he *wasn't* a prodigy. He was a grad student.

"What if I don't want to?" he challenged.

Tricia blinked.

"I mean, I'm an adult. I haven't got much to do in my free time except read or watch TV. I thought I might just interview a few people. Get their take on the guy."

"I don't think that's a good idea."

"Why?" A crooked smile crossed his lips. "Will I cramp your style?"

"No!" Tricia felt a flush rise once more. "You're an adult. You can do as you please on your time off."

"Would you like to accompany me?" David asked.

"Absolutely not."

He eyed her critically. "Are you sure?"

"I'm sure," she lied. She wasn't about to admit that all this talk about investigating Sanjay's death had sparked her inquisitive nature.

"If you *were* to investigate, where would you start?" he asked.

Tricia shrugged. "With the people who knew him."

"His co-workers?"

Tricia nodded. "But don't expect them to cooperate. You're a stranger in town—and a transient. You'll be here today and gone in August."

He nodded. "Better they take their wrath out on me than someone like you."

"Why do you assume they'd be violent?"

"I don't . . . It's just that you may have to deal with these people in the future—I won't."

Tricia shrugged.

"I've already uncovered a tidbit," he teased.

Tricia squinted at him. "And that is?"

"His surname. It's Sanskrit for 'noble one' or 'noble person.'"

"It's not pertinent to his death."

"No, just an interesting piece of information."

Tricia's cell phone pinged. She glanced at the text from Angelica.

*Where are you?*

Tricia glanced at the clock.

"Oh, dear. I was supposed to be at my sister's place fifteen minutes ago."

"I'm sorry I kept you," David said, straightening. "I thought I might try out the other Ms. Miles's eatery Booked for Lunch tomorrow. It's basically a diner, right?"

Tricia nodded. "Yes, but the cook also makes excellent desserts. They're all made in-house. The carrot cake is to die for."

"I hope I don't, but I'd like to try it. What are you doing for lunch?"

"Well, as it happens, I usually have it with my sister *at* Booked for Lunch."

"Maybe I'll see you there."

"I don't go at noon."

"So you said."

Her phone pinged again. "I'd better at least answer my sister before she sends out a posse."

"I'm going, I'm going," David said, picked up his purchase, and headed for the door. "See you soon."

"Right."

She watched him go.

Tricia didn't like the idea of David going all amateur sleuth on her, but as he said, he was an adult. And, if she was honest, she wouldn't refuse to listen to anything he had to report.

# SEVEN

**Angelica seemed** quite annoyed when Tricia finally arrived at her apartment only twenty minutes late. She tossed Angelica's dog, Sarge, a biscuit to quiet his joyful barking and sidled up to the kitchen island. Already the room was filled with the aroma of roasting pork, and the chilled, stemmed glasses clunked against the top of the granite kitchen island as Angelica practically flung them onto the counter.

"Whoa! Don't break them," Tricia warned.

"I'm sorry. I guess I'm just a little tense," Angelica admitted.

Since her sister was in such a foul mood, Tricia decided not to share her most recent conversation with David with her. They could talk about it some other time.

"What's got your knickers in a twist?" Tricia asked as she watched her sister plunk the olives pierced by frill picks into the glasses.

"Becca Chandler," Angelica growled, and reached for a pretzel twist, dunked it into a small bowl of mustard, and popped it into her mouth, chewing viciously.

"Dare I ask why?"

Angelica swallowed. "When we spoke at lunch, you didn't mention the woman wanted to interview me."

"Did she use that word?"

"No, I did. She wants to pick my brain."

Tricia waved a hand in dismissal. "Oh, that. She told me she wants to pick mine again, too. The thing is, she nags and badgers you, and then she'll blow off everything you say."

"I got that feeling."

"Why would speaking with her make you tense?"

"Because she wants to speak with Nigela, too. Luckily, I can circumvent her on that," Angelica said as she retrieved the sweating pitcher of martinis and set it on a tray. She nodded toward the living room and picked up the tray. Tricia dutifully picked up the bowls of pretzels and mustard and followed. They took their customary seats.

Tricia knew what her sister meant when it came to avoiding Becca—at least for her Nigela persona. She'd successfully built an impenetrable wall where no one could contact the elusive Nigela without going through Antonio. So far, her virtual fortress had held. When she wanted to speak with her NR Associates underlings, she did so via Zoom with a corporate logo for a photo and used a device to change her voice. So far, so good. Tricia suspected a few people in the village had guessed the identity of Nigela's alter ego, but no one spoke of it. Nigela had been too good to the citizens—and many business owners—of Stoneham. It wasn't worth it to them to betray her.

"So, did you speak to Becca for long?" Tricia asked as Angelica poured their drinks.

"No. She wants to have lunch. I'd just as soon have a tooth pulled."

"She wants to have lunch with me, too."

"What did you tell her?" Angelica asked, passing a glass to her sister.

"Soon. How *soon*? That's anyone's guess."

Angelica frowned. "As I'm one of the Chamber presidents, and she's a member, I don't see how I can beg off. I mean, I'm supposed to be available to everyone in the organization who's looking for help, contacts, or even just a little moral support."

She'd been that and more to the members, during both her stints as Chamber president.

Angelica sat back in her seat and took a long sip of her drink. She sighed. "I needed that."

Tricia took a much smaller sip of her drink. "What's going on in the village?" She didn't consider discussing the usual goings-on as gossip. And as Chamber co-president it was her duty to keep on top of things, right?

"You mean mundane things like the village's street cleaning machine blew its engine or more on Sanjay's murder?"

"Well, I think you know my preference," Tricia said, and reached for a pretzel, dunked it into the mustard, and tasted it. Mmm . . . honey mustard, and probably made by the Harvicks, owners of the Bee's Knees just down the street.

"Patti Perkins at the *Stoneham Weekly News* is working on the obit for Sanjay," Angelica said, and toyed with the frill pick in her drink.

"Did he have any family?"

"He told Antonio he was single and that his parents were doctors in Boston. I don't know if he had any siblings."

"Wow, isn't it unusual for the son of physicians to be a construction worker?" Tricia asked.

"From what I hear, yes. That said, construction work can also be quite lucrative. And Sanjay wasn't a common laborer. He was Jim

Stark's right-hand man. He did things like estimate lumber and other supplies for their jobs—that's a math-heavy task right there, so it's not like he wasn't capable of following in his parents' footsteps. Maybe he was just rebellious."

"Or he wanted to do something more with his hands other than performing surgery," Tricia suggested.

"Maybe," Angelica agreed.

"Are you worried that the renovations on the mansion might be delayed because of Sanjay's death?"

"Not just the mansion. Stark Construction was already stretched to the max before this happened. They're juggling way too many jobs, and Sanjay was the glue who was keeping it all together."

Tricia nodded. "How does it affect you personally?"

"I wasn't going to move into the new offices, but Ginny and her staff need to be out of their current office by the end of July. It was going to be a squeaker whether the work was completed by then. Now . . ."

"Can't you get a month's reprieve?"

Angelica shook her head. "The building's owner wants to turn the office back into an apartment for his daughter. I wish he'd just let NR Associates buy it. We offered the moon, but couldn't come to an agreement."

"What will your people do if they have to leave?"

Angelica shrugged. "If it wasn't high tourist season, they could camp out in either the Brookview or Sheer Comfort Inn. As a last-ditch effort, we might try to rent a conference room in one of the bigger motels on Route 101." She sighed. "That would be inconvenient and possibly detrimental to morale."

Tricia was glad she wasn't facing the situation. Another reason to run just one business at a time. She took a moment to mull over her most recent conversation with David, deciding Angelica had calmed down enough to hear what she had to say. Still, she took a sip of her drink to fortify herself.

"It seems David is very interested in Sanjay's death."

"Isn't everybody?" Angelica said.

"He looked up the meaning of Sanjay's surname. It's Sanskrit for 'noble one' or 'noble person.'"

"How apropos."

"Yes. And that's not all he told me."

Angelica looked up. "Oh?"

"He wants to look into Sanjay's death." Tricia gave a nervous laugh. "Have you ever heard of anything so silly?"

Angelica leveled a penetrating gaze at her sister. "Yes—and you're the reckless fool who's done it on numerous occasions."

Tricia silently fumed.

"You *are* going to discourage him from doing that, aren't you?" Angelica pressed.

"Of course. In fact, I already have."

"And were you successful?"

"I doubt it. But I'm going to keep my eye on him," Tricia said point-edly.

"To keep him out of trouble or to aid and abet him?"

"Angelica!" Tricia chided her.

"It's a fair question. When is he going to have time to do all this sleuthing, anyway?"

"He didn't say, but I would assume it won't be on the Chamber's clock."

"We'd better make sure of that by keeping him busy. Did you say his parents wouldn't be happy if they knew the village's reputation as New Hampshire's Death Capital?"

She had.

Why was Angelica getting all bent out of shape over this? It wasn't as though she hadn't participated in many of Tricia's forays to fight crime. She winced at that descriptor. She did not wear a catsuit and cape, nor was she a real-life Miss Marple. She didn't have nearly enough gray hair for that!

"What's for dinner?" she asked, hoping to change the subject, but it was obvious from Angelica's expression that she had no such intention.

"We're not done talking about David, and how he's *not* going to investigate Sanjay's death."

"How do you propose we stop him?" Tricia asked.

"Threaten him with his job!"

"Are you kidding? He was the best candidate we had—at this late date, I doubt we'd be able to sucker, er, I mean convince anyone else to help out for the next two months."

Angelica scowled. "*I* will speak to him about this."

Tricia nearly cringed. When she applied herself, Angelica could scare the bejeebers out of a serial killer and never even raise her voice. But then Tricia steeled herself. "I thought we agreed that I would be David's main contact at the Chamber since you're so busy with your other obligations."

"I could make time for that."

"Are you insinuating that I can't handle the situation?"

Angelica didn't even blink. "Yes."

"Angelica!"

Angelica set down her drink and threw her hands into the air. "All right. Handle it. But I want his investigative impulses shut down—as of tomorrow. Do I make myself clear?"

Much as she detested her sister's tone, Tricia meekly answered, "Yes," and fought the urge to stick out her tongue. Honestly, sometimes Angelica brought out the worst in her. "Now can we talk about dinner? What smells so good?"

"Pork tenderloin with garlic mashed potatoes, gravy, and a big salad I made especially for you."

"Thank you."

"You're welcome," Angelica said coolly.

The sisters finished their drinks, each of them focusing on another corner of the room to avoid looking at each other. It was Sarge who broke the tension by leaving his little bed and trotting over to sit in the space between his owner and auntie. He barked three times, looking from one sister to the other.

Angelica's anger seemed to melt away as she looked at the little dog and his soulful brown eyes. "Do you want your mommy and aunt to stop bickering?" she simpered.

It was more likely he wanted another dog biscuit or two. Tricia didn't voice that opinion lest she have her head bitten off.

Angelica drained her glass and poured herself another. "We'll have to finish our second drink with our dinner."

"That's okay with me," Tricia said, and poured the last of the mixture into her glass. At that point, she didn't feel inclined to stay any later than necessary. And she felt the urge to rebel against her tyrant of an older sister.

So, it wasn't any wonder that upon arriving home Tricia picked up her cell phone and tapped the newest contact. It rang four times before it was answered. "Hi, David. I was wondering . . . did you want some help with your investigation into Sanjay Arya's death?"

# EIGHT

**Tricia arrived** at the Dog-Eared Page and found David in one of the back booths, nursing a Guinness. As she approached, he stood, something she wasn't sure most young men his age knew to do when a lady arrived, then he pulled out the chair for her to sit. Another bonus point in his favor.

"Thank you."

"Can I get you a drink?"

Tricia glanced over his shoulder, raised a hand giving a victory sign, and Bev, the server, gave her a nod and turned toward the bar, which didn't escape David's attention.

"You're well known here."

"I get around," Tricia said, modestly. "Now, what have you got so far?"

David's eyes sparkled in anticipation.

"Well, I've spoken to a couple of his work crew and they were split on his likability."

"Oh? Everyone I've spoken to seemed to like him."

"That's just it. He was either a friendly, great guy or a pri—"

Tricia raised a hand to stave off that descriptor. "I get the picture. What made him unfriendly to some people?"

David raised his glass. "Apparently, he could be a mean drunk."

"Who said that?"

"One of Stark Construction's carpenters."

Tricia hadn't visited the pub lately, but she could have sworn she'd never seen Sanjay Arya darken its door and said as much.

"Apparently, he did most of his drinking in Milford. They've got more bars than little old Stoneham."

"Do you think we need more?"

"It couldn't hurt." He looked around the quaint pub. "This is a great spot—for the older crowd."

"Do you know what the demographics are for the citizens of our quaint little village?"

"Old, older, and oldest?"

Tricia sighed. He wasn't that far off.

"What would you suggest we do to attract a younger clientele?"

"You're asking the wrong person. I happen to like places like this. I love all the little bookstores and gift shops. My dad thinks I should have been born a girl because of the way I dress and the things I enjoy."

"What about your mom?"

He smiled. "She likes me just the way I am."

Good for mom.

"Was she the one who got you interested in costume jewelry?"

"That was my grandmother. That pin I had on yesterday . . . it belonged to her. When she died, nobody in the family wanted any of that. I thought they were interesting and attractive so I took them." He frowned. "My dad and uncles got upset when I started wearing them. Considering they had belonged to *their* mother . . ." He let the sentence trail off.

David had ditched the pendant and wore a different brooch that evening. Tricia nodded toward the silver-and-green-stone pin that currently adorned his chest. "And that one?"

"It's a penannular brooch made of Connemara marble. I don't get many occasions to wear it. I thought an Irish pub might be the appropriate place."

"Did it belong to your grandmother, too?"

He shook his head. "Estate sale find. Don't you love it?"

She did very much like it.

"But you didn't come to talk about my taste in accessories," David said.

"No," she agreed. "I suppose you've collected all the mundane facts about Sanjay."

"His address, where he went to school, checked out his social media pages. As you say, the mundane stuff."

Tricia figured she ought to have a look at Sanjay's online presence as soon as she returned home.

Bev arrived with a tray and a gin and tonic with a slice of lime in a sweating glass, along with a bowl of potato chips. She set the items down before Tricia. "Let me know if you need anything else."

"Thanks, Bev."

Bev smiled at them and turned away.

"I didn't get a bowl of chips," David said quietly.

Tricia pushed the bowl forward. "We can share."

"Thanks," David said, and grabbed one, popping it into his mouth and crunching it.

Tricia grasped the piece of lime, squeezed it into her drink, and then picked up the glass and took a sip. "What's next on your investigation schedule?"

David shrugged. "I thought I might go on a pub crawl in Milford tomorrow evening. Want to come along?"

"I might be available. When would you need to know?"

"After lunch tomorrow? I thought I might get a bite to eat at one of them."

Tricia frowned and shook her head. She didn't have a reason to cancel on Angelica that early in the evening. Canceling or leaving early might give Angelica the idea that Tricia was doing something she wouldn't approve of. And she'd be right. "I might be able to join you later at one of the establishments."

"That's better than nothing, I suppose."

"I don't have to be there at all," Tricia said, with just a hint of impatience.

"I know. But I thought you wanted to work with me on this."

"I do. But . . . my sister doesn't think it's a good idea."

"Did that ever stop you before?" he asked.

Tricia let out a breath. "No."

"Then why should it stop you now?"

She frowned at him. "You *are* a bad influence."

He smiled. "That I have any influence on you makes me happy."

The hairs on the back of her neck prickled. "But I'm serious. Angelica does not approve of it, so be warned."

"I can handle her."

Tricia stifled a laugh and shook her head. "Never, *ever*, underestimate Angelica Miles." David looked nonplussed at her warning and she decided to change the subject. "Let's talk about what you hope to gain with your little pub crawl."

"A better idea of who Sanjay the man was."

*Obviously.* This kid really was a rookie when it came to sleuthing.

"Have you visited his home?"

"Not yet. I don't have a car," he reminded her. "Which also means that I guess I'll just have to wait until you're available tomorrow night to go to Milford. It's not that far. I guess I could walk, but—"

Tricia sighed. "I can be available after seven thirty tomorrow night. Is that too late for you?"

"It'd be just about perfect," David said.

"Good."

Tricia stared down at her drink. She'd barely made a dent in it, which made her think about a pub crawl the following evening. "I guess I'll have to be the designated driver." And what would Angelica make of her if she begged off her usual happy hour martinis? She'd have to think of something. In the meantime, she was determined to enjoy the drink before her. After all, she only had to walk across the street to return to her home—no operating heavy machinery involved.

"I heard the dead guy's boss showed up right after the cops yesterday morning. Doesn't that seem suspicious to you?" David asked

"No." Maybe. "Why?"

David shrugged. "If Sanjay was in charge of the project, why would the boss show up? Didn't he have faith in his second-in-command?"

"Maybe he'd been trying to call Sanjay and got no answer and decided to check up on the project himself."

"Would that automatically mean he would show up at the jobsite the guy managed? I mean, no work happened on Sunday, did it?"

Probably not.

"I assume, like a lot of people in this village, that Jim Stark keeps a police scanner going and that's how he heard about the body being discovered. When he came bursting past the police barrier, he said he'd heard about it. How else would he know?"

"Well, if he killed the guy he sure would've known." David looked skeptical. "How well do you know Stark?" David asked.

"He worked on my store and my apartment. Twice for both."

"And your assessment of his character?"

Tricia shrugged. "I thought he was a pretty straightforward kind of guy. His crew did the work, on time, and stuck pretty much to the original quotes."

"But you never worked with Sanjay?"

Tricia shook her head. "If he was working for Jim at the time, it was probably on another project. Do you know how many crews Stark has?"

"Not yet. Is it important?"

"Maybe. Maybe not."

David nodded, looking thoughtful.

Chasing that information down would give him something to do on his own time. And she had better make sure he wasn't doing this independent study when he should be working. She asked the question.

David laughed. "I promise"—he crossed his heart with his right index finger—"my first loyalty is to the Stoneham Chamber of Commerce. In fact, I'm already coming up with shortcuts to do things."

Tricia's eyes narrowed. "Such as?"

"I reformatted the mailing list so that there are no blanks on the template. It's just a small thing, but over time it'll save labels."

Tricia had despised that job when she'd volunteered for the Chamber three years before—it was so fiddly. She should have just let Pixie do it, but she also felt she couldn't dump a job she hated on an underling to get out of the work.

Tricia sipped her drink and winced. And here she'd been plotting to dump the Chamber newsletter on David. It could also be looked at as an opportunity. Something to fill out his résumé. Yes, that was her plan, and then she wouldn't *have* to feel guilty about it.

David tipped his glass back and finished his beer. Tricia had only a few sips left in her own glass. "We should probably call it a night," she suggested.

David glanced at the clock on the wall near the bar and frowned. "I guess."

Had he been planning on something else?

"You don't have to leave if you'd rather stay."

"And let you walk home alone?"

Tricia stifled a laugh. "I'm a big girl."

David stood. "It wouldn't be right."

"Have it your way," she said, and rose, digging in her purse to leave some bills on the table. David didn't jump in to offer to pay. Well, she hadn't expected him to.

They left the pub, looking both ways before jaywalking across the street and heading north up the sidewalk until they reached Haven't Got a Clue. Tricia scrounged in her purse for her key ring. "Thank you for walking me home."

"Happy to do it," David said.

They stood there for long seconds, just staring at each other. Tricia gave a nervous laugh as a smile crept onto David's lips, and she could have sworn his eyes twinkled. A shiver ran through her and for a moment she was afraid he might lunge forward and kiss her, so she quickly turned and, with a shaking hand, unlocked the door. "I'll see you tomorrow."

"I'll wait with bated breath," David said.

Tricia nodded and hurried inside her shop, closing the door and locking it behind her. She gave David a quick wave before she stepped deeper into the store and set the security system for the night. She hurried up the stairs and entered her apartment without turning on the lights. She quickly crossed her living room to look out the bay window down to the street in time to see David enter the building where he was staying, and she felt confused. He didn't offer to pay for their drinks, but he was chivalrous enough to want to make sure she arrived home safely.

She shook herself, considering (a) the Chamber job wasn't paying him much and (b) he probably escorted her home because he was aware of the number of murders that had taken place in Stoneham. But he also knew that most of them were premeditated. It wasn't often someone had been randomly killed in what was apparently New Hampshire's most dangerous, if picturesque, village.

And why on earth would she have thought he'd be interested in kissing her? She must be getting delusional in her old . . . well, middle . . . age.

Still . . .

Miss Marple jumped up on the windowsill and looked out the window, apparently seeing nothing out of the ordinary. Tricia petted her cat and frowned.

Why did David Price make her feel so disconcerted?

# NINE

**Tricia was** early at the Chamber of Commerce office the next morning. She figured it was best to stick to business where David was concerned and he arrived five minutes before his set work time. She was determined to give him his training and assignments for the morning and head out for her morning walk. She was pleasant, but her attitude was no-nonsense despite their chumminess the night before. Yes, that was the approach she was going to take with him from here on out.

"What are you doing for lunch today?" he asked as Tricia gathered up her things to leave.

"Uh," she managed, taken aback by the question. "As I told you, I'm having lunch with my sister."

"How about tomorrow?"

"I'm having lunch with my former store manager. It's a weekly thing."

"Oh. Okay."

Tricia resisted the temptation to ask why he'd asked. Probably because he didn't know anyone else in the village and didn't want to eat alone. Given the circumstances, Tricia would have felt the same.

"I'll see you this evening. Shall we meet in the municipal parking lot at seven thirty?"

"I'll count the hours," David said, grinning.

Would he really do that? Maybe if he was bored with the simple tasks he'd been trained to do. Perhaps she and Angelica should try to come up with a big project for their intern to accomplish. She'd speak to her sister about it.

"See you later," Tricia said, and headed out the door. Minutes later, she was back at Haven't Got a Clue just in time for the ritual coffee klatch with Pixie and Mr. Everett, who were discussing the latest Stephen King novel. Mr. Everett thought Mr. King's books were in dire need of severe editorial intervention, while Pixie loved every excess word, sentence, and chapter. It was a familiar discussion Tricia stepped away from.

When the first customer arrived, the coffee break broke up and everyone assumed their usual positions to make it yet another phenomenal sales day at Haven't Got a Clue.

The morning passed quickly and between spates of customers, Pixie and Mr. Everett continued to spar over King's novel, with much laughter and teasing. It pleased Tricia how well her employees got along. They were still going at it when they left for lunch and seemed to have carried on the conversation upon their return. That is until Pixie changed the subject.

"Hey, guess who Mr. Everett and I shared a table with at the Bookshelf Diner?" Pixie asked.

"June from the Cookery?" Tricia ventured, turning to retrieve her purse before leaving for her own lunch with Angelica at Booked for Lunch.

Pixie shook her head. "Try again."

Tricia sighed. She wasn't a fan of this type of guessing game. "Grace?"

Again, Pixie shook her head.

"Young Mr. Price from the Chamber of Commerce," Mr. Everett volunteered.

"That was nice," Tricia said. "And what did the three of you talk about?"

"Mostly tag and estate sales," Pixie said. "You must have told him about how I spend my Sundays. He hinted very broadly that he'd like to go with me to a sale or two this weekend."

"Wouldn't you like a thrifting buddy?" Tricia asked. Pixie's husband, Fred, often accompanied her on such forays. It was during football and basketball seasons that he begged off.

"Oh, sure," Pixie said, but somehow she didn't sound quite as enthusiastic as her words might imply. "He even offered to give me a few bucks for gas, as he hasn't got any wheels."

"That was thoughtful of him."

"Yeah. He seems like a nice guy."

"Will you take him with you?" Tricia asked.

Pixie shrugged. "I guess. I mean, you can vouch for him, right?"

"So far he's been great for the Chamber. He picked up the job's tasks in no time."

"He seems an admirable young man with well-thought-out plans and ambitions," Mr. Everett chipped in. "He seemed very enthusiastic about completing his studies in library science. It's a noble profession. And his specialty—children's literature—will serve him well to influence a new generation of readers."

That was quite a mouthful for the usually reticent Mr. Everett.

"Yes," Tricia agreed as she scurried around the counter, giving up her place to Pixie. "After lunch, I'm going to hit the bank, so I might be back a little late."

"Take your time. We've got everything covered. Haven't we, Mr. E?"

"Indeed we do," he said.

"See you in an hour or so," Tricia said, and flew out the door.

Booked for Lunch was still crowded as Tricia threaded her way around the tables and sat down in the banquette across from her sister. "What looks good today?" she asked, bypassing the usual chit-chat.

"The soup-and-half-sandwich special is a Reuben and corned beef and cabbage soup."

"That's a lot of protein, isn't it?"

"You won't complain when you taste that soup," Angelica said.

Tricia shrugged. "I'm game."

Angelica dumped a packet of sugar into her coffee cup, picked up her spoon, and stirred, her expression imperturbable. "So, I heard you had a drink with our protégé at the Dog-Eared Page last night."

"I did," Tricia answered. There was no point in denying it as there'd been at least twenty patrons in the pub who'd seen them sitting at a table together.

Angelica seemed to be waiting for a further explanation.

"The poor kid has no friends in the village. I expect that'll change over the coming weeks," she said neutrally.

"I suppose," Angelica only half agreed. "So, what did you talk about?"

"What's going on in the village. He told me about the jewelry he received after his grandmother passed. Just the normal kinds of things one talks about."

Angelica raised a skeptical eyebrow.

"Have you heard about when work is supposed to resume at the Morrison Mansion?" Tricia asked.

"No, and I'm pretty annoyed about it. No one seems to be answering the phone at Stark Construction."

"That's strange."

"It sure is," Angelica agreed.

Molly the server came by, topped up their coffee cups, and took their twin orders before heading for the kitchen.

Tricia decided she'd better try to control the conversation so that Angelica didn't start in on her about David once more. "So, how is Sofia getting along now that she's back in preschool?"

It was the right decision. Angelica couldn't stop talking about her favorite girl, and they'd finished their soup-and-sandwich combo before she began to wind down.

"Have you got time for dessert?" Angelica asked.

Tricia glanced at her watch. "Sorry, no room. Besides, I've got to run to the bank."

"I'll see you this evening," Angelica said. It sounded more like an order than an invitation.

"Until then," Tricia said, and got up from her seat, quickly making her escape.

Only two other customers were in the bank when Tricia arrived, and she made her deposit and had just left the building when she saw Toni Bennett, wife of Jim Stark, heading in her direction.

"Hi, Toni," Tricia said brightly, but she was not greeted in kind.

"That intern you've got working at the Chamber is an impertinent little twit," Toni practically spat.

"Sorry?" Tricia said, her mouth agape.

"He came into my shop a little while ago and started asking all kinds of questions about Sanjay Arya."

"What kind of questions?" Tricia asked innocently.

"How well did I know him? Did he have any enemies? The kind of questions only the police should be asking," Toni said tartly.

Tricia sighed but said nothing.

"Well?" Toni demanded. "What are you going to do about it?"

"What time of day was this?" Tricia asked, already knowing the answer.

"The noon hour."

"He was on his own time. The Chamber can't dictate what he does on his own time."

"Why not? He's the Chamber's emissary—the face of the organization. Surely that gives you the right to manage his movements."

"Not really. And he isn't the face of the organization. Angelica and I are."

"Well, you're not the ones sitting in the Chamber's office eight hours a day—the primary person in the organization dealing with the members and the public."

Tricia pursed her lips. She didn't want to fight in a public place about David and what he did in his free time.

Toni didn't back down. "If you won't do something about this—this . . ."

Tricia was almost sure she was about to call David a whippersnapper.

"—person, then I'll go straight to the top."

"I'm the top," Tricia pointed out.

"Of course you're not. Angelica is in charge of the Chamber—and she never should have left it."

Tricia straightened to her full height. "I'm sorry you don't see any value in my contributions to the organization."

Toni crossed her arms across her chest, her lips curled into a sneer. "You do the newsletter, which is just a recap of the meetings. It's hardly inspiring."

Tricia didn't need to stand there and be insulted. "I'd better let you go on with your errands." She turned on her heel and started walking.

"I mean it," Toni called after her. "I'm going to call Angelica!"

Tricia didn't turn or bother to acknowledge the threat. Still, her stomach roiled. She'd be in deep doo-doo with her sister. Now she needed to figure out how to defuse her sister's seldom-seen ire.

By the time Tricia returned to Haven't Got a Clue, she was no longer seething but she had a few questions for her staff. Unfortunately, she had to wait until several customers had completed their purchases and exited the store before she could speak freely.

"Hey, Pixie," Tricia said, desperately trying to keep her voice neutral. "I thought you said you shared a table with David Price at lunch?"

"Yeah, we did. And then he left to check out the Antiques Emporium. He's really into costume jewelry, you know."

Yes, she did know.

"I told him that Sarah Kelly has a twenty percent sale on some items in her booth," Pixie explained.

"He seemed quite enthusiastic," Mr. Everett put in.

So, he'd had a legitimate reason to visit the shop. Had he just gotten a little too enthusiastic about his task and sought out the enterprise's owner to pick her brain about Sanjay's death? Tricia would have to speak to him about it later that evening when they met to go on their pub crawl.

She still hadn't decided if she was going to mention it to Angelica. It would probably be best to stay mum, as already Angelica seemed to feel threatened by David's presence, although for the life of her Tricia couldn't figure out why.

Still, she'd said she'd be the designated driver. That was going to take some finagling, opting out of her usual double-martini happy hour with Angelica.

Still, she'd figure it out.

She had to.

# TEN

**Summer had** always been the season Tricia enjoyed most. After the long, dark winter and chilly spring, the warm, gentle evening breezes of late June were a balm to her soul. The month was creeping ever closer to July and the long holiday weekend ahead.

Her posture might have said she was relaxed, but she felt anything but. She had too many things on her mind. David . . . Toni . . . Becca . . . and the complex mix of emotions the three of them inspired. And the summer's biggest holiday approached. Fourth of July always meant a surge in tourists visiting Booktown and a register filled with cash and credit card receipts. Tricia hadn't had that holiday free since opening her shop and, truthfully, she didn't miss it, either.

After closing up shop for the day, Tricia dutifully reported to Angelica's abode for dinner. Upon her arrival, her sister ushered Tricia out onto the balcony to wait while she finished getting their drinks and happy hour snacks ready. Tricia stretched out on the chaise longue and gazed at the bucolic churchyard over the fence that hemmed in the alley behind the buildings on Main Street, yet was unable to relax. The muscles in her neck were so tense, she feared they might snap.

Angelica swooped onto the balcony with a polished silver tray in hand and set it down on the little table that sat between the chaises. She plopped onto her own chaise, poured the concoction into the chilled glasses, and handed one to Tricia. They raised their glasses. "*Salud.*" Angelica took a sip.

Tricia wet her lips but didn't partake of that fine English spirit.

Angelica looked down at the tray. "Oh, darn. I forgot the cheese slices to go with the crackers," Angelica said.

"I'll get them," Tricia said, still clasping her glass and jumping up from her seat, hurrying into the kitchen. She snatched the frill pick from her glass, dumped the contents in the sink, and turned on the tap to refill her glass with water before she found the plate of cheddar and returned to the balcony. She sat down again bolt upright, pushing the plate toward her sister.

Angelica scrutinized her sister's face. "You seem on edge tonight."

"Not at all," Tricia said, and slid one of the olives off the frill pick with her teeth and chewed it. Being soaked in the water had diluted its briny taste. "It may feel like summer, but I feel like I'm suffering from spring fever."

"Me, too. If only I had more free time," Angelica said wistfully.

"What would you do with it?"

"Time?" She shrugged. "Probably take on another work project."

"Is that what you'll be doing this evening?"

"Sadly, yes. I'll be reviewing a proposal to partner with the Milford Nursery and Flowers. A lot of their orders come from here in Stoneham. They'd like to expand and have a satellite shop here on Main Street, if possible."

"But they're only a hop, skip, and a jump down the road," Tricia said.

"Yes, but they have enough orders to warrant expanding. If they want a partner, why shouldn't it be NR Associates? We supply the capital, they supply everything else, and we share in the profits. It's a win-win for everyone."

It certainly sounded that way.

"So, you won't get to relax on the balcony anymore tonight?" Tricia asked, her tone innocent despite her actual intention.

"I wish, but the light isn't good enough. I'll just have to stay inside to work."

"That's too bad," Tricia said, but it gave her an excellent opportunity as well. "Can I help you get dinner on the table?"

"We've barely touched our drinks," Angelica protested.

Tricia forced a laugh. "So right." She took a sip of her tap water, lamenting the loss of her more potent cocktail.

Angelica glanced at the clock on the wall. "Yes, it'll be ready by the time we set the table."

Tricia gladly helped with that task. And she found herself speed-eating.

"Are you in a hurry?" Angelica asked.

"I just don't want to keep you from your work."

Angelica didn't look convinced, but she didn't comment, either.

Tricia finished her meal and was on her feet, tidying the kitchen while Angelica pushed what was left of her dinner around her plate.

Tricia glanced at her watch. Again. And. Again. Time seemed to have slowed to a painful halt.

Finally, Angelica wiped her mouth with her napkin, giving Tricia a chance to swoop in and snatch the plate and cutlery out from under her. She rinsed the dishes in the sink and loaded them in the dishwasher.

"Well, gotta go," she said cheerfully, when she actually felt more like a sneak. A lying sneak. Then again, she was a grown woman. She didn't owe Angelica an explanation of where she went, or with whom, and what she did. It was just that Angelica expected Tricia to respect her requests. It wasn't often she pulled the big-sister-so-I'm-the-boss card. "I'll let you get on with your work and see you tomorrow."

"Good night," Angelica said, sounding just a little weary as she closed the apartment door behind her sister.

Tricia felt more than a little guilty as she left the Cookery, entered her store, and then immediately exited through the back door. She looked up to make sure Angelica hadn't foiled her by going back out on the balcony, didn't see her, and followed the alley to the municipal parking lot, where she found David loitering next to her car. He snapped to attention upon seeing her.

"Right on time," he said cheerfully.

And he had no idea how difficult it had been for her to perform that little trick.

"Let's go." She pressed the button on her key fob and the door locks in her Lexus jumped up, allowing them entrance.

The shadows were beginning to lengthen as Tricia pulled out of the parking lot and headed north toward Stoneham's nearest neighbor.

"I've scoped out all the menus at all the bars and it sounds like Bar None has some cool appetizers."

"You wouldn't want an entrée?"

"I *might* go for the fish tacos. I'll have to wait and see when I get there."

"And you think Sanjay might have frequented this place?" Tricia asked.

"It's a shot."

"Have you thought about how you're going to approach his possible friends?"

"Sort of."

That didn't sound very encouraging.

David peppered her with questions about the village during the short drive to Bar None. At least he seemed interested in his temporary home. She wished he'd asked for pointers on how to approach potential sources of information.

The parking lot was only half-full when they arrived at their destination. The place was more upscale than Tricia would have thought as a hangout for construction workers. Its facade included a large picture window that overlooked the parking lot. Upon entering, she saw that the window with stained glass appliquéd accents was the backdrop for the bar, which was decorated with stuccoed walls, faux grape leaves, and wine racks filled with what may or may not have held the real thing. A small dining room was connected to the bar area, which was populated with faux leather stools with no customers warming their backsides on them.

Tricia and David took seats as a tall, thin bartender who must have been in his midthirties turned to face them. The name badge pinned to his chest said TED. "What'll you have?" he asked David, as though Tricia wasn't even there.

"I'll have a Guinness."

"We only sell American beers," the bartender growled.

David let out a breath. "Okay, what's on tap?"

"You can read, can't you?" the bartender said, pointing to the logos on the taps.

David frowned. "I'll have a Sam Adams."

"Patriotic of you," the bartender muttered, and grabbed a glass, filling it with the amber liquid.

"And you?" he asked Tricia.

"I'll have a Shirley Temple."

"A what?"

She sighed. "A ginger ale with a maraschino cherry."

The man rolled his eyes, but he grudgingly made the drink.

"You'd have thought I'd asked him to spike it with gold," she muttered.

"That's Goldschläger, isn't it?" David asked.

Tricia nodded.

Moments later, the bartender delivered both drinks and growled the amount due. David looked away. Tricia sighed and brought out her wallet, tossing several bills on the bar. "Keep the change," she said.

The bartender looked at the bills on the bar and scowled. "Thanks." He turned and walked away.

"This doesn't seem like a very welcoming place," she commented.

"Think we should ask the bartender if Sanjay was a regular?" David asked.

"Only if you want your head bitten off. And if we aren't all that welcome . . ." She let the sentence dangle.

"Then someone with Sanjay's complexion might not be, either?"

"It's a thought," Tricia said.

David looked discouraged. "And I had my heart set on fish tacos."

"Booked for Lunch often has them as a special on Fridays. Tommy's an excellent short-order cook. You won't be disappointed."

"I'll remember that." David looked down at his beer. "As you already paid for our drinks, we may as well finish them."

They hadn't even started.

While they sipped their refreshments, they studied the bar's clientele—younger people out for dinner and a drink and sparsely attended for a Wednesday night. Tricia wondered if the waitstaff was friendlier than the bartender.

"What exactly *did* you hear about Sanjay frequenting the bars in Milford?" she asked.

David shrugged. "Only that he'd been seen in a couple of bars along the main drag."

"Drinking? Socializing? Remodeling?"

David averted his gaze. "Uh . . . I'm not exactly sure."

Tricia leaned in closer and lowered her voice. "Then why are we here?"

"To ask about him."

Tricia got the feeling David was operating under wishful thinking.

Meanwhile David's gaze had drifted up to the other end of the bar where Ted was washing glasses in the small sink. "Why would someone employ such a surly guy like him?"

Tricia looked over her shoulder at Ted. "Nepotism?"

David sized the guy up. "It would have to be."

"Why don't we take our drinks into the dining room and you can order an appetizer before we grill the server," Tricia suggested.

"The cauliflower steak sounds interesting."

Only, Tricia decided, if it was covered in some amazing sauce or a river of melted cheese.

They picked up their glasses and ambled into the dining room, where the hostess directed them to a booth near the back of the restaurant where the lights were dimmer, setting two menus on the table. They sat down and Tricia looked around. "Are you going to be able to read the menu in this light?"

"I've always got the flashlight in my phone," David said.

He was serious. Tricia watched as he pulled out his cell phone and activated the light. He quickly perused the appetizers and closed the menu. "I think I'll just stick with an order of fries and onion rings." They decided they'd try to strike up a conversation with the server when she brought the food.

A woman wearing dark slacks and a white shirt with *Bar None* embroidered on it arrived at their table. "Hi. I'm Candace. I'll be taking care of you this evening. What can I get you?"

"Nothing for me, thank you," Tricia said.

David ordered.

"Be right back," she said, and winked.

He waited for her to be out of earshot before speaking. "She seems nice."

Would she be as accommodating when he started asking questions? Tricia decided not to coach him when it came to interviewing a possible source of information and to sit back and let him take the lead.

They chatted about mundane Chamber tasks until the server returned with David's sides. She set them in front of him.

"Hey, another southpaw," he said.

She offered a wan laugh lifting her gaze toward the bar area. "It's a bigger club than you might think. Can I get you anything else?"

"Uh, yes. I was wondering if you knew Sanjay Arya."

The smile drained from the young woman's face as her eyes darted toward the bar. "W-who?" she stammered.

"Sanjay Arya. Indian fella. Worked as point man for Stark Construction in Stoneham," David said.

"No, I didn't," she said coldly, and turned.

"Wait. You didn't? Does that mean you also didn't know he turned up dead the other day?"

"I'll bring you your check," she said in the same dead tone, and stalked off.

David frowned. "Hmm, that didn't go over too well."

Tricia shook her head.

"Do you think she knew him?"

Tricia nodded.

"Then why would she say she didn't?" he asked, sounding puzzled.

"Eat up. Your fries are getting cold," Tricia directed.

"What did I do wrong?"

"You started out great with the icebreaker, and then blew it by jumping in with the heavyweight question before she had a chance to warm up to you."

David frowned and grabbed the bottle of ketchup that sat on the far side of the table, shaking a substantial puddle of it onto his plate, taking care it didn't hit the onion rings.

"Where should we go next?" he asked.

Tricia glanced at her watch. "Home."

"But we haven't come across any information on Sanjay."

"And we're not likely to."

"Why do you say that?"

"You picked the right place, but now that you've alienated the server, she isn't likely to talk and will undoubtedly tell her co-workers not to give you the time of day, either."

David dunked a french fry into the ketchup, covering at least three-quarters of it before popping it into his mouth. Tricia watched as he chewed. At least he didn't speak with his mouth full.

"How should I have handled it?" he asked once he'd swallowed.

"First, you don't just leap into a conversation by interrogating someone. You want them to like you. You do that by being nice. By saying things like, 'Wow, that was fast service. Thank you,' or asking what she'd recommend. 'Is there live music on any particular day?'"

David frowned. "I hadn't thought about that." He picked up another fry and ate it. "So, what happens next?"

"Next, we go home."

"Together?" he asked, and smiled.

Tricia scowled. "Yes, in my car."

David picked up another fry and chomped on it, swallowing before he spoke again. "Does this mean it's the end of my investigation?"

"For tonight, it does."

He frowned and picked up an onion ring, taking a bite, but the onion became separated from its crunchy coating and he ended up sucking it into his mouth like a long strand of spaghetti. "Oops."

Oops indeed.

Once he'd swallowed, he said, "I guess I need to read more than one mystery to get the hang of these things."

"I think so," Tricia said quietly.

"I *don't* want to give up. I'm not a quitter."

"But you *are* a student—"

"And apparently I've got a lot to learn."

As promised, Candace returned with the check, slapped it on the table, and turned without another word.

"Have a good evening," David called cheerfully.

He got no response.

Tricia took the last sip of her drink just as David consumed his last onion ring.

"That hit the spot," he said. His gaze traveled to the check, then back to his empty, ketchup-splattered plate.

"Why don't I get this," Tricia suggested, growing just a little weary of David's reluctance to pay for anything, and then she felt like a bit of a rat when he next spoke.

"That's very generous of you," David said. He gave her another sweet smile.

Tricia grabbed her wallet from her purse, placed several bills on the table, and stood. David pushed his plate back and got up, then followed her out of the restaurant. Their server and the bartender both gave them the evil eye as they passed.

Twilight was upon them as they crossed the parking lot to Tricia's car.

"Thanks for dinner."

"It was hardly a dinner." But then Tricia was speaking to a college student. One might think a grad student—especially one studying the wonderful world of books—might have more nutritional smarts . . . but then she'd lived on tuna salad and lettuce for far too much of her adult life and was in no position to judge. "You're welcome," she amended.

Tricia unlocked the car and they got in. The conversation was nil as they traveled back to Stoneham. Tricia pulled up in front of the building housing David's new apartment.

"That was fun," he said.

"It wasn't," she countered.

"I'm sorry. Can I come buy another book from you tomorrow?"

"You don't have to buy books from me."

"Yeah, I checked out the library and they have a pretty good selection of mysteries."

"I didn't mean that."

"I know you didn't. I was hoping you might make a few more author suggestions."

"That's my job."

"Is it just a job to you?"

"It's my chosen career."

"And you love it?"

"Every minute," she agreed, and managed a smile. "And as much as you're going to love your life's work."

"Maybe," he said, shifting his gaze to the dashboard.

Was David having doubts about library science?

"Well, I suppose you could change majors and go into law enforcement," she said lightheartedly.

He turned to look at her, unsmiling.

"It was a joke." One he'd obviously not found funny.

"I guess I'll see you tomorrow at the Chamber."

"I'll try to get there," Tricia promised.

He nodded. "Thanks for the company."

She smiled and watched as he got out of the car. He paused at the door and turned back to face her. Was he waiting for her to leave? She did, and he waved.

Tricia looked in her rearview mirror and saw he watched her drive away. She turned left at the end of the street and turned into the alley that led back to the municipal parking lot, ruminating over the hour she'd just spent with the Chamber's intern.

One thing was for certain: David wasn't going to outshine Tricia when it came to being an amateur sleuth.

# ELEVEN

**Miss Marple** seemed particularly glad to greet her owner that evening, and spent the rest of the night close to Tricia's side. Was she trying to convey that she was lonely or just that she was determined to stick to Tricia like glue? The little gray cat was the first one to bed and the first one up the next morning. Too early. But it gave Tricia time to bake some cookies for her staff and customers. Sugar cookies. She knew Sofia would enjoy them, too, and filled a container with them to take with her to Ginny's home later in the day. With that task done, she still had time to go for her morning constitutional.

Tricia stepped out of Haven't Got a Clue and started north on Main Street—her usual route—when suddenly someone approached from behind and fell into step with her.

"Hey, Tricia," David said, only slightly out of breath.

She gave him an annoyed sideways glance. "You could give a person some warning," she groused, but didn't break her stride.

"Sorry." They walked past the Cookery, just as the door to the Patisserie up ahead opened and Mary Fairchild stepped out with a white bakery bag in hand. "I wanted to also say sorry about last night," David continued.

Mary stifled a giggle as she passed them on the sidewalk. "Morning, Tricia," she said, and let out another giggle. "Sorry," she added, and hurried along.

This time, Tricia stopped to watch her neighbor scurry away.

She frowned at David, noticing that he'd donned a different brooch. This time, it was a sparkling green dragon. "Thanks for that. Now Mary's going to spread it around that you had something to be sorry about, and it won't be to my—and especially your—benefit."

"What do you mean?" he asked innocently.

Tricia rolled her eyes and turned north to charge ahead once more.

"What?" David insisted, trying to keep up.

"Never mind."

"Anyway, about last night," David said. "Like I said, I realized that just reading one rather dated mystery does not an amateur sleuth make."

"You've got that right."

"I woke up early this morning and thought about what you said about befriending people before asking them questions. If you ignore that lapse, was what I said to the waitress so wrong?"

"These days, they like to be called servers. And it wasn't so much the words, but you didn't even ease into the subject—you just charged ahead."

"I figured the direct route might be the fastest way to get the information I want."

"Subtlety is not your middle name."

"You gave me the impression you didn't think I'd be able to find out anything else about Sanjay's death."

Tricia didn't comment.

"What's the first thing you would have done—in my place?"

Tricia shrugged. "I might walk by the mansion and look at the neighbors' homes. If anyone was out, I might try to engage them in conversation."

"What would your opening be?"

"Anything. *My, that's a lovely garden. May I pet your sweet dog? Isn't it grand to see the old mansion coming back to life?*"

"Aha! Icebreakers."

"Exactly."

"And are you going to walk by the mansion this morning?" David asked.

"I hadn't planned on it."

"Why not?"

"It's not on my usual route."

"You ought to shake things up once in a while."

"I shake things up plenty," she remarked.

"That I'd like to see." Again David gave her what she was beginning to think of as a flirty smile.

Tricia ignored it—wondering why she let him get away with it. As she'd already told herself, she was old enough to be his very young mother. Maybe she ought to tell him that.

Maybe.

"So, what do you say?" he badgered her.

"About what?"

"About deviating from your usual circuit and passing by the mansion?"

Tricia frowned, knowing it wrinkled her forehead and wishing she hadn't done it. "You're not going to let this go, are you?"

"What can it hurt?" he asked reasonably.

Tricia let out a long breath. "Oh, all right." They walked up to the corner, looked both ways, and crossed Hickory Street, turning west.

"Pretty day, isn't it?" David asked.

They'd had several pretty days in a row, but the forecast for that evening called for showers. That would mean no cocktails on Angelica's balcony. Well, at least she'd get to drink her martini that night instead of tossing it into the sink. Such a waste of good gin.

"So, what should I be doing in the meantime?" David asked.

"Paying attention to your Chamber job," Tricia said.

"Apart from that. What would you do?"

"I should listen to my sister and not get involved."

"But you said you'd help me."

Yes, she had.

"Well, for one thing, I'd want to know what Sanjay was doing at the mansion on a Sunday night. Who did he meet? Did a burglar sneak up on him? Was it a friend? If it was an enemy—who?"

"All good questions. And?" David said, pushing for more.

"It's a good place to start," Tricia said as she looked both ways before crossing Poplar Street.

"What other kind of people would he have known, besides his tight-lipped co-workers?"

Tricia shrugged. "He might be known to the people who man the contractor registers at the big home improvement store on the highway."

"Yeah. I wouldn't have thought of that."

"I think there's a lumberyard in Milford, too. But you'd have to visit during working hours."

"That's what lunch hours are made for," David said, his eyes bright.

"There's only so much you can do during that time," Tricia said.

"Yeah," he admitted. "Not having wheels is a big problem. I thought when I took the job I'd only be going places within walking distance. Except for the grocery store, that is. Speaking of which, I should have asked if we could stop there last night. I'm already running out of grub."

Tricia sighed. David was her charge, after all. "I'd be glad to take you. How about this evening? Can you make it through the day?"

"Oh, sure. Thanks."

"You're welcome."

They walked half a block in silence before David spoke again. "So, where's this mansion you don't want to walk by?"

Tricia gave him a sour look. "You're like a terrier with a bone—you don't give up, do you?"

"It's not in my nature. I could go by myself, but I don't know the lay of the land."

"The Chamber has maps," she told him.

"Oh? I must not have run across them. You'll have to let me know where they are. I might have to give them out as early as today."

Yes, he might.

"They're in the top drawer of the far-right file cabinet. In a folder marked—of all things—'Stoneham maps.'"

"Advertising maps?"

"Yes, but it's pretty comprehensive because of landmarks like the Historical Society, and there are several other businesses on side streets where the merchants have bought ads—like Griffin Photography. The mansion itself isn't listed, but the street it's on is."

"Good to know. I'll study it. I want to know these streets like I'd lived here all my life."

"Do you like the village?"

"Like? I love it. Who wouldn't want to live in a place this charming?"

"I'm glad you think so."

"So, which way to the mansion?"

Tricia sighed and pointed. "Up the next block." As they walked side by side, Tricia realized something. "Didn't you say you'd spoken with some of Sanjay's co-workers?"

"Uh, yeah."

"Where and when was that?"

"Um . . ."

Tricia stopped dead. "You were at the mansion, weren't you?"

"Me?"

"Yes, you."

"Well, sort of," he said sheepishly. "I mean. I didn't *know* I was going to go there, and I didn't pay attention to *where* I was going."

"How could you not pay attention to where you were going?"

"I was reading a book at the time." It seemed plausible to Tricia. Better a book than staring at his phone.

"Then how did you find your way back to Main Street?"

"I just kept walking—and reading—until I came back to familiar territory. I figured I eventually would."

"But you didn't pay attention so you could find your way back to the mansion?"

David held out his hands and shrugged. "I was caught up in the story."

Tricia let out an exasperated breath and she looked both ways before they crossed the street, not trusting David to be as safety conscious. Half a block farther, they paused in front of the imposing stone Morrison Mansion.

"Looks abandoned," David commented as they eyed the yellow crime scene tape fluttering in the light breeze. "There were trucks and workers here when I walked by on Tuesday."

"What time was that?"

"Around seven."

"In the evening?"

David nodded.

Tricia frowned. "Why would they be working so late?"

"The guy I spoke with—a guy named Foster, who said he was now in charge of the work crew—said they were trying to catch up after losing the whole day's work on Monday."

It was well after eight and there was no sign of anyone working on the project. Tricia wondered if Angelica knew what was up. Or perhaps Antonio would have a better idea. She retrieved her phone from her pocket and sent him a quick text.

"What next?" David asked.

Tricia glanced across the street, where an elderly woman was watering the plants that hung from chains below the eaves on her house. Without a word, she looked both ways and crossed the road.

"Hello!" she called cheerfully. "Those are beautiful flowers."

"Thank you," the woman said, lowering her little blue watering can.

David joined her and Tricia spoke again. "I know absolutely nothing about flowers. What kind are they?"

"Fuchsias. They are pretty, aren't they? But they're a pain in the butt to keep alive when it gets hot," the woman said, and laughed. "My daughter gave them to me for Mother's Day. If I forget to water them for just a day, they start to wilt and I have to cajole them back to life."

"Do you think talking to plants really helps?" David asked.

"Of course it does. A kind voice is soothing to all plants and animals. Wouldn't you agree?" the older woman asked Tricia.

"Absolutely. Hi, I'm Tricia and this is my friend David. We're on our morning constitutional and thought we'd take a different route this morning."

The old woman nodded. "Lots of people have walked or driven by since—" She nodded in the direction of the mansion, which at one point must have had acreage around it, but was now wedged in a residential neighborhood.

"It's a shame," Tricia said. "And this is such a quiet neighborhood."

"I hope it stays quiet. With so many businesses going into that old house, it'll be as busy as Main Street around here. Did you know that the entire green space behind the house will be a parking lot?" She shook her head. "All that asphalt is going to mess with the street's drainage. Most likely the people on Maple Avenue will be flooded out every time it rains."

"I'm sure the new owner must have taken that into account. I mean, wouldn't that be part of the zoning regulations?"

"There've been offices in there before. It's probably grandfathered in. I'm just glad my home is on *this* side of the street."

Tricia's gaze traveled to the home's front door, which had a video doorbell attached to its right side. Had it recorded the time Sanjay's truck arrived at the mansion—or perhaps whom he'd met there? Chief McDonald surely had looked at whatever footage had been captured. But it wouldn't hurt to ask. Now to figure out how.

"Has there been any trouble on the street—other than that poor man's death—since the construction began?" Tricia asked.

"Just noise." The woman looked across the street and frowned. "They usually start work before this. I wonder if they're just going to give up."

Tricia hoped not. Angelica had too much riding on the work's completion by the end of the month.

"I don't suppose you saw anything out of the ordinary on Sunday night."

"No, but my camera did," the woman said, and jerked a thumb over her shoulder toward the door.

Aha! Problem solved.

"Really?" David said, all innocence.

"It picked up the dead man's truck pulling into the driveway about midnight, but nothing else of interest."

"Wow," David said.

That meant that whoever had killed Sanjay was either already at the house or arrived on foot, and possibly through the back of the property. Tricia had no doubt McDonald and his force had already canvassed the neighborhood to find out.

Tricia looked back at the hanging pink flowers amid the green foliage. "They sure are pretty. Do you know where I can get a couple of pots of these fuchsias?"

"Sure. The greenhouse section at the big hardware store on the highway. Well, it's getting kind of late in the month. But they might still have some."

"I think I'll drive over there later today and have a look. Thanks for the tip. And thanks for speaking with us."

"Have a nice day," the old woman said, and turned back to her watering. Tricia walked over to the sidewalk and headed east once again.

"Gee, you handled that well," David muttered under his breath.

"Practice makes perfect," Tricia said, but there was no triumph in her voice. She didn't see this kind of information gathering as a game.

"Why aren't you going to talk to other neighbors?"

"It would look suspicious. Besides, the police will have already spoken to everyone. It's part of their job." She glanced at her watch as she walked.

"You don't have to open your store for another ninety minutes," David commented.

"I do have other chores to attend to—and you've got to open the Chamber office."

"Oh, yeah. I almost forgot about that."

"Well, don't forget about it. If Angelica hears that we've been snooping around—"

"There'll be hell to pay?"

"Hell hath no fury like Angelica on the warpath," Tricia warned him.

"Then we'll just have to keep a low profile. Speaking of which, what are you doing for lunch today?"

"Do you call that keeping a low profile?"

"I'm lonely." Was he?

"As it happens, and as I mentioned yesterday, I have a standing lunch date with my former store manager on Thursdays."

"You must be good friends."

"She's like a niece to me," Tricia said, when in fact, Ginny *was* her niece by marriage.

"She must be pretty special to you."

"She is. And her whole family, too."

"Then will I see you tonight?"

"What for?"

"To brainstorm about Sanjay's murder . . . among other things."

"What other things?"

"Do I need to make a list?" he asked.

Again Tricia sighed. "No."

They approached Main Street. "I guess this is where I peel off," David said.

"I'll see you later."

He smiled and pointed an index finger at her. "And I take that as a promise," he said, and pivoted, breaking into a jog.

Tricia let out a breath and shook her head. She was letting this kid get under her skin.

*Better that than your heart.*

# TWELVE

**It wasn't** often that Tricia turned off her phone, but as this was Ginny's last lunch at home, she didn't want anyone to interrupt their celebration.

Tricia parked her car near the home's back door, got out, and jostled with the brown paper bags of food she'd only minutes before picked up at Booked for Lunch, as well as the container of cookies she'd baked earlier that day. She'd asked the short-order cook, Tommy, to make something fabulous—and a surprise—for her and Ginny's last lunch at the Barbero home before Ginny returned to the Nigela Ricita Associates workforce the following Monday.

The door to the house was open, with just the screen door in between her and the home's utility room. "Ginny!"

"Coming," came a voice from farther inside the house. In seconds, Ginny appeared with baby Will slung over her diaper-covered shoulder. "I was just burping this little guy. When I'm done, I can put him down for a nap. Let me help you with at least one of those bags."

"I've got them," Tricia assured her.

Once inside the kitchen, Tricia set the bags on the counter. "Could you keep an eye on Sofia while I get Will settled?"

"Sure thing."

"Hi," Sofia greeted her great-aunt. She sat at a little white table in the kitchen's corner, playing with blocks.

"Hello, little one. What are you making?"

"A pwincess castle." Sofia was dressed in a Cinderella blue dress, pink slippers (they didn't make glass ones for toddlers), and a plastic tiara with faux gems adorning her tawny curls. She looked absolutely adorable.

Tricia unpacked the cardboard cartons of food, setting them on the counter. After visiting Ginny every Thursday for the past two months, she knew just where to retrieve the plates and cutlery for their meal.

In no time, Ginny returned. She looked relaxed in her drab gray sweatpants and a tank top that perfectly matched her daughter's costume. "What have we got today?" she asked.

"It's a surprise."

"Oh, come on," Ginny chided her.

"No, really. I have no idea what Tommy made. I asked him to surprise me. It sure smells good."

"Well, let's open one of the cartons and find out. I'm starved!"

"I'm stouved, too, Mama," Sofia said, turning in her seat.

"You can do the honors," Tricia said, handing Ginny a serving spoon.

Ginny opened the carton's lid and squealed with delight. "It's his famous homemade mushroom tortellini. He doesn't normally serve it, does he?"

"No. It's time-consuming, so Angelica only has him make it for our family dinners."

Ginny opened another bag, which held a fresh loaf of Italian bread; the other carton held undressed salad greens. "Oh, boy. This is a feast. And it just so happens I've got a bottle of white wine chilling in the fridge."

Tricia laughed. "Better than a picnic."

"I'll say." Ginny noticed the container on the counter. "And cookies, too!" she cried joyfully.

While Tricia laid the plates and placed the flatware beside them, Ginny retrieved the wine, glasses, a cutting board, and a serrated knife. "There's butter in the fridge," she told Tricia, who easily found it hiding under a glass dish.

Tricia took over cutting the bread while Ginny got Sofia settled in her high chair.

"Hello," came a male voice from the vicinity of the utility room, and seconds later Antonio entered the kitchen. "*Amore mio,*" he called to his wife as he approached, and gave her a quick kiss on the lips. "Darling, Tricia. So good to see you."

Tricia never got over how much she enjoyed hearing her nephew's soft Italian accent.

"I apologize for not answering your text this morning. I've had my secretary phoning Stark Construction every half hour and still have not been able to speak with anyone."

"That's too bad."

"Mama is not pleased."

She wouldn't be.

"Ah, what have we here?" Antonio asked, looking at the cartons on the counter and sounding intrigued.

Ginny gave him a fishy glance. "You know perfectly well that Tricia has been bringing me lunch every Thursday since I went out on maternity leave."

Antonio feigned innocence. "Really?"

"Yes, really."

"Don't worry," Tricia said, and stepped over to the cupboard to retrieve another plate. "Tommy always makes enough for leftovers."

"Which has saved us from eating mac and cheese on more than one occasion," Ginny said, and laughed.

"I like mac and cheese," Sofia opined.

Ginny grimaced. "I think Sofia would eat it for every meal if I let her." Instead, she took out a peanut butter and jelly sandwich she'd made earlier for her daughter's lunch. Sofia was over the moon.

Once she was set, the adults sat down at the island and started serving themselves.

"What brings you home for lunch?" Ginny asked her husband.

"I may have heard about the tortellini from *mia madre*," he explained. "Is better than a PBJ."

"And how," Ginny agreed.

"I had an ulterior motive as well," Antonio said, doling a portion of salad onto his plate as Ginny jumped up to fetch a couple of bottles of salad dressing from the refrigerator.

"And what was that?" Tricia asked.

"I knew you would be interested to hear about"—he paused and glanced toward his daughter—"the unfortunate happenings at the mansion the other day."

That she would.

"I did not think it would be wise to speak of such things at our family dinner on Sunday. They always upset dear Mr. Everett."

Yes, they did.

"Where would you like me to start?" Antonio asked as he poured wine for the three of them.

"How well did you know Sanjay Arya?"

"Enough to converse freely about the work at hand. We did not speak much of personal things. We were not friends." Which wasn't surprising. "He seemed a very efficient person. The repairs on the mansion were on time and on budget. You cannot ask more of a contracting firm."

"What happens now that he's no longer managing the project?" Tricia asked.

"I'm worried that on my first day back on the job I'll be calling looking for temporary office space when I'd much rather jump back into real work," Ginny groused. She stabbed a tortellini, shoved it into her mouth, and chewed. The taste brought back her usual sunny grin. Tricia had a bite and experienced the same reaction.

"Have you spoken to Jim Stark about a revised schedule?" Tricia asked.

"As I said, I have not been able to contact him—or anyone in his office," Antonio said, sampling the wine. "Yesterday his receptionist told me he will return my calls, but so far it hasn't happened. Today no one picked up."

"That seems weird," Ginny commented. "NR Associates is paying him a lot of money to get that project finished on schedule."

"I assume there are penalties if the work isn't completed on time," Tricia remarked.

"But of course. Angelica drives a hard bargain," Antonio said with a hint of a smile.

"She can't blame Jim's company while knowing his project manager was killed," Tricia said.

"That is true. But she may ask for other concessions. We will have to discuss it further."

Angelica was known for treating her employees and vendors well. Surely she would be reasonable about this situation, too.

"Angelica mentioned that Patti Perkins was writing Sanjay's obituary for the *Stoneham Weekly News*. Do you have any idea what it'll say?" Tricia asked Antonio.

"Now that my role at the newspaper has diminished, it is Patti's call for most of what is in each issue. She's doing a very good job, too."

Tricia had no doubt all along that would be the case.

"Why don't you give her a call and ask," Antonio suggested.

Tricia's eyes widened. Angelica might want her to keep her nose out of this business, but Antonio seemed to be actively encouraging her.

"Of course, by the time it sees print next Friday, it'll be old news," Ginny remarked.

Maybe. But Patti might have some information Tricia hadn't yet come across. She thought she might make a side trip to the village's fish wrapper before returning to Haven't Got a Clue.

They finished their lunches and Ginny broke open the cookie container. "Multicolored jimmies," she said, practically squealing with delight, and handed the first one to Sofia, who squealed in kind.

"I made them just for you," Tricia said. And Mr. Everett and Pixie and anyone else who walked through Haven't Got a Clue's door. But little Sofia didn't have to know that. She ate her cookie with great gusto and didn't turn down a second one.

**Upon parking** her car in the municipal parking lot, Tricia wasted no time in hurrying to the *Stoneham Weekly News*.

Though it had been only a few weeks since she'd visited the village newspaper, the office had undergone a complete transformation. The pea green walls were now a soft peach. The shabby furniture had been replaced, and new computers sat at each station. Framed copies of past issues graced the walls. Best of all, the three women who ran the paper had smiles on their faces.

"Hey, Tricia," Patti greeted. "What do you think of our updated digs?"

"The place looks beautiful."

"It's a pleasure to come to work," Ginger said. "And we got to pick the colors."

"Then I take it you're all enjoying working for Nigela Ricita Associates."

"You bet."

"Have you met Kara? She's our new part-time employee and works with customers on the ads and cold calls potential clients, while Ginger is now our graphic designer," Patti said.

"Very nice to meet you, Kara," Tricia said.

"And you," the young woman answered.

"Well, what brings you in today?" Patti asked Tricia.

"Antonio said you were working on Sanjay Arya's obituary."

Patti's smile faded. "Obits can be seen as the worst part of the job, but I like to think it might be a person's last opportunity to shine."

"And did Sanjay have a lot to shine about?" Tricia asked.

Patti looked just a little uncomfortable. She sighed. "Why don't we go into my office and talk."

Tricia's eyes widened, but Patti gestured for her to enter the small room and closed the door behind them.

Like the outer office, the new office had also undergone a similar transformation. The walls featured front pages—probably facsimiles—of famous headlines from the past. The *Titanic* disaster, Kennedy's assassination, and the Twin Towers falling. They were a sobering reminder of how important a free press is.

Patti sat behind her desk and indicated Tricia should sit in the chair before her.

"So, what can I tell you about Sanjay Arya?"

It turned out Tricia already knew most of what Patti intended to include in his obituary.

"Have you spoken with his family?"

"They haven't returned my calls. Part of me can understand why. Of course, they want their privacy at this trying time, but we might be able to help the police with their inquiries."

Patti wasn't a trained journalist, but she'd picked up a lot during her more than eight years working at the village's only news source.

"Who have you spoken to locally?"

"His boss, Jim Stark, who had only praise for his protégé. Called his loss a terrible blow to the company. I spoke to his former landlady, who called him a model tenant. Always paid his rent on time and . . ." Patti paused.

"And?" Tricia prompted.

Patti shook her head. "I'm not about to print gossip. We're a family newspaper, after all. And I intend to send a copy of the obit to his family."

"There's something scandalous in his past?" Tricia asked innocently.

"His present," Patti said, lowering her voice, her expression coy.

"What did it involve?"

"S-e-x," Patti spelled.

Tricia hadn't thought Patti was a prude, but maybe she was wrong. "And?"

"Isn't that enough?" Patti asked, wide-eyed.

"Well, surely it was with another consenting adult."

"Adults," Patti clarified. "And not in his graduating class, if you catch my drift."

Tricia wasn't sure she did, but it was interesting nonetheless.

"Anyone I know?" Tricia asked.

Patti pursed her lips. "I don't think it would be appropriate for me to speak further on the subject."

"But . . . could one of these lovers have found out about the other? It *could* be a motive for murder."

Patti nodded sagely.

"Have you shared this information with Chief McDonald?"

"Of course. I'm a good citizen."

"And what did he say?"

"That he'd look into it."

Tricia knew better than to ask McDonald to give her information on Sanjay's lovers. But who were they? And how could she unearth that information?

Should she seek out the waitress at Bar None? Maybe. But Tricia didn't know where to find her—except at work. She knew only the woman's first name. Would Sanjay's landlady be inclined to tell her about the man's lovers? Did she know or did she just speculate? Had Sanjay brought his lovers to his home? Could the landlady describe them—or perhaps their vehicles?

It was a thread she might want to investigate.

Tricia rose from her chair. "Thanks for speaking with me, Patti. I'll look forward to next week's edition to read the full obituary."

"It's always good to see you, Tricia. You've been a good friend to the staff here at the *Stoneham Weekly News*—especially when we couldn't count on anyone else."

It was a stinging reminder that Patti's first boss had treated his workers with disdain—and their second boss had only just met them when he'd suddenly passed away. Antonio had guided the paper for only a couple of weeks before he left the women to carry on by themselves, and it looked like they were doing just fine without male intervention.

"You flatter me," Tricia said, but she was pleased nonetheless.

"Just speaking the truth. Don't hesitate to visit at any time," Patti said with what sounded like sincerity.

Maybe Tricia was jaded, but whenever anyone initiated an invitation of that sort, she found it was soon rescinded. She hoped this one wouldn't suffer that fate.

"I'd better get back to work," Tricia said.

Patti rose and walked Tricia through her office door to the paper's exit.

"See you soon," Tricia said.

"Bye," the three women chorused as the door closed behind her.

Tricia walked to the corner, looked both ways, and crossed the street, heading for Haven't Got a Clue, wondering what she would do with the information she'd just learned—and if she should share it.

# THIRTEEN

**It was** after four when Tricia returned to Haven't Got a Clue. Mr. Everett was attacking the shelves with his lamb's wool duster, while Pixie stood behind the glass display case/register and greeted her with a blue Post-it note attached to her right index finger. "Message for you to call Ms. Becca Chandler. She wants to have lunch with you tomorrow."

"Did she actually add the Ms. to the message?"

"No, I'm just being polite," Pixie said matter-of-factly, but Tricia sensed there was more to the story.

"And?" she prompted.

Pixie sighed. "She was adamant that I give you the message the absolute moment you walked through the door and to make sure you called her immediately. She's a *very* busy woman."

"And we aren't?" Tricia asked, a little annoyed.

"Apparently."

"Then I guess I'd better call her."

"Why didn't she just call you on your cell phone?" Pixie asked.

"Um . . . oops. I seem to have turned it off."

Pixie smiled and nodded. "Good decision."

"Did I miss anything important while I was gone?"

Pixie shrugged. "We had a few good customers. You'll probably need to take another trip to the bank."

"It's a hardship, but I think I'm woman enough to handle it. Unless you want to go."

Pixie shrugged. "I don't mind."

In fact, upon reflection, Tricia thought she'd prefer Pixie run the errand. She didn't want to take the chance of running into Toni Bennett once again. "Okay. You get the deposit ready and I'll call Becca. Oh, and you can just head for home after going to the bank."

Pixie grinned. "Great. I'm going to make a special dinner for Fred tonight. I've gotta cut up a lot of vegetables. That's the worst part. This way I can have most of it done before he comes home." She emptied the till of all but a few bills and the change, and headed for the basement office to get the bank bag and deposit slip. Meanwhile, Mr. Everett continued to dust and Tricia picked up the heavy receiver on the store's vintage phone and dialed Becca's number. She answered on the second ring.

"About time you got back to me," Becca complained.

"I didn't know a possible lunch tomorrow would be an emergency," Tricia said.

"Are you available?" From her tone, it seemed Becca expected Tricia to drop everything to *be* available.

"Yes. What's your plan?"

"A picnic," Becca said excitedly. "I'm having it catered by the Brookview Inn."

"And where will this picnic take place?" Tricia asked.

"It's a surprise."

As Becca now owned half the available land around Stoneham and the zoning board had turned down her request to build on the main drag, it stood to reason she'd picked an alternate spot for her tennis venue.

"I can hardly wait," Tricia said, feigning enthusiasm.

"Good. I'll pick you up at your store at one o'clock *sharp*."

"I'll be ready," Tricia promised.

"Great. See you then." Becca didn't wait for Tricia to answer and hung up.

Tricia replaced the receiver on its hook just as Pixie returned. "I'm having lunch with Becca tomorrow. She's picking me up at one o'clock. On. The. Dot."

Pixie laughed. "I'll be sure to be here to hold the fort."

"Thank you."

Pixie grabbed her purse from behind the cash desk and headed for the door. "See you tomorrow," she called.

"Bye."

No sooner was she gone when the store's phone rang. Tricia picked up the receiver once again. "Haven't Got a Clue. This is—"

"Tricia," David said. "I've been trying to reach you all afternoon. Did you lose your phone?"

"No, I turned it off."

"Why would you do that?" He sounded genuinely puzzled.

"So no one could bother me."

"Am *I* bothering you?"

"Not yet, but there's still time."

Silence greeted that remark.

"It was a joke," she said.

"Oh. I was calling to make sure we're still getting together tonight. I want to talk about what we've learned about Sanjay's death today."

"I thought I was going to take you to the grocery store."

"No need now. I got a couple of loaves of day-old bread at the Patisserie. It was half-price. I'm set for a few days."

Stale bread was good for a number of things: croutons, stuffing, French and regular toast. Would he use it for sandwiches? She didn't ask. And what could he have possibly found out about Sanjay's death that she didn't already know?

Tricia bit her lip, considering his proposal. "Can do. Where do you want to meet?"

"How about my place?" David suggested.

The optics of that wouldn't look good. Nor would it look ideal if he came to her home. Tricia turned and lowered her voice so that Mr. Everett couldn't hear. "I'd prefer a public place."

"Why? Do you think I'm liable to attack you or something?"

"No. But, technically, as one of the Chamber presidents, I *am* your boss."

"I still don't see the problem."

*That's because you're so terribly young.* Or did she mean just inexperienced in the ways of the world?

"The Dog-Eared Page?" he suggested.

After two martinis with her sister, Tricia really didn't want to imbibe another drink. "I don't think so. People might get the wrong idea."

"Then how about we just go to the Chamber office?" he proposed.

Then, to passersby, it would look like they were just working late instead of . . . what? They weren't fooling around. They were playing detective—only no one had to know that.

"That sounds good."

"What time?" he asked.

"Seven thirtyish?"

"I'll be there. See you then."

Tricia said good-bye and hung up the phone, turned, and found Mr. Everett standing before her.

"Going on a date?" he asked neutrally.

"Uh—uh," she stammered. It was highly unusual that Mr. Everett would ask such a question. "No. David Price wants me to advise him on a project I want him to take over at the Chamber," she fibbed.

Mr. Everett nodded. "Such a hardworking young man. And taking on a task on his own time—that's initiative for you."

"He's certainly ambitious," Tricia agreed.

"They say young people today are apathetic workers, but young David seems to be an aberration."

His words make her feel as though she and David were sneaking around. If she was honest, they were, but not for the reasons most would think.

Mr. Everett sighed. "I'd best shake out this duster and put it away for the day," he said.

Tricia nodded and watched as the older man headed for the back of the store, then she turned and glanced out the window. The only people visible were an older couple who ambled along the sidewalk on the opposite side of the street. She watched until they paused in front of the Dog-Eared Page to consult its posted menu before entering the pub.

Suddenly she wished she'd agreed to meet David at the bar. Was she getting a little bored spending all her evenings with her sister? Had she limited her life these past few years and kept others out of it? If she hadn't spent so much time with Angelica would she have married Marshall Cambridge and settled into a quiet life?

No, she decided, it was just as well she hadn't. He'd lied to her— for his own self-preservation—about nearly every aspect of his life. That he'd kept up the deception with so many people for so long was rather astounding. That *she'd* had no clue was unnerving.

Tricia shook herself to clear her mind of unsettling thoughts and then she and Mr. Everett went through their daily end-of-day ritual of vacuuming and mug washing.

Finally, it was time to shutter the store for the evening. "Have a good day off," Tricia told Mr. Everett.

"Oh, I will. Grace has convinced me that we need to establish a weekly date day and we decided Fridays would be it. Tomorrow is our first."

"That sounds lovely. How will you celebrate it?"

"I shall take her to the Brookview Inn for lunch and spoil her," he said, his blue eyes practically twinkling.

"I hope you have a wonderful time. And may it be the first of years and years of celebrations."

"Thank you, Ms. Miles. I hope one day you'll find someone to give you the same kind of joy Grace has given me."

Warm happiness coursed through Tricia. "Thank you."

"Well, I'd best be on my way. I wouldn't want Grace to worry about me."

"See you on Saturday," Tricia called as Mr. Everett passed through the door and it closed behind him.

It had been more than twenty-four hours since Toni Bennett had confronted Tricia in front of the bank. If she'd spoken to Angelica, surely Tricia would have heard about it by now. That meant either Toni was bluffing, or she just hadn't yet had a chance to speak with the older Miles sister.

After the tongue-lashing she'd received the previous evening, Tricia decided she'd better get moving and head for Angelica's place.

June had left for the day and Tricia unlocked the Cookery and headed for the stairs that led to Angelica's living quarters above. It never ceased to please her to hear Sarge's joyful barking at her arrival. Once inside, she rewarded him with three biscuits, which thrilled the dog and annoyed his owner.

Angelica furiously stirred the concoction in the sweating pitcher. "Stop overfeeding my dog. He'll be as fat as a—"

"Now, now," Tricia warned. "Fat shaming is just not allowed in this house."

"It's *my* house," Angelica pointed out.

"And you know just how hurtful such comments can be."

Angelica frowned. "He's a dog."

"And dogs are very perceptive."

Angelica shook her head. "Okay. You've got me there. However, there's something serious we need to talk about."

Tricia recognized that tone. "Can we at least pour the drinks first?"

Angelica scowled but complied. Tricia could tell by her posture—and the fact that her sister didn't suggest they retreat to the balcony or living room—that Angelica was about to pull some kind of guilt trip. And Tricia had a pretty good idea of what the subject would be.

"Cheers," Tricia said, hoisting her glass.

Angelica merely glared at her.

Tricia took a healthy swig of her martini.

"I heard from Toni Bennett this afternoon," Angelica began, not looking at all pleased.

"And?" Tricia inquired cautiously. She'd been dreading this moment.

"She said David has been going around asking prying questions of not only her, but other Chamber members and that you refuse to rein him in."

"I did have a brief conversation with her yesterday and I assure you—"

"You're covering for that boy."

Tricia frowned. "He's hardly a boy. And what he does on his own time—"

"Reflects on the Chamber—especially if he's being obnoxious."

"I can't imagine him acting that way."

"Well, I can."

"Angelica!"

"We've talked about this and you agreed to get him to stop his Sherlock Holmes impersonation."

The sisters seldom argued, but it looked like this time they weren't going to agree on anything.

Tricia tried again. "I did speak to him. Whether he listens . . ." She let the sentence hang. She wasn't about to confess her complicity. Instead, Tricia needed to change the subject, and fast.

"Just before he left this evening, Mr. Everett told me he and Grace are going to the Brookview Inn tomorrow for lunch. It's their inaugural celebration of a weekly date day."

"Date day? How sweet," Angelica said, her sour expression lightening in an instant.

"I was wondering if you could pull some strings to make their first-ever date day truly memorable."

"Like what?"

"I don't know, a special flower arrangement on a reserved table overlooking the brook. Maybe have Chef Keenan make something special for them. Send champagne to the table."

"Mr. Everett doesn't drink," Angelica pointed out.

"Grace does," Tricia countered. "How about a decadent dessert? Candy?"

Angelica frowned. "Let me think about it. Did they make a reservation?"

"I don't know. He didn't say."

"Hmm . . ." Angelica looked thoughtful, and Tricia knew she'd been successful in diverting her sister from their previous conversation. "Yeah, let me think about it," she reiterated.

"There's something else I wanted to mention to you," Tricia said. "On my walk this morning, I met a woman who lives across the street from the Morrison Mansion. Is it true the entire backyard will be converted into an asphalt jungle?"

"That's the plan. Why?"

"It seems a shame, that's all. I mean, the building isn't going to be restored to its former glory—and neither is the garden."

"What do you know about gardening?" Angelica asked.

"Nothing. But I like looking at them. It might be something nice for Ginny and her marketing team to look at while they're coming up with new plans to promote NR Associates. And there's plenty of street parking."

"Expanding the lot was a decision made to appease the neighbors who objected to said on-street parking," Angelica said bluntly.

Tricia nodded. "Just how many people will be working in the building?"

"At least ten, maybe more. And they'll all have cars. We have to accommodate their clients, as well."

"Could you give your employees some kind of incentive to walk to work?"

"That wouldn't work in the winter."

"I suppose you're right," Tricia admitted, feeling defeated.

"But I like your idea," Angelica said thoughtfully. "I'm sure Ginny and the others *would* prefer to look out on a beautiful garden instead of a parking lot."

"Put a picnic table out there and they could have lunch—and even meetings in the yard in good weather."

Angelica looked thoughtful. "Hmm. I'll see what I can do."

Tricia allowed herself a smile. If Angelica said she'd think about it, she would. In fact, it was already almost a done deal.

Tricia changed the subject. "So, what's for supper?"

"Spaghetti. Unfortunately, it's only store-bought sauce. You know,

I've missed cooking from scratch so much, but these days I'm so busy . . ."

Tricia let her sister wax on about her hunger for meaningful food prep. As long as she was on that tangent, Tricia was prepared to listen.

Before Tricia knew it, dinner was over and they were clearing away the plates and loading the dishwasher. Tricia made a big deal out of checking her watch. "My goodness, is that the time? I've got so much paperwork to catch up with tonight. I simply must fly."

"Have a good evening," Angelica said sweetly, but then her expression turned hard. "And don't forget what I said about encouraging David Price."

"Me? Encourage him?"

Angelica's glare was penetrating. "Yes."


**The sun** still had a ways to go before it dipped below the horizon, but the west side of Main Street was deep in shadows as Tricia walked toward the Chamber's temporary headquarters. The lights were on and David sat at his desk, his computer glowing.

"Hey, there," he called as she entered.

"Hey, yourself."

David placed his elbows on the desk, resting his head on his clenched fists. "What have you got for me?"

Tricia took a seat that had been provided for visitors. "Before we get into any of that, I think we should talk about your investigative procedures."

"Why?"

"It seems your speaking with Ms. Bennett at the Antiques Emporium struck a rather unpleasant chord. Not only did she berate me outside the bank yesterday, but she spoke to Angelica this afternoon and got her all riled up, too."

"So, what does the erstwhile Mrs. Stark have to hide?" David asked.

"I'm wondering the same thing."

David nodded. "So, how do we get her to confide in us?"

"We don't. We get someone who knows her—and what her beef is—to spill the beans."

"Who would that be?"

"I'll have to think about it. Maybe poke around a little bit."

"Why can't I do that?" David asked, sounding just a bit like a petulant kid.

"Because according to Toni, you're about as subtle as an elephant in a tearoom."

David frowned. "I just need a little more practice—and how am I going to get it if I don't talk to people."

*Maybe observe a master,* Tricia thought. Of course, she was too modest to say it out loud.

"Now, what was it you wanted to talk to me about?" Tricia said, and got up, moving to sit behind her desk when the door opened. She cringed as Dan Reed entered. Dan owned the Bookshelf Diner, formerly with his wife, who was now sitting in a cell awaiting trial for murder. Because of her incarceration, the diner had lost its short-order cook and Dan had lost whatever affection Nadine had had for him—which had not been much the last time Tricia had spoken to her.

David stood. "Excuse me, sir, but we're closed."

"The lights are on, and the door was unlocked—how can you say you're closed?" Dan demanded.

David pointed to the temporary sign they'd taped to the door giving the Chamber's expanded summer hours—hours when he was available to run the office.

"I'm here, so you may as well talk to me."

David sighed. "How can I help you, sir," he said, sounding infinitely patient.

Dan's gaze zeroed in on the dragon pin attached to David's shirt and he seemed to rear back, looking offended. "Who are *you*?"

"I'm the summer intern." David offered his hand. "David Price."

This time Dan took an actual step back, not accepting the offering. Instead, he turned his gaze on Tricia. "What's it take to get some service around here?"

"David just offered to help you," Tricia said.

"I don't need help from a snot-nosed kid—"

"I'm hardly a kid," David defended himself.

"What is it you want, Dan?" Tricia asked pointedly.

"I wanted to report that the Brookview Inn has been hiring illegal aliens."

"Little men from Mars?" David asked under his breath.

"What did you say?" Dan snapped.

David sobered. "Nothing, sir."

"That's a pretty serious accusation, Dan. Where's your proof?" Tricia asked.

"They was all speaking Spanish in the kitchen."

Tricia scrutinized Dan's face. "When was the last time you were at the Brookview Inn?"

"Recently," he hedged.

Tricia knew for a fact that Dan never patronized the Brookview Inn because he was working at his own restaurant during the same hours of operation. And he rarely attended Chamber events—such as the monthly breakfast meetings at the inn's dining room.

"That doesn't mean they're illegally in this country—it means they're bilingual," she pointed out.

"The police won't do anything about it—I've reported it. It's up to the Chamber to clean up our village."

"Clean it how?" David asked.

"Get *rid* of those foreigners," Dan shouted.

"I happen to know that the Brookview workers are *not* illegally here in this country," Tricia said with certainty.

"How?"

"Because I personally know Antonio Barbero, the CEO of Nigela Ricita Associates, and know they vet all their employees."

"And why should I believe anything he's got to say? He's Eye-talian—probably in this country illegally, too!" Dan practically shouted.

Tricia was in no mood to spar with the man, but it looked like she wasn't going to be able to avoid it. "Unless you're a Native American, *you're* descended from immigrants. We all are," she pointed out.

But Dan wouldn't listen and started on yet another rant about Sanjay. "At least someone in the village had the good sense to take out yet another foreigner."

Tricia rose to her feet in indignation. "Dan Reed, you should be ashamed of yourself!" she chided him.

"Why?"

"That man was murdered—and he *wasn't* a foreigner. He was born in this country."

"Well, his people were foreigners and they should go back to where *they* came from."

Tricia had had enough and started moving in Dan's direction, causing him to step back. She stepped forward and he took another step back. It was almost a dance until his back was pressed against the heavy plate glass door.

"I'm sorry, Dan, but David and I have Chamber work to do—on our own time, I might add. We'll finish this conversation at some other time." She leaned against the metal bar in the center of the door, putting her weight behind it and pushing it open, forcing Dan to step onto the sidewalk before he fell.

"Talk to you later," Tricia said, immediately pulling the door closed and locking it.

"Hey, I'm not finished with you!" Dan shouted, but Tricia walked away and David followed her into the small storeroom.

"Are we just going to hide in here until he goes away?" David whispered.

"That's my plan," Tricia said.

"What's wrong with that guy?" David asked.

Tricia sighed and shook her head. "He's just full of hate and conspiracy theories. His wife is in jail for murder and not only did he not stand by her, but he's also divorcing her so he won't have to pay her attorney fees. That's just one example of his true character."

"Nice guy. You really shouldn't even bother engaging in conversation with a person like that. You're wasting your breath," David said. "And after hearing that tirade, I don't think I'll patronize his diner again."

Tricia rarely darkened the diner's door for much the same reason. They waited a full minute before Tricia peeked around the corner and saw no sign of Dan, so she moved to sit behind her desk once more. David came out to join her. "Now, what was it you wanted to tell me about?" Tricia asked.

"To be honest, I don't have anything new to tell. I didn't have time to snoop. I was busy here all day taking reservations for the upcoming breakfast meeting."

Good.

"What have you come up with?" David asked, and perched on the edge of her desk.

Tricia sighed. She may as well share what she'd most recently learned. "It seems that Sanjay was a bit of a ladies' man."

David raised an eyebrow. "Interesting. Do you know who he was running around with?"

"No, but apparently they weren't in his age group."

David looked thoughtful. "Could it be that Ms. Bennett—aka Mrs. Stark—was one of his lovers and that's why my talking to her raised her hackles?"

Tricia hadn't considered that, but it made perfect sense. "Could be."

"How can we find out?"

"*We* shouldn't do anything."

"You're not going to cut me out of this now, are you?" David asked, sounding hurt.

"We should just let Chief McDonald and his team look into this."

David frowned, looking distinctly annoyed. "Well, I'm not giving up. That is unless you forbid me to ask questions."

"You know very well I can't forbid you to do anything."

"You could fire me."

Good grief, the man had been on the job only three full days. "That's not an option."

"Because you wouldn't be able to find someone to work as cheaply as me and on such short notice," he said, looking her straight in the eye.

He was right about that.

"You're not going to let this go, are you?" Tricia asked, feeling weary.

David sighed. "I could back off . . . I suppose," he said grudgingly, tapping his fingers on the desk, quite near her own hand.

Tricia pretended not to notice. "If you insist on pursuing this, please just take it slow. There's no hurry."

"Someone *killed* Sanjay."

"But it's not likely that person will kill again," she pointed out reasonably.

"Is that what you said after Marshall Cambridge's death?"

Tricia felt her cheeks grow hot. Marshall's apparently accidental death had set off a string of killings that had shocked the area's citizens and traumatized her, as well. She could tell that David realized he'd hit a nerve with his last statement. Had he already done enough digging to discover the whole sordid story?

She stood once again. "It's been a very long day and I've got another busy one ahead of me tomorrow," she said, thinking about her lunch meeting the following afternoon with Becca Chandler. Any encounter with the former tennis star tended to raise Tricia's blood pressure.

"I'm sorry. I shouldn't have said that," David apologized.

Tricia shook her head. "You made a valid point. But suddenly, I just don't have the heart to talk about death anymore."

David stood as well. "Okay, I'll walk you home and we won't speak about Sanjay's death anymore tonight."

"Thank you."

They closed up the office, locked the door, and started south down Main Street, neither of them speaking.

As usual, traffic was practically nonexistent at that time of the evening, and they crossed the street at the light. It took only a minute more before they stood outside of Haven't Got a Clue. Tricia retrieved her keys from the pocket of her slacks, choosing the proper one.

"I'm sorry if I upset you," David said quietly.

Oh, he'd upset her, all right, but she also realized she'd probably overreacted. Not enough time had passed to heal the wounds on her soul from the whole chain reaction of events that had occurred after Marshall's death and Tricia wondered if she'd ever truly get over it.

If nothing else, she had to try.

Tricia turned the key in the lock. "Good night," she said over her shoulder.

"Pleasant dreams," David said.

Tricia turned back to look at him and something inside her seemed to melt. He seemed so young, and yet when she looked into his eyes she saw an old soul. Was that assessment a way to justify the feelings she didn't want to admit owning? She wanted to say something, but the words wouldn't come—or was it that she couldn't trust what she might blurt?

She turned away.

"Good night," Tricia said again, entered her store, and closed the door behind her.

# FOURTEEN

**Tricia was** so rattled by her conversation with David that she found she couldn't concentrate enough to read her beloved vintage mysteries. She didn't want to think about murder and mayhem. Instead, she streamed a movie from her childhood while she made another batch of cookies for Pixie and her customers. The small-town antics of Pollyanna Whittier played in the background while she focused on measuring and baking and the heavenly aroma of maple syrup cookies filled the apartment—made with syrup from just down the road in Mason, New Hampshire. They were sure to be a favorite.

By the time the movie ended, the cookies had cooled and she packed them into an air-tight container. By then Tricia was tired enough to sleep. Except her dreams were riddled with the screech of tires and the nerve-shattering sounds of gunfire that awakened her more than once. Heart pounding, she'd found it hard to get back to dreamland, and as a consequence slept right through her alarm.

Hauling herself out of bed, Tricia realized she didn't have time for her usual morning walk, and after showering, dressing, and making a quick breakfast for both her and Miss Marple, she went straight down to Haven't Got a Clue to begin her workday.

Pixie arrived just before opening, cheerful as ever, but she paused to give Tricia a hard once-over. "You look like hell."

"Oh, thanks."

"No, really. Is everything all right?"

Tricia shook her head. "I just had a bad night's sleep."

Pixie glanced over to the beverage station and the plate piled with cookies. "And you must have been busy, too."

Tricia managed a laugh. "My lost sleep was your gain."

"Too bad Mr. Everett's going to miss this," Pixie said as she stowed her purse behind the counter.

"I'll bake more."

Pixie laughed. "I know you will. And I approve. My waist might not, but the rest of me does."

They enjoyed a cup of coffee and a few cookies together before Tricia ran upstairs to reassess her makeup. Pixie was with a customer when she returned and the morning quickly disappeared. Pixie went to lunch a few minutes early and was back well in time for Tricia's lunch with Becca.

David hadn't appeared.

Becca's minivan pulled up in front of Haven't Got a Clue at five minutes before one, and Tricia hightailed it out the door, giving Pixie a wave. She hopped into the passenger seat and Becca took off before she'd even fastened her seat belt.

"Hello," Tricia said.

"Yeah, yeah. Glad you could make it," Becca muttered, concentrating on her driving.

During the ride, Becca dominated the conversation, diving right in with her plans for the new tennis facility. Her attitude toward what she'd deemed misfortune only days before had done a complete one-eighty. Now that her tennis club wasn't going to be confined to a small lot on Main Street, she could expand the building to include a spa and a gift shop, which would naturally feature a new line of tennis equipment she was about to launch, as well as sportswear for men, women, and children. "Catch them while they're young and they'll be tennis enthusiasts their entire lives," she babbled. She wasn't wrong. It had worked for Tricia and Angelica. Even these days, people knew not to bother the older of the Miles sisters when Wimbledon or the French Open was being broadcast.

Becca tapped her turn signal and braked, waited for oncoming traffic, and then pulled onto a dirt road, letting the van bump its way to where a large and silent excavator was parked in the middle of a field. The van rolled to a halt and Becca shoved the gear shift into park before turning off the engine. "Well, what do you think?"

Truthfully, Tricia thought it a shame that such a beautiful meadow was going to suffer the blight of a pole barn structure. There'd be no outdoor tennis courts, not when a building could accommodate students and enthusiasts year-round.

"It's a beautiful site."

"And it'll be even more attractive once the building and landscaping are complete," Becca said with pride. "I thought about a field of cosmos. They look so pretty swaying in the breeze."

"Are you sure you shouldn't have started this endeavor in a bigger city? I mean, while Stoneham is a destination for book lovers, it's hardly a tennis mecca," Tricia remarked.

Becca grinned. "Yet! Besides, it makes sense to try the whole concept out in a smaller market. If it can sustain itself here, it'll do even better in bigger venues."

"Is that what you think—or what your marketing team thinks?" Tricia asked.

"We're all on the same page," Becca said authoritatively.

Becca's page, no doubt.

Tricia's stomach growled. Becca had promised there'd be food. Were they going to harvest some of the wildflowers and dandelion greens for their lunch?

"Hungry?" Becca asked.

"It is that time of day," Tricia said, not wanting to sound too eager.

"Hang on." Becca opened the driver's side door and got out, opened the van's side door, and rummaged behind the seat, coming up with two white cardboard boxed lunches. They'd been a staple at many of the working, lunchtime meetings Tricia had held back in the days when she'd been in charge of a large nonprofit back in Manhattan. It was hit-and-miss. Somehow, the ham or roast beef sandwiches were always grabbed before she had a chance to choose and she was left with cheese or bland tuna, with none of the crunchies Tommy at Booked for Lunch included. It was well known that Becca liked to frequent the Bookshelf Diner. Their food was okay—typical diner fare, but not as good as Booked for Lunch or anywhere else in the village.

Tricia forced a smile. "How nice."

Becca seemed to read Tricia's mind. "These are from the Brookview— *not* the Bookshelf Diner," she deadpanned, and she climbed back into the van and handed one of the boxes to Tricia. She adjusted her seat to give herself more room. Tricia did the same.

"I've got to get a picnic table out here—not just for myself, but for the construction workers. A happy crew gets the job done faster." She opened her box and looked inside. "Speaking of which, have you heard anything about the Sanjay Arya murder?" Becca asked, her voice just a little higher than normal.

"I didn't think you'd be interested," Tricia said, and opened her own boxed lunch. Roast beef on seeded rye. Yum! A small container of horseradish was nestled beside it. What looked like two chocolate chip cookies were wrapped in cellophane and tied with a yellow ribbon. The Brookview knew how to make any meal special.

"Oh, I'm *always* interested in what goes on in the village. As a businesswoman, I'd be a fool not to be."

"Well, yes and no," Tricia answered, and looked for a knife to spread the horseradish onto her bread.

"The yes part?" Becca prodded.

"He was killed with his own hammer."

Becca shuddered. "That's terrible." She set her boxed lunch on the console and actually seemed shaken by the information.

Having found the plastic knife, Tricia unwrapped her sandwich and liberally spread the bread with the horseradish.

Becca eyed her. "Laying it on a little thick, aren't you?"

"I love horseradish. Clears your sinuses." She took a bite of her sandwich and coughed, tears filling her eyes. She chewed and swallowed. "Now, that's a great sandwich," she whispered hoarsely.

Becca handed her a sweating water bottle. "You're welcome."

"Thanks."

Becca looked out the driver's side window for long seconds before she picked up her boxed lunch once again. She unwrapped her sandwich, which appeared to be ham and cheese. "Do you know any of the Board of Selectmen members?"

"Personally?"

Becca nodded.

"I guess so. Not that we're buddies or anything. Why?"

"Because I have it on good authority that it was one of them who blackballed my tennis club being built on Main Street."

"I thought it was a zoning decision."

Becca shook her head.

"Who was the good authority who tipped you off? And if they're so good, why didn't they just flat out tell you who was against your club?"

"They had their reasons," Becca said, although she didn't sound at all convinced. "But if I know you, you could find out."

Tricia didn't want to confirm or deny that statement.

"Am I right?" Becca pushed.

Tricia bit into her sandwich again. This time, her cough attack wasn't sincere, but she figured it might help to change the subject.

"Do you need the Heimlich maneuver or something?" Becca asked.

Tricia shook her head and uncapped her bottle of water, taking a healthy sip.

Becca bit into her sandwich. They ate in silence for a long minute before Becca spoke again.

"Honestly, I should probably thank the person who black-balled me."

"Why's that?"

"Because ultimately, this *is* a better location. There'll be windows everywhere but the tennis courts."

The view *was* spectacular. Tricia could see where it would be a distraction for those playing tennis or taking a lesson.

Becca sighed. "I'm only sorry that . . ." But then she didn't finish the sentence.

Had she been going to mention Eugene/Marshall? Tricia didn't want to talk—or even think—about him.

"So, what are you going to do with the lot on Main Street?"

"I haven't decided yet."

"Have you considered selling it?"

"Not on your life. Main Street real estate is worth its location in gold."

Tricia was afraid she might say that. But it gave her something else to mention to Angelica that evening during happy hour.

On the way back to Stoneham, Becca yammered on and on about her plans for her tennis club empire. Tricia only half listened, wondering if she ought to pursue finding out who the person on the Board of Selectmen was who'd tried so hard—and succeeded—to keep Becca from opening her new business on Main Street. And she knew just who to ask. Too bad she'd have to wait until the next day to do it.

**It was** after three when Tricia arrived back at Haven't Got a Clue and was pleased to see that a Granite State tour bus had arrived during her absence. Still, between customers, she had all afternoon to ponder Becca's problem . . . except, it really wasn't a problem anymore since moving the location of the new tennis facility would be an improvement on all levels. But it bothered her that Becca had been blackballed by the village's governing body and possibly just one person was behind it.

It was nearing closing time when the foot traffic slowed to a halt.

"We haven't had time to think, let alone talk," Pixie said as she came back from the washroom after tidying up the beverage station and washing the employee mugs.

"Anything interesting happen while I was at lunch?" Tricia asked.

"Your little friend David Price dropped by."

"To see me?"

Pixie shook her head. "Nope. He wanted to horn in on my Sunday thrifting."

"I'm sorry. When he mentioned that going to tag and estate sales was a hobby, I naturally thought of you. I'm sorry that I—"

"Don't be sorry. Fred's already planned to change the faucet in our bathroom on Sunday and he doesn't want me hanging around to give him advice. Besides, I felt sorry for the kid not having a car. I figure if he needs to go to the grocery store, I can give him a lift there, too."

"Thanks for your kindness."

Pixie waved a hand in dismissal. "Eh, it ain't kindness. I been in the same situation and figured I'd cut the kid some slack."

"Thanks again," Tricia said.

"Uh, he was here for at least fifteen minutes shootin' the breeze and asked a lotta questions about you."

Tricia blinked in surprise. "Me? What kind of questions?"

Pixie shrugged. "What's your background, where were you born, when's your birthday?"

"And you answered them?" Tricia asked, raising an eyebrow.

"I told him he should ask you. But I did throw him a few tidbits of info," Pixie admitted.

"Such as?"

"How good you are to me and Mr. E. How much fun it is to work here. That kinda stuff."

Tricia heaved a sigh of relief but then wondered why she felt so inclined. "It's very nice of you to speak so well of me."

Pixie giggled. "Don't you sound fancy-schmancy?"

Tricia smiled. "I can pull it off when I have to."

They both laughed, but then Pixie became practical. "Do you want me to vacuum or dust before I head out for the weekend?"

"No, Mr. Everett enjoys it. We'll save it for him to do tomorrow."

"Righto." Pixie glanced at the clock. "Okay, I'm going to hit the trail. If I find anything worth getting at the weekend sales, I'll see you on Sunday afternoon—otherwise, first thing Monday morning."

"Have a great weekend!"

Pixie waved as she headed out the door.

Miss Marple jumped up on the sales counter and said, "*Yow!*"

"Yes, you can have a treat before I leave for Angelica's." Tricia sprinkled a few crunchy bits into the cat's snack bowl before grabbing her keys and locking up.

As usual, Sarge was ecstatic to see Tricia, and she tossed him a couple of dog biscuits before settling at the kitchen island, where Angelica was putting the finishing touches of parsley sprigs on bruschetta.

"The parsley is a bit much, isn't it?" Tricia asked.

"Food should look as good as it tastes," Angelica said.

"It does."

"Would you like to sit out on the balcony again? It was so pleasant the other night—and thank goodness I don't have to rush off to work tonight."

"Great."

Angelica pushed the platter of appetizers at Tricia. "Take these and I'll bring the drinks."

Sarge had polished off his biscuits and, tail wagging, happily followed Tricia out onto the balcony. Angelica joined them only a minute later.

"So, how did your lunch with Becca go?" Angelica asked, setting down the tray and taking her seat on one of the twin chaises.

"Not bad. Of course, she never asks me what *I'm* up to or what *I* think about anything."

"I thought that was the reason you got together," Angelica said, and poured the drinks.

"Yakking at me was the reason *she* wanted to get together. You'd think I'd know better by now."

"Well, you must have learned *something* of interest during the time you spent together."

"Becca says she isn't interested in selling her lot on Main Street."

"Of course not. I wouldn't, either. Depending on what she puts in there, it could be a gold mine."

"What would you build?"

"More retail space," Angelica said without hesitation.

Of course.

"I've been thinking . . . we ought to brainstorm with our summer intern about that," Angelica added.

"About what?"

"Recruiting more booksellers. If that's what the majority of Chamber members want, that's what we ought to do. Only I'm not looking to take on another project in that vein. Are you?"

"Not particularly. I've spent far too much of my time this week devoted to the organization," Tricia said, toying with her olive-speared frill pick.

"Oh? I thought you enjoyed spending time with your little protégé," Angelica said smugly. "You seem to spend more than just Chamber working hours with him."

Who'd spilled the beans?

Tricia waited. She knew Angelica wasn't going to leave that conversational thread hanging. "What do you mean?" she asked innocently.

"I saw the two of you last evening walking along Main Street."

Tricia thought fast. "Oh, that. We had a little conversation with Dan Reed."

"You opened the Chamber after hours for *him*?"

"No, David wanted some additional instruction," she lied. "Dan

barged in spouting more of his vitriol about the illegal aliens *you've*—
oh, pardon me—*Nigela* has working in the Brookview's kitchens."

"Those workers are *not* in the US illegally," Angelica protested.

"I know that and I told him so, but you can't reason with a man
like him—and that's precisely what David said to me. It takes all my
charm-school training not to pick up the nearest heavy object and
brain Dan—not that it would knock any sense into him."

"The thing is, he claims he heard them speaking Spanish in the
kitchen, but he never darkens the inn's doors so how would he know?"

Angelica shrugged, not at all interested in hearing about Reed.
"Dan's just an old blowhard. Let's not waste any more breath on him.
I'm more interested in what you and David were doing at the Cham-
ber last evening."

"In addition to Chamber protocol," she fibbed once more, "he
wanted to talk about Sanjay."

"Oh, not that again!" Angelica protested.

"I think I set him straight," Tricia said, and mentally crossed her
fingers. Then again, he'd come to Haven't Got a Clue that day know-
ing she wouldn't be there to pump Pixie for information about her.
Thank goodness Pixie listened to but didn't spread gossip. And if
David was smart, he'd never mention Marshall Cambridge's name in
Tricia's presence again.

"He came into the shop today to ask if he could go thrifting with
Pixie on Sunday." That, at least, was true.

"Is she going to let him?"

Tricia nodded. "I thoroughly approve. If he makes new friends,
he'll feel less dependent on us."

"You mean on *you*."

"I guess." But, if she was honest, Tricia rather liked his attention—
not that she would admit that to Angelica . . . or anyone else. Not
even David.

"How's the dinner coming?" Tricia asked, hoping the change of subject would stick.

"It'll be ready in about twenty minutes. Let me top up your glass," Angelica said, and reached for the pitcher.

Tricia picked up another piece of tomato-encrusted bread and took a bite. Perfection! And then she chose to steer the conversation toward Becca's intentions. As a potential business rival, Angelica listened intently. And Tricia was glad not to mention David Price's name again during the conversation.

# FIFTEEN

**Saturday was** Pixie's day to work at Booked for Beauty, where she had quite the following giving manicures and crafting pretty and unique acrylic nails. Mr. Everett always arrived early for work, so Tricia wasn't surprised when she came down from her apartment that Saturday morning to find that her employee and friend had arrived and already had the beverage station up and running, ready for their first shared cups of coffee of the day and for the customers who'd be coming in throughout the morning. They sat down in the reader's nook and Miss Marple immediately jumped on Mr. Everett's lap, purring happily as he stroked her long, silky fur.

"I wanted you to know what a delightful lunch Grace and I had at the Brookview Inn yesterday for our first official date day," he said.

"I'm so glad to hear that."

"They lavished a lot of attention on us, including champagne cocktails."

"Did you have one?" Tricia asked, knowing Mr. Everett seldom imbibed.

"I did have a sip or two," he admitted, albeit sheepishly. He cocked his head in Tricia's direction. "Did you arrange for the special treatment?"

"I just put a bug in someone's ear," Tricia admitted.

"Well, I appreciate the gesture, and Grace was over the moon," he said happily.

Just what Tricia had hoped. But she also had something else she wanted to discuss with her friend and employee. "You keep up with local politics, don't you?" she asked as an opening.

"It's a habit I picked up when I had my store," he admitted.

"Do you know who the current Board of Selectmen members are?"

He smiled. "These days, they're not all men."

"That's a good thing," Tricia said.

"Indeed. And yes, I know *of* them, but not personally. Why?"

She told him about Becca being forced to change the location of her tennis facility.

Mr. Everett frowned. "I would hope none of the members would be petty enough to vote against Ms. Chandler out of spite." He sighed. "But it's not unknown to happen, either." He rattled off the names of the members, some of whom Tricia had heard of, and one in particular: Toni Bennett.

Well, well, well.

Tricia had spoken to Toni on many occasions, but she couldn't be called anything but an acquaintance, and after the haranguing the woman had given Tricia days before, Tricia wasn't sure she could even count her as that. She didn't know much about Toni, either. That might need to change.

They finished their coffee just as the first of the day's customers arrived. Mr. Everett was only too happy to make some book recommendations while Tricia stationed herself behind the register, her thoughts traveling back to Toni Bennett.

At one time, Angelica's former Cookery manager, Frannie Armstrong, could be counted on to report all of the village's gossip, but she, too, was now sitting in a cell in the New Hampshire State Prison for Women after accidentally poisoning someone. Those things happened, Tricia supposed, and while she didn't miss Frannie, she did miss the espionage system the woman had fielded during her years living in Stoneham.

Donna, one of the Bank of Stoneham's tellers, could often be a good source of information. At least she had been of late, but she and Tricia knew each other only on a very casual "say hello"-upon-a-transaction kind of basis and Tricia only ever seemed to hear Donna's gossip secondhand.

And then Tricia remembered where she'd heard quite a bit of juicy gossip being swapped: Booked for Beauty, Angelica's hair-and-nail salon and day spa.

Tricia stroked the hair on the back of her head and decided she needed a trim as soon as possible.

Tricia waited until after Mr. Everett's lunch break and canceled her own with Angelica before she flew out the door and power walked up the block to Booked for Beauty, hoping they'd be able to squeeze her in.

"Tricia! It's been ages since you've been in here," Randy Ellison cried from behind the salon's reception desk. The salon manager inspected her shaggy mane and tut-tutted her.

"I know—I know. I'm just so busy what with running my own business and being Chamber co-president . . ." she began.

"And you're stunningly successful at both," Randy praised her.

"You flatter me," Tricia said.

"Not at all. Now, what can we do for you today?"

"Just a trim."

Randy's gaze traveled across the spa's open landscape. "We have an open chair. Clarice!" he called. A woman with magenta hair, dressed in the shop's uniform of black slacks, blouse, and flats, who'd been sitting in the lounge area, reading a magazine, stood at the sound of her name. "Can you please help Tricia here?"

The woman nodded and moved to one of the empty stations along the south wall.

"Clarice is one of my best stylists—we've been together for years," Randy gushed by way of an introduction. It was just the recommendation Tricia wanted to hear. Clarice was sure to know all the local gossip. Tricia just had to hope she'd be willing to spill it.

"Thanks, Randy," Tricia said, and headed to the chair where Clarice waited.

"Have a seat," the stylist said.

Tricia sat and settled her purse on the floor in front of a full-length mirror.

"Now, what can I do for you?" Clarice asked.

"I'm feeling a little shaggy. A trim should do it."

"Do you want a wash?"

"No, you can just wet it. I'll need to get back to work pretty soon."

"No problem."

With a flutter of the lightweight black cape, Clarice settled the cloth around Tricia, pulling it taut around the back of her neck.

"I don't see Pixie Poe here today," Tricia commented, looking around the salon.

"Oh, she finished her last appointment half an hour ago and headed out the door in a flash. Something about a big sale in Litchfield."

Tricia nodded. Pixie lived for the thrill of the hunt for vintage clothes, books, and anything else that tickled her fancy.

"Going anywhere nice on vacation this year?" Clarice asked as she retrieved her scissors.

"Sadly, no. I own one of the bookshops on Main Street. I can't possibly leave during the tourist season."

"Oh, yeah. You own Haven't Got a Clue, right?"

"That's right. Have you been to my store?

Clarice shook her head as she picked up a plastic spray bottle and began squirting Tricia's hair. "I don't have time to read."

"Not even just before you go to bed?" The idea of not reading before she turned off the light at the end of the day was totally foreign to Tricia.

"Nah. I hate reading. When I was in school, they made us read *the* most boring stuff. I vowed I'd never read another book again—and I haven't," Clarice bragged.

Tricia was horrified by the confession. Not reading for pleasure? What a sad life this woman must lead not to be enriched by the written word. And how many children had been turned off of reading by a curriculum that they didn't enjoy or couldn't identify with? Still, Tricia tried not to judge Clarice's pitiable existence. She had come here for a specific reason, after all.

"So, how's life treating you?" Clarice asked as she used an index finger to tilt Tricia's head up, inspecting what she had to work with.

"I'm just a little blue," Tricia admitted. "My sister and I found that poor man Sanjay Arya on Sunday at the old Morrison Mansion."

"Oh, yeah, it's been the talk of the village," Clarice whispered.

If it was, Tricia had been excluded from that clique. "Do tell," she encouraged.

"No one seems to find it odd that the young man was killed."

"He had enemies?" Tricia asked with faux surprise.

"At least one. Otherwise, he'd still be alive," Clarice said pointedly.

That wasn't a helpful observation.

"He didn't have that reputation," Tricia insisted.

"Says who? It seems Mr. Arya liked the ladies and was seen around the area with more than one."

"Anyone we know?"

"Well, I don't know her personally. She gets her hair done in Nashua—wouldn't lower herself to patronize a local business like us, which is just as well. I've heard she's a terrible tipper," she said conspiratorially. "But I'll bet she expects the locals to visit *her* shop."

"Really?"

"Oh, yeah. Not me. That place of hers sells just a whole lot of junk. And her—she struts around the village with her nose in the air. I'm surprised she doesn't fall off her Jimmy Choos."

"Just who are we talking about?" Tricia asked innocently.

Clarice bent lower and snipped the hair around Tricia's ears. "Toni Bennett—otherwise known as Mrs. James Stark. Mr. Arya's employer. You can't get saucier than that, can you?"

Tricia's eyes widened. Sanjay and Toni were lovers?

It took Tricia a moment to recover from the confirmation of that news. But then, this wasn't the first time it had been intimated that Toni stepped out on her husband. There'd been rumors three years before that Toni had had a relationship with murder victim Pete Renquist. It was said her husband was a big supporter of the Second Amendment and had an arsenal. That Stark considered his wife his property and was prepared to shoot anyone who looked sideways at her.

Tricia answered Clarice's question. "No, you certainly can't. Just . . . how did they get away with it?"

"Obviously they didn't—I mean, not if everyone's talking about it."

But who was everyone? And how accurate was this tidbit of information? And Sanjay hadn't been shot—he'd been bludgeoned to death.

Snip. Snip. Clarice had started cutting in earnest.

"Did Toni's husband know?" Tricia asked.

Snip. Snip. Snip.

"It's been said it was going on for a while, so maybe not. Everyone knows Stark works late most days of the week in that junky-looking construction trailer."

It *was* a bit of an eyesore wherever it landed within the village limits, with its faded blue paint and rust pocking the corrugated metal sheathing.

"Do you think Mr. Stark found out?"

"Isn't the spouse *always* the prime suspect in a love triangle?" Clarice asked as she squinted at Tricia's bangs and began to snip once again.

"So I've heard. But you hinted Sanjay had more than one lover."

"They say he'd been seen in Milford hanging around the bars." Which David had received corroboration on from at least one of Sanjay's co-workers. And who was the *they* she kept mentioning?

She asked.

"I *don't* gossip," Clarice replied, sounding offended.

"I'm sorry, I didn't mean to imply—"

Clarice sniffed and continued snipping. An awful lot of hair seemed to be accumulating on the floor. At this rate, Tricia wondered if she'd be as hairless as a sphynx cat.

Tricia wasn't sure how to get Clarice talking again. Asking if she'd read any good books was out. "Uh, have you lived here in Stoneham long?" she tried.

"I *live* in Litchfield. I *work* here in Stoneham," Clarice said tersely.

"But you've been in the area all your life?"

"Mostly."

"I've only been here seven years, but it feels like home to me."

"*You* have quite the reputation, too."

"Oh?" Tricia asked innocently.

"As being terribly unlucky."

Tricia supposed it was better than being called a jinx to her face.

Clarice kept snipping for long minutes. Other women were getting their hair cut, nails done, pedicures, and facials. Many voices added to the chatter. How could Tricia get Clarice talking again—even if it wasn't anything she wanted to hear? Maybe she should change the subject to something else that might be the talk of the town.

"It's too bad that the big tennis club won't be built on Main Street."

"Are you kidding? It's the best thing that could have happened," Clarice declared.

"Do you think so?"

"Of course. We need more service-oriented jobs in this village."

"Such as?"

"Higher-end restaurants wouldn't hurt. People who frequent them need to get their hair and nails done. Maybe they could get some spiffy clothes stores in, too."

Did Clarice, O hater of the written word, realize Stoneham's nickname was *Booktown*? Then again, was Tricia beginning to think like Dan Reed and his ilk, who thought the village should allow only book-related shops to set up a business?

"Would you patronize those businesses?" Tricia asked.

"Do I look like I could afford them?" Clarice said. "But the people who *can* would bring in money and jobs."

That *was* great—if they also didn't price out the people who were hired to work in such places.

Clarice picked up the blow-dryer and put an end to any more conversation, which was just as well, as Tricia felt they weren't likely to agree on much of anything.

Finally, Clarice turned off the dryer, fussed at Tricia's hair with a comb, and turned the chair so that Tricia faced the mirror. Her mouth dropped as she inspected the carnage. Her hair was short. Really short in the back. Maybe a quarter of an inch long—if that—with a long swag that had been combed from the back to droop over her forehead like a horse's forelock. She swallowed several times.

"What do you think?" Clarice asked smugly.

Tricia had asked for a trim. Looking at what was left of her hair made her feel like she'd been scalped.

"It's . . . a little daring," she said, her voice wobbling.

"And so are you," Clarice said with zeal.

Tricia felt the heat of a blush rise up her neck to stain her cheeks. Good grief! She was going to have to walk back to Haven't Got a Clue for all the village to see what she could barely stand to look at.

"I . . . I need to get back to work," she said, her voice more than a little shaky. Her legs were unsteady, as well, as she followed Clarice to the reception desk where the cash register and credit card machine resided. Clarice told her the bad news, and Tricia handed over her card. The slip cranked out of the little thermal printer and Clarice handed it and a ballpoint pen to Tricia. By the hard look on her face, Tricia felt as though the woman was daring her to skimp on a tip— just like Toni Bennett. Tricia quickly calculated 20 percent and added that to the bottom line before handing the slip back.

"Thank you," Clarice said with just a hint of triumph in her voice.

Randy rushed up to the reception desk. "Tricia, darling, you look fabulous! It's so bold of you. Isn't Clarice a genius?" he gushed.

Clarice was something, all right.

"I—I need to get back to work," Tricia said in a strangled voice, and wished it was raining so that she could cower under an umbrella on the way back to her store. If only she'd thought to wear a hat to the salon, no one would have to see the mangled mess atop her head. She thought about the mirrors scattered around her apartment and wondered what it would take to cover each and every one of them.

She stepped out of the salon and onto the sidewalk, looking right and left. Thankfully, no one she knew was in view and she practically ran south, heading for the village's only traffic light, where she could safely cross the road, fully aware that she had to pass shops and storefronts where people she knew were bound to notice her hair—or lack thereof. She didn't dare let her gaze stray from the path in front of her.

She made it all the way back to Haven't Got a Clue without meeting any familiar faces, darted into her store, and slammed the door behind her, breathing fast.

Mr. Everett stood behind the big glass display case. He glanced up at Tricia's arrival and did a double take. "Oh, my! What happened to your hair?"

"I don't want to talk about it," Tricia said. Well, wail about it, more like.

"It's . . . it's very striking," Mr. Everett said, still looking shell-shocked. His words were fine. The delivery sounded more than skeptical.

"It's horrible," Tricia said, trying not to cry.

"Is *that* what you expected?" Mr. Everett asked.

Tricia shook her head.

"Well, it *will* grow back," he said, but sort of winced as he said it and then added under his breath, "eventually." He squinted at Tricia. "Perhaps you can style it differently?" he suggested.

Tricia looked at her reflection in the door's glass panel. No. That wasn't going to work, either.

"I think I'll go up to my apartment and sulk," Tricia said.

"For what it's worth, most of the people who patronize Haven't Got a Clue are strangers. I'm sure they won't think anything of the style," Mr. Everett said, quite uncharacteristically.

Tricia tried to smile but felt sick.

As the Chamber of Commerce's co-president, she was destined to talk—face-to-face—to at least one of its members (if not more) on a daily basis.

Tricia dragged a hand through the mop of what was left of her hair and thought again about the Kentucky Derby's most recent winner. Her head was virtually a buzz cut in the back and shaggy in the front. She'd never felt defined by the hair on her head. She'd had bad cuts before, but nothing like this.

And it seemed so silly that something as trivial as this could bring her to tears.

Trivial?

No. But it wasn't the worst thing that could ever happen to her, either.

The door to the shop opened and a customer entered.

Tricia cleared her throat and stepped forward. "Welcome to Haven't Got a Clue. I'm Tricia. How can I help you?"

The man looked her straight in the eye and didn't even seem to notice her hair. "Have you got any books by Rex Stout?"

Tricia's gaze darted to Mr. Everett, who gave her a thumbs-up. "Yes. Let me show you." She led her customer to the proper shelf.

And with that, she thought she just might live after all.

# SIXTEEN

**Tricia wasn't** sure how she made it through the rest of the afternoon. Avoiding any reflective surface seemed to be her best bet. Mr. Everett finished dusting and headed out for the day with an encouraging smile and "I'll see you tomorrow."

"Good night," Tricia said, and closed the door behind him, heaving a great sigh. Now the hard part began. Showing her face—or rather her hair—to those she knew. And the first on her list was Angelica.

But first, Tricia donned a sun hat. She might have to walk only a few feet to get to the Cookery, but she wasn't yet up to facing any of her colleagues. It was best to get Angelica's reaction first.

Thankfully, no one she knew was on the sidewalk and Tricia quickly let herself in. June had already left for the day, and Tricia re-locked the door and headed for the door marked PRIVATE and the stairs up to Angelica's apartment. Sarge barked cheerfully and Tricia hung up her hat on one of the pegs that held the dog's leashes.

"Hello!" Angelica called from the kitchen. Tricia ambled over to the island and took a seat, her stomach churning. "Did you have a good day?"

"Oh, I had a day, all right," Tricia said, sidestepping the question.

"So did I. It was lunch-with-Becca day," Angelica said, her back to Tricia as she removed the chilled pitcher and martini glasses from the refrigerator.

"How did that go?"

Angelica heaved a dramatic sigh. "Tedious. If she wanted to pick my brain, she might have let me get a word in edgewise."

"She does seem to do that with everyone."

Angelica stirred the pitcher's contents. "Just being with her was so upsetting, I barely ate a bite of my quiche."

"What are we having for dinner?"

"Quiche."

"You brought it home in a doggy bag?"

"Of course, and Sarge ate it for his dinner. He loves quiche. I still wanted some," Angelica said as she took a ready-made pie from the fridge and thrust it into the oven. "It'll reheat beautifully." Finally, she looked up and started, her mouth dropping open. "Oh, Tricia! Your hair!" For a moment Angelica seemed flummoxed. "It's—it's stunning." She sounded stunned, all right.

"Yeah, I was pretty stunned when I saw what *your* Clarice had done to it."

"Clarice at Booked for Beauty?" Angelica asked.

"She's the perp," Tricia said, and not at all kindly.

"What did you ask for?" Angelica asked, looking more than a little appalled.

"A trim."

"That's not a trim," Angelica conceded.

"Tell me about it. Luckily, I've got a very big hat that will hide it until it can grow out."

"I can get you a cap from the NR Associates softball team—that is, if you don't mind promoting them until you can grow it out."

"I was thinking I might have to visit a wig shop in Nashua."

Angelica reached out and touched the bristly back of Tricia's head. "You can't even wear extensions with it that short in the back. What in the world made her do this to you?"

Tricia sighed. "We were talking about Sanjay's murder, and—"

Angelica scowled. "And of course, *you* brought it up."

"I was just trying to find out what people in the village were saying about it," she said defensively.

"And that is?"

"That Sanjay was a womanizer."

Angelica seemed taken aback. "He was?"

Tricia shrugged.

"But what's that got to do with Clarice butchering your lovely hair?" Angelica asked.

"The conversation diverged. She was saying how we needed more service-related businesses in the village, and when I asked if she'd patronize them, she seemed to take offense. And, by the way, her answer was a definite no."

Angelica shook her head. "What do you want me to do; fire her?"

"No. But I won't be patronizing your beauty salon again anytime soon."

"But that will reflect badly on me!" Angelica protested.

"No, it won't. I'm a dissatisfied customer. I won't speak out about this chop job to others, but I certainly won't patronize any place that makes *me*, their customer, feel disrespected."

Angelica scowled. "I have to tell Randy about this. If she could do this to you—the owner's sister—she might do it again to someone else whose opinion she happens to disagree with, and I can't have that."

"Do what you feel is right," Tricia said, feeling utterly defeated.

Angelica looked distinctly unhappy. "What will you do in the meantime?"

"Hide."

"You can't do that." Angelica scrutinized her sister's hair. "It might not be to your taste, but you can't deny the cut is striking."

"So is a bowling ball, but I wouldn't want to be classed as one."

"A bandanna could be your new best friend."

"Only if I was wearing Daisy Duke shorts and a halter top, and that's hardly business attire."

Angelica didn't comment and commenced pouring their drinks. Tricia assembled crackers on a plate and carried them into the living room. They settled into their usual seats. Tricia picked up her glass and chugged half its contents.

"Tricia!" Angelica admonished.

Tricia wiped her mouth with the back of her hand. "After the day I've had, I needed that. But besides that, I wonder if other villagers share Clarice's opinion on bringing in more high-end personal service businesses."

"Our constituents are Stoneham's business owners—not their help."

"The booksellers want one thing and the others want something—*anything*—else. So whom do we try to please?"

"It's a crapshoot, all right," Angelica said, and sipped her drink. "What camp are you in?"

"If I'm honest, I'd like to see more booksellers."

"And I'm with Clarice. The better experience we can deliver to a variety of tourists, the better. Let them go to the sweet shop after they've gone to all the bookshops. And let them eat or have a drink on Main Street."

"So says the owner of two restaurants and a lunch cart."

"They haven't hurt the tourist trade."

No, they hadn't.

"We'll compromise. When you speak to David on Monday—and I assume you'll go into the Chamber office then—get him started on finding new booksellers, or at least brainstorming *how* to get more of them to relocate to Stoneham."

"I can do that."

"And I'll speak to Antonio about more partnerships for Nigela Ricita Associates."

"That's not fair."

"Oh, all right then. I'll look into finding some independents to check us out. Wouldn't it be nice to have an ice cream parlor—or better yet, another Ben and Jerry's type of outfit? They've made Waterbury, Vermont, a tourist destination. Why shouldn't some other outfit have the same luck here?"

"New Hampshire has fewer cows?" Tricia suggested.

"I'll find out and get back to you on that," Angelica said, and took another sip of her drink. She eyed Tricia's hair, making her feel self-conscious.

"Do you have to stare at me?"

"I'm getting used to it."

She sure didn't sound it.

Tricia polished off the rest of her drink. Drinking to forget her haircut might be her only option just then. At least she was willing to give it a shot . . . or two . . . or three. . . .

# SEVENTEEN

**Tricia skipped** her usual walk the next morning. Instead, she headed down to her basement office, which doubled as an exercise room on stormy days, and walked her miles on the treadmill, while Miss Marple watched from her office chair. Afterward, she headed back up to her apartment to shower and change. As she was running out of flour, she decided to make a three-ingredient peanut butter cookie recipe she'd been meaning to try for some time. It helped pass the time and they tasted pretty darn good.

Before heading down to her store, Tricia tried on several hats and scarfs, finding nothing that pleased her, and decided to at least start the day without a head covering. As Mr. Everett had said, most of the people who darkened her door didn't know her and would think her rather severe hairstyle was just a part of her persona and ignore it. And he'd been right. The customers who entered the store the day before hadn't even blinked at seeing her hair.

Sundays at Haven't Got a Clue differed from the rest of the week with shorter hours. Mr. Everett arrived just before noon and they began their workday.

Before long, Tricia forgot about her hair. A steady stream of customers kept her and Mr. Everett busy until nearly four thirty, when a familiar car parked outside of Haven't Got a Clue and Tricia watched as Pixie climbed out of the driver's side of the vehicle. She moved to the trunk of the car and retrieved a box. Tricia hurried to the door to open it for her assistant manager.

"Well, it looks like you had a good day of picking," she told Pixie.

Pixie turned to face Tricia and actually flinched. "Your hair!" she cried. "Who did that to you?"

"Someone at Booked for Beauty."

"One of Randy's girls did *that*? I can't believe it!" Pixie cried. "When?"

"Yesterday. You'd already left for the day. . . ."

"Who?"

"Clarice."

Pixie's expression hardened.

"You know her."

Pixie nodded and shook her head sympathetically. "Good grief, if I was there I would've stopped her. I mean . . . you didn't *want* your hair to look like that, did you?"

"No," Tricia admitted, feeling exposed, hanging out of the doorway. "Can we take this stuff inside?"

"Oh, sure," Pixie said, as though sensing her boss's discomfort.

"Did you have fun thrifting?" Tricia asked, longing to change the subject.

"Oh, yeah," Pixie admitted. "Wait'll you see the bounty. And I've got another box out there, too. Hang on while I get it."

Less than a minute later, Pixie retrieved the carton of books and closed the lid on her trunk. Again, Tricia held the door for her and followed Pixie to the cash counter. Pixie pulled the box's interwoven tabs to reveal the contents.

"Wow, it looks like you hit the jackpot!" Tricia said as she began to unpack the goods. Someone had collected pristine editions of Nancy Drew books dating back to the 1940s, most with their original dust jackets. Several vintage Hardy Boys editions rounded out the collection. "How much did you have to pay for these?"

"A song. Well, nearly. David charmed the woman out of them for a buck apiece."

"What?" Tricia asked, astonished.

Pixie nodded. "He spoke to the daughter of the person who'd passed away. Told her how he remembered reading the same books at *his* grandmother's home. If he'd'a talked a few more minutes, he probably could have gotten them for free."

Really? He hadn't mentioned reading mysteries as a child.

Tricia did a quick tally. "There're more than twenty books here."

Pixie nodded. "I woulda missed them completely. David saw them squirreled away in an attic. I don't usually go in attics when it's this hot out. It would melt my makeup."

"Did he buy anything for himself?"

"Did he," Pixie said, her eyes wide. But when she didn't say anything more, Tricia had to prod her.

"And? What kind of stuff?"

"Dishes. Silverware. Costume jewelry."

"What does he need dishes for? The apartment he's staying in came furnished with everything he needs."

"He collects the stuff. He looks for Limoges. Says he's a Francophile. He got a nice porcelain dresser set of hand-painted forget-me-nots."

"Do you know what a dresser set is?" Tricia asked.

Pixie stared at her boss. "I do now."

"Did you enjoy your time with him?"

"Yeah. He's got an even sharper eye than—" Pixie stopped speaking, and swallowed.

"Edward," Tricia supplied, her voice quiet.

Pixie's late son. Her eyes filled with tears, but then she cleared her throat, stood straighter, and nodded. Like Mr. Everett, Pixie wasn't comfortable showing her emotions—even to someone she considered a friend.

"Did you drop David off?" Tricia asked, changing the subject.

Pixie nodded. "He had three boxes of stuff. Said he was glad he'd waited to spend his cash today, as it wouldn't have gone as far at the Antiques Emporium. Gotta love the last few hours at an estate sale," Pixie declared, in almost her usual cheerful tone. "That's when the sellers practically throw the stuff at you."

"How much do I owe you for all this?"

"Thirty-five bucks."

Quite the haul. Tricia frowned. "I wish you'd let me pay you for your time."

"And I've told you a hundred times that I do this for the thrill of the hunt. I get to buy all kinds of neat stuff for you and the other booksellers and it doesn't cost me a dime."

Come Sundays, Pixie must be enduring a heavy load of endorphins. But the effort seemed to do her good, as her smile had returned.

Tricia retrieved the cash from the register, while Pixie wrote out a receipt for her.

Mr. Everett, who'd been keeping his distance, finally approached the cash desk. "It looks like another fine addition to our stock."

"You bet," Pixie agreed. "I'd better hit the road. It's my turn to make supper."

"What are you having?" Tricia asked.

"Spaghetti and meatballs with a nice salad and garlic bread." Pixie lowered her voice. "I could eat the whole loaf of that bread and just forget the rest but Fred likes his meatballs. What are you guys having at Ginny's?"

"Sunday surprise," Mr. Everett said, his blue eyes twinkling.

"You'll have to tell me all about it when I see you next."

"I shall," Mr. Everett promised her.

"Bye!" Pixie called, and headed out the door.

Tricia and Mr. Everett just had time to send the boxes of new books down the dumbwaiter to the basement for inventorying and pricing before they had to leave for Ginny's house for dinner. Angelica was already there when they pulled up the driveway, as she had either cooked the feast or had it catered for the family and its honorary members.

"Sunday is my favorite day of the week," Mr. Everett confessed. "Grace and I love to see the children and the dinner conversation is always enjoyable, as well."

"I'm pretty partial to Sundays myself," Tricia said.

As they entered the house, they were warmly greeted with excited calls of "Gamma" and "Poppy" from Sofia and a welcoming committee of Ginny and Antonio.

Angelica must have warned the Barberos about Tricia's hair, for neither Antonio nor Ginny said a word about it. At two years old, however, Sofia hadn't yet learned tact.

"You chopped off your hair," she declared as Tricia bent down to talk to her great-niece.

"I got it cut," Tricia admitted sheepishly.

Without warning, Sofia reached out and grabbed the forelock, giving it a sharp yank.

"Sofia!" Ginny admonished.

Tricia removed the little fingers from her hair and forced a smile. *Kids will be kids*, she thought.

Grace hadn't mentioned Tricia's hair, either, which suited Tricia just fine.

As it was a perfect late-June evening, the family gathered on the patio, where they were to have a barbecue with Antonio doing the honors at the grill, but first, they sat down for some socializing and to spoil little Will, who got passed from lap to lap for some more love from his honorary grandparents, too. Angelica offered everyone nachos and chips and dip while Ginny made sure everyone had their favorite wine or soft drink. Tricia tried the nachos—nice—and took a seat between the Everetts.

"William tells me the new Chamber intern is working out well," Grace said.

"A little too well," Angelica muttered under her breath, and swirled the wine in her glass.

Tricia shot her sister an annoyed glance. She turned to Grace. "Yes, he's a fine young man."

"'Young' is the operative word," Angelica said as though in warning.

Tricia ignored her. "It's hard to believe he's only been on the job for four days."

"And how long will he be with the Chamber?" Grace asked.

"Until the end of August when he'll be going back to grad school."

"Hopefully, by then, we'll have found a full-time older lady for the job so he can train her," Angelica said.

"What makes you think it *has* to be a woman?" Tricia asked.

"We only got one man to interview for the internship, but I'm an equal-opportunity employer," Angelica said. "If the best man for the job is a man, it's fine with me. But let's face it, that kind of work mainly goes to women."

"But we're going to be competitive and pay what the job is worth," Tricia said.

"Of course."

Grace looked like she wished she'd never brought up the subject. She cleared her throat. "I'm sure that will take a lot of pressure off of you ladies."

"David's already done that," Tricia said.

"He went thrifting with Pixie this afternoon," Mr. Everett put in. "I think he's charmed her, as well."

Was that a veiled comment aimed at Tricia? No, Mr. Everett was the kindest person Tricia knew. He would never cast aspersions on anyone, least of all her.

"Has anyone heard anything new in the Sanjay Arya case?" Grace asked.

Tricia shook her head. "Just rumors about his character."

"Oh, dear," Grace said, sounding upset. "Nothing from Chief Mc-Donald to say he's closing in on a suspect?"

"Not that I've heard," Tricia said.

"And why should you be listening for such when you promised you weren't going to get involved in this one?" Angelica asked.

"One what?" Sofia asked innocently.

"Nothing, darling girl," Angelica said, and held out her hand to the toddler. "Come with Nonna and help her put the salads in bowls and she'll let you lick the spoons."

Sofia had gotten to lick beaters and spoons before and knew it was a good thing. She accepted Angelica's invitation and they left the patio and headed indoors.

"I'd better go help them," Ginny said, getting up from her seat. "Otherwise Sofia is liable to spill or break something. She loves to help—and that usually means a *lot* more work for me."

Tricia was just as glad Angelica left the area. Now she wouldn't have to watch everything she said—at least when it came to David Price *and* Sanjay Arya.

Grace looked concerned. "Are you poking into that poor man's death?"

"I wouldn't say *poking*, but I have heard things." Yes, and hearing about Sanjay and Toni had cost her most of her hair. Maybe Angelica was right. Maybe she should just butt out of this one. But how could she when David was insisting on looking into things? The fact that they hadn't spoken in two days was probably a good thing. Maybe he'd settle into the job and his short-timer's life in the village and he'd be gone before the end of August.

The thought made Tricia feel more than a little blue.

*What is wrong with you?*

Tricia felt her cheeks grow hot. Her emotions were just as unsettled as a middle schooler's.

"Would you like another glass of wine?" Antonio asked Tricia.

Tricia looked down at her empty glass. She hadn't realized she'd practically guzzled its contents. She smiled at him. "Thank you."

When he left the area in search of another bottle, Grace leaned forward. "I didn't want to say anything while everyone else was around, but I do know something about Mr. Arya."

"Grace," Mr. Everett warned as he gently rocked little Will.

Grace ignored him. "Well, not about him, per se, but the company he worked for—Stark Construction."

"Oh?"

"It seems they've been selling off a lot of their heavy-duty equipment."

"I hadn't heard."

"I hadn't, either. That is until we got a request at our foundation from a nonprofit that wanted to buy an excavator."

"Is that something you'd normally consider?"

"We take every request seriously. It just seemed odd to me that

Stoneham's most sought-after contractor would be selling off his equipment."

"Perhaps he's going to replace it with new machinery," Tricia suggested.

Grace threw a look in her husband's direction. Mr. Everett had stopped rocking the baby and looked upset.

Grace seemed to think over what she wanted to say. "Perhaps," she said at last. She stood. "I wonder if Angelica and Ginny need any help in the kitchen. I'd best go see." Grace picked up her glass and disappeared into the house.

Mr. Everett looked embarrassed and began rocking the baby once again. Little Will had fallen asleep.

Tricia sat back in her chair. So, why would Jim Stark be selling off equipment? Was he just upgrading, or did he need the money? And why would someone that successful—and in demand—need money? It was something to ponder.

And . . . maybe Tricia might just poke around, after all.

But only a little bit.

# EIGHTEEN

**When Tricia** returned home later that evening, she checked the Internet to see if she could find heavy-duty equipment for sale and tie it to Stark Construction. The firm's website had no pages devoted to such sales, and none of the phone numbers listed for machinery for sale matched any of those listed for Stark's company. She sat back in her chair and bit her lip, thinking.

Now, why would Stark be liquidating his equipment—especially when he had so many jobs lined up? Jobs that were contracted—like Becca's tennis club. If he was going out of business, surely the company wouldn't be taking on new work.

Grace hadn't said when she'd received the request for funds. Had it been something that just came up or had this request happened in recent months? Tricia wasn't sure she wanted to ask. As it was, she was sure Grace would not be in her husband's good graces after speaking about it. Tricia was sure Mr. Everett would have considered such a disclosure as gossip. He'd made his disapproval quite clear without saying a word.

Would Becca Chandler know?

It was just after nine, and Tricia was sure that Becca would not have retired for the night. On impulse, she grabbed her phone and made the call.

"What's up?" Becca answered with no other preliminaries.

"You've got a contract with Stark Construction to work on your tennis club, right?"

"Well, yes and no," Becca admitted.

"How's that?" Tricia asked.

"Now that the Board of Selectmen shot down my first location, I've got to get all the permits for the new one. I mean, it shouldn't be a problem as they were the ones who suggested the alternate location, but that's going to put construction back at least six months—maybe longer. I am *not* pleased about that."

"So, that means you've got to renegotiate your contract with Stark Construction, right?"

"Yes, but it shouldn't be a big deal. Why are you asking?"

"It's just that there's a rumor going around that Jim Stark's selling off some of his heavy equipment. A lot of it." Okay. Tricia wasn't sure of that—but she had a gut feeling it might be true.

Silence greeted that statement.

"Becca?" Tricia said.

"I'm here . . . just trying to digest what you said."

"Are you already in talks with Stark Construction on the new timeline?"

Again, it took long moments before Becca spoke again. "As it happens, my attorney said that Stark had put him off—twice—when it came to rescheduling to talk about the new timeline. What do you think's going on?"

"I don't know. I was hoping you might."

"I will definitely get my lawyer on it first thing in the morning. If Stark is stalling me, I want to know why. And if Stark can't deliver in a timely basis, I'll be on the phone in a heartbeat to find someone who can."

Of course, that was a lie. Becca had people who did that kind of thing, but Tricia did not doubt that Becca was a hard negotiator.

"As your Chamber co-president, I'd appreciate it if you'd keep me informed. Other members are relying on Stark Construction to start or complete their projects."

"You mean Nigela Ricita Associates, right?"

"Among others," Tricia bluffed.

Again, a long silence followed before Becca broke it.

"I appreciate you calling me and giving me a heads-up, Trish."

Tricia cringed. She only allowed her sister to use that familiar form of her name.

"I'll get back to you as soon as I know anything."

"Thanks."

"Talk to you soon," Becca said, and ended the call.

Tricia set down her cell phone wondering what she should do next. She really had no excuse to talk to Jim Stark—if she could get hold of him. She'd wait to see what the next day brought. After all, there wasn't a hurry.

Unless the killer decided to strike once again.

**Monday dawned** overcast, but the local meteorologist promised there'd be no rain that day. Tricia wasn't sure she believed him and decided to take an umbrella with her on her morning walk. She spent the time thinking about what she'd learned the day before but came to no conclusions. She needed to bounce her thoughts off someone else. Luckily, David was waiting outside Haven't Got a Clue when Tricia returned from her walk.

"Oh, you got your hair cut," David said in lieu of a greeting and sounding more than a little disappointed.

Tricia touched the back of her head. "The stylist got a little carried away, but it was time," she said, hoping the lie might at least sound plausible.

David shook his head. "I think you'd look really nice with long hair. Have you ever worn it long?"

"Back in high school. It's a lot easier to take care of when it's short," she said. Boy, would it be easy to take care of this whack job. "How about you? Have you ever had *really* short hair?"

"My grandfather wanted me to have a buzz cut. He said long hair was for girls but my parents and grandmother are fine with it longer. I like it this way. Besides, it's hard to find anyone who can cut curly hair."

Tricia had heard that from friends who'd suffered the same problem.

They were conspicuous standing outside her shop. Tricia retrieved her keys, unlocked the door, and beckoned David to follow her in. "Would you like some herbal tea?"

"Hate the stuff. And I don't have a tea bag on me right now. Have you got any instant cocoa?"

"Yes."

"I could go for that."

"Sit down in the reader's nook while I get the beverage station up and running," Tricia directed.

Minutes later, Tricia served him a mug of cocoa while she poured herself a second cup of coffee. She wasn't sure she wanted to share what she'd learned the evening before from Grace and Becca, but she did have something else on her mind.

"You know, it's always bothered me that Sanjay was robbed of his wallet and keys before he was murdered," Tricia said.

"Was it to throw off the police? They might chalk it up to a robber instead of someone Sanjay knew."

"It gives a plausible reason for murder, but I don't think that's why he was killed."

"You think it was one of his lovers or one of his lovers' husbands or boyfriends, right?"

"That's an obvious conclusion, but not necessarily the correct one."

"It seems to be the only motive anyone is considering."

Tricia nodded, but it didn't feel right to her. There must have been more to Sanjay Arya than just a ladies' man with as many females of the species as he could charm.

"What do you think the killer did with the keys and wallet?" David asked.

"If he or she was smart, dumped them. Keeping them would be an admission of guilt."

"So, where would someone get rid of something like that?"

"As far away as possible."

David nodded. "If it was you, where would you get rid of them?" he persisted.

"I'd drive to the ocean, get on a ferry to anywhere, take a walk on the deck, and then fling them into the sea."

"That's what a smart person would do. But don't you think some people would want to keep souvenirs like that?"

"Definitely. And that's why they get caught with damning evidence."

"So, let's assume we have a semi-smart killer. What body of water around here would swallow up a wallet and keys?"

"There's a pond in the village square. It's not very deep, but I wouldn't want to go wading in it. It's probably full of duck poop."

"I can't say I'd want to go wading into it, either. Anywhere else?"

Tricia shrugged. "The stream that goes through the Brookview Inn's property. There's a little bridge in the back garden. Most people who stay there probably don't visit the garden. I did when Angelica was staying in one of the bungalows after she broke her foot."

"Why didn't she just stay home?"

"Her home was in Connecticut at the time. It was just before she moved here permanently. She can come on a little strong at times, and I was her caregiver. Believe me, I used that garden as my own private sanctuary."

"What are the chances our killer would have known about that garden?"

"Probably zero to none."

"That's too bad." David looked thoughtful. "What are the chances the police searched the mansion's yard for the wallet and keys?"

"Fairly good. They'd have taken at least a cursory look around."

"Maybe we should do it, too. The killer might have buried them there." David looked thoughtful. "Do you know anyone with a metal detector?"

"No, and it would be absurd to think someone would dump the keys there."

David was quiet for a moment. "Maybe I'll take a walk over there anyway."

"When?" Tricia asked.

"This evening. Maybe after it gets dark."

"It would look mighty suspicious."

"What time of day *wouldn't* it look suspicious?"

"Well, no one blinked an eye when Angelica and I turned up there at six in the morning—before the workmen showed up."

"But you said no workmen had been showing up to work."

"Nigela Ricita Associates needs that office space finished before the end of July. I'm sure communication between Antonio Barbero and Stark Construction is getting hot and heavy."

"You've got an in with RN Associates, don't you?"

"You could say that. Antonio is a dear friend of mine."

"Yeah, you have dinner with his family every Sunday."

"You heard?"

"Those dinners are legendary. I've heard they even closed the Brookview's dining room for a couple of them."

"Don't believe everything you hear."

"See if you can get permission for us to search and then let's go do it," David said.

"It's a waste of time."

"I'm not doing all that much productive work between the hours of six and seven a.m. How about you?"

"When you put it that way, no," she remarked.

But, knowing how Angelica felt about Tricia snooping around, she also knew that there was no way Antonio would give them permission to search the grounds.

Then again, it was always easier to ask for forgiveness than permission.

"What say we meet outside my shop tomorrow morning at six for a walk around the village? And if we just happen to stop in front of the Morrison Mansion . . ."

"Sounds good to me," David said, giving her a toothy grin, the sight of which made something inside Tricia melt. She gave herself a mental shake and an order to *stick to business*.

Speaking of business, she told him about Angelica's request that he brainstorm ways of getting new booksellers to locate in the village.

"Challenge accepted," he said, and downed the last of his cocoa.

"Oh, and one more thing."

David looked quizzical.

"I thought you said you weren't familiar with mysteries."

"You mean the genre?"

Tricia nodded.

"I'm not."

"Pixie said you told the woman at the estate sale that you'd read those Nancy Drew books you spotted."

"I have. More than once. But those are kid books. They don't involve murder."

"You think there's a difference?"

"Sure there is."

Tricia waited for him to elaborate and when he didn't she decided to give up on the subject. "Thanks for spotting the books. We really need them to stock our shelves." Or, more likely, to offer them online to find a potentially bigger audience.

"You're welcome. I aim to please." He reached out, grabbed her hand, and squeezed it. It wasn't clammy as it had been the day she'd met him. His fingers were warm and the touch sent a tingle up her arm.

Tricia stood there for long seconds, not knowing what to say or how to react. But then she caught sight of the clock on the wall. She cleared her throat. "Hadn't you better get to the Chamber?"

David released her hand and looked at his watch—a vintage Omega. Her father wore a similar one that had belonged to her maternal grandfather, although given what she now knew about her father, Tricia wondered if he'd pawned the watch and was wearing a knockoff. Perhaps David was wearing one, too. Maybe she'd ask . . . someday.

At the risk of being patronizing, Tricia waved her hand in the direction of the Chamber office. "Shoo! I'll see you tomorrow."

David smiled. "You bet."

Tricia watched him until he was out of sight and wondered how she would feel weeks from now when he returned to school.

She turned and picked up their mugs.

She didn't want to think about it.

# NINETEEN

 **Mondays always** seemed a little melancholy without Mr. Everett at Haven't Got a Clue. Tricia suspected Pixie missed him as much, especially as she had to have lunch by herself, and often just brought a brown-bag meal that she ate in the store's basement office, her nose planted in a book. Tricia felt just a little guilty as she left the shop to have lunch, as she did most days, with her sister. And she knew the café would be full of people—including those who knew her. They were going to see her hair. As she reached for the door handle, she steeled herself for the worst.

As usual, Angelica was already seated in Booked for Lunch's back booth. She always had a notebook at the ready, preferring old-fashioned paper and pen to make notes on rather than her phone or a tablet. She was just so full of ideas she couldn't bear to waste a single moment of the day. It sometimes made Tricia feel like a slacker. She frowned. Guilty for Pixie eating alone, and good-for-nothing be-cause she had interests beyond just running her bookstore. She needed to have a good talking-to . . . that or an intervention. But from whom?

Angelica looked up as Tricia approached the table. "So, what have you been up to today?"

"Not much," Tricia admitted, and slid into the booth. "It's just a typical slow Monday."

Angelica scrutinized her face. "Not planning anything nefarious, are you?"

Had someone overheard her conversation with David that morning, or was Angelica just speculating based on past history?

"I'm one of the good guys—or gals, if you prefer."

"Mmm." Angelica set down her pen and let out a breath. "I've spoken with Randy over at the day spa."

Tricia felt every muscle in her body tense.

"He was horrified that you're so unhappy with the cut Clarice gave you. He said he's going to give her a stern reprimand."

That and a couple of bucks would get Tricia a lousy cup of fast-food coffee. "Is that supposed to make me feel better?"

"I imagine she'll show up at your store sometime in the next day or so to apologize."

"That won't be necessary," Tricia said, although that wasn't how she felt.

"Yes, it is. I won't have the people in my employ pulling stunts like that. What if, instead of cutting your hair, she'd given you a chemical burn while tinting it?"

Tricia didn't tint her hair but got the message. "I can see your point."

"How will you handle the situation?"

"I don't know." Tricia considered herself to be a decent person, but she wasn't sure she could forgive Clarice for what she'd done to her hair.

Angelica changed the subject. "Did you see your little protégé this morning?"

"He's not my protégé, and yes, he stopped by my store before he went to work. It's only a few steps out of his way," Tricia pointed out.

"On the wrong side of the road," Angelica muttered, and lifted her water glass to take a sip.

"We spoke about recruiting booksellers to the village."

"Good."

The bell over the café's door rang.

Angelica looked up. "Speak of the devil."

Tricia twisted in her seat to see that David Price had just walked into Booked for Lunch.

"My, but he's late for his midday meal today, isn't he?" Angelica asked with more than a little snark.

David looked around the small restaurant, caught sight of the Miles sisters, and waved, heading in their direction.

"Oh, please," Angelica muttered.

"Hey, ladies." David glanced at the table and only the cups before them. "Do you mind if I join you for lunch? Separate checks, of course," he amended.

"I'd love it," Tricia said, and scooted over to the far edge of the booth to make room for him.

Angelica forced a smile. "Having a late lunch?"

"Yeah. I got tied up with talking to the catering staff at the Brookview about next month's meeting, but everything's all straightened out now. I hope it isn't a problem shutting the office later than usual," David said.

"You were doing exactly what you needed to do, and you're certainly entitled to your full lunch hour," Tricia said. "Isn't that right, Angelica?"

Angelica grinned. "Absolutely."

Tricia knew that pseudocheerful tone but resisted kicking her sister under the table.

"That's a lovely pin," Angelica said, noting the glittering jade frog that graced the front of David's button-down shirt.

"Thanks. It's one of my favorites. So, what's the special today?"

"Liver and onions," Angelica said, her voice flat—and not knowing David would enjoy the meal.

"It is not," Tricia told their guest, and this time she did give Angelica's calf a tap with her foot and received a glower in return.

"Have you started thinking about ways to bring in new booksellers to the village?"

"Yes," David said, "and I've spoken to a couple of booksellers in Rutland and Stowe who might want to open satellite locations here in Stoneham."

"That was quick," Tricia said.

"They know my parents. They also said they'd spread the word."

Tricia eyed her sister, but Angelica merely nodded, looking just a tad annoyed. "And have you come up with anything else?"

"Mostly the tried-and-true. Advertise, but also I made a list of booksellers in a hundred-mile radius and worked up a rough draft for a pitch letter. Would you like to see it?" he asked, already reaching for his back jeans pocket. He withdrew a sheet of copy paper folded in quarters and handed it to Angelica. She quickly scanned the lines.

"Hmm. It needs work," she said. She handed the paper back to him. "Perhaps you could polish it up . . . when you're not working to discover Sanjay Arya's killer."

"All my working hours are devoted to the Chamber. It's a great place to work. I only wish I could stay on after my stint is done. I'm really beginning to like this little burg."

"Despite all the killings?" Angelica asked innocently.

He shrugged. "It seems to me they're more an aberration than anything else."

"One might say that," Angelica muttered.

Tricia was glad to see Molly the server approach the table to take their orders.

"Hey, you got your hair cut, Tricia," she said in greeting.

"All of them, actually," Tricia said, and self-consciously smoothed the near-stubble at the back of her head.

Molly rattled off the day's specials and Tricia was shocked to find that Angelica had been telling the truth. One of them actually was liver and onions. Only David ordered it, while Tricia and Angelica made it easy on Molly by ordering the soup-and-half-sandwich special, which, on that day, was vegetable soup and ham salad.

Angelica launched into a tirade about how Stark Construction was going on its second week without touching the work on the mansion, leaving poor Ginny to scramble looking to sublet alternate office space to occupy in a matter of weeks.

David ate his lunch without contributing to the conversation, and if his warm thigh hadn't been resting against hers in that tight little booth, Tricia might have forgotten he was even there.

As soon as Angelica finished her lunch, she was up on her feet. "I must get back to work. Time waits for no one," she quipped. She leveled a severe glare at Tricia. "I'll see you this evening." It sounded more like an order than an invitation.

David polished off the last of his liver, wiping his mouth with his napkin, and signaled to Molly, who nodded in his direction but turned away.

"I need to get my portion of the check," he told Tricia.

She shook her head. "It's taken care of."

"But—"

"Lunch is always free to anyone who joins the boss at this table."

David shrugged. "I'll have to thank Angelica the next time I see her. Or should I send a written note? Would that have made her like me more?"

"She doesn't dislike you," Tricia fibbed.

"You could have fooled me," he said. "Are you ready?"

Tricia pushed her empty plate away. "Yes."

David walked Tricia back to Haven't Got a Clue. "We seem to say good-bye a lot in front of this door."

"Why don't you come in and say hello to Pixie."

"Oh, yeah. I could thank her again for chauffeuring me around yesterday. She gave me a lot of thrifting tips, too. She's a gem."

"Yes, she is."

Tricia opened the door and they found Pixie waiting on a customer. They waited until the woman left, with quite a hefty bag of books, before stepping up to the counter.

"Hey, Pixie. Thanks again for letting me tag along with you yesterday," David said.

"It was my pleasure," Pixie said, sounding more formal than usual. "We should do it again—soon," she said, but didn't invite him to accompany her the next Sunday.

David glanced at the clock. "I'd better scoot. I'm sure there'll be a ton of messages on the Chamber's voice mail. There usually are."

"I'm glad you could join us today," Tricia said, meaning it.

"We'll have to do it again sometime," he said, smiled, and headed for the door. "See you tomorrow, Tricia."

The women watched as David left the shop.

Pixie sighed. "What a good kid. I'm sure his mother must be very proud of him. Once he graduates, he's gonna have a great career—books day in and day out, year in and year out." She swallowed hard and her eyes became watery. "Meeting a nice kid like him just reinforces the fact that my son was such a loser," Pixie said with a tremor in her voice.

"David's led a very different life than Edward did," Tricia said sympathetically.

"And that's all my fault," Pixie said bitterly.

"Don't say that. It was merely a matter of circumstance. You did what you thought was best for both of you."

"And I was wrong."

"You can't second-guess yourself."

"Who says?"

"Me. And Edward wasn't a loser. He was a hero—*my* hero. He saved my life."

"Well, it was a life worth saving," Pixie agreed, giving her boss a watery smile.

"Thank you for that."

Pixie nodded and scraped the back of her hand across her eye, smearing her mascara. She pulled a dainty handkerchief from her skirt pocket and blew her nose—loudly. While she was gathering herself, the door opened and an older couple entered the shop. Tricia greeted them, but Pixie was soon back to her usual cheerful self and took over. The rest of the afternoon was uneventful.

As Tricia had made no plans for that evening, she hosted dinner and happy hour for Angelica. Her sister started by making snarky remarks about David before she switched to her concern about delays with the Morrison Mansion renovations. Tricia didn't add much to the conversation and ended up nodding so much that her neck began to ache and she started counting the minutes until Angelica headed for home.

One hot bubble bath later and Tricia was ready for dreamland. She set her alarm but was awake before it went off at five o'clock. She dressed and fussed with her makeup—not for David's sake, but since her disaster of a haircut, she felt the need to look her best when she stepped outside Haven't Got a Clue.

Sure she did.

Once ready, she and Miss Marple descended the steps to the shop to wait for David's arrival. Tricia found herself pacing up and down the aisles, with various things flitting through her mind. One thought seemed stuck on repeat . . . the idea that she and David might be caught on the neighbor's door camera. But did it really matter? They could be guilty of trespass, but not breaking and entering, and that was because Antonio was sure to vouch for her, even if she didn't have permission. She hoped.

*Oh, crap!* Tricia forgot to get Antonio's official blessing to search the mansion's grounds. Was it forgetful or willful amnesia? Tricia didn't like to think about it.

David showed up on Tricia's doorstep at 5:55.

"Ready?"

"Of course."

Tricia locked the door and they headed out in the morning's chill. The temps were predicted to rise in a matter of hours, but Tricia was glad she'd donned a light sweater in the interim.

They walked in companionable silence until they reached Maple Avenue. That's when Tricia's hackles began to rise.

"Are you okay?"

"Fine," Tricia lied, wondering if an unpleasant conversation with Chief McDonald might soon be on her list of things to do.

That day, David wore his hair in a man bun—but no brooch. It was just as well. She worried that some creep might decide to pick a fight with him over them. The thought of that possibly happening disturbed her. She would be terribly upset if someone hurt him.

*Stop it!*

Upon arriving at the mansion's backyard, they decided to walk the yard in a grid pattern, with Tricia pacing the length of the property and David walking its breadth. David had a habit of humming, which

Tricia found just a little annoying, but then it was better than just listening to the buzz of traffic or the roar of a chainsaw. And she recognized most of the tunes . . . standards sung by the likes of Frank Sinatra, Ella Fitzgerald, Bing Crosby, and others.

"Don't you know any newer tunes?" she asked as their paths crossed.

"What?"

"You're humming 'Stardust.'"

"Oh, yeah, it was one of my grandfather's favorites. One hell of a romantic, that old guy. If you're so into today's music—"

"Who said I am?" Tricia countered.

But David plowed on without listening, "I could hum something else. How about Lady Gaga's 'Shallow'?"

"That won't be necessary."

"So, how do you know 'Stardust,' anyway?" he asked.

"Because my grandmother used to have a record player and *she* played it all the time."

"She had good taste," David said. "So, what's your favorite music?"

"I like all kinds," Tricia said impatiently. This little chat was holding up their search.

"Then if you won't commit, I'll continue to serenade you with my favorites."

Tricia wasn't all that keen on humming and changed the subject as a distraction. "We should pick up the pace of searching this property if we want to get to the Chamber by eight o'clock."

"Right," he said, and they split up once again.

They'd covered most of the overgrown grass, but Tricia had to admit it was probably a hopeless task. She thought about ticks and was glad they'd both worn heavy pants and good shoes.

Finally, they met at the southeast corner of the yard with nothing to show for their efforts.

"Well, I guess that's it," David said, sounding disappointed.

"Are you kidding?"

"What do you mean?"

"We haven't checked the border garden looking for disturbed soil. Someone could have buried Sanjay's phone, wallet, and keys on the grounds."

"I suppose. But don't you think the cops have already looked there?"

"Cops sometimes miss things," Tricia pointed out.

David frowned. "Did you bring anything to dig with?"

Tricia pursed her lips. "No."

"So, what if we find that disturbed dirt? What do we do then?"

"We dig with our hands."

David wiggled his fingers and Tricia noted how clean his nails were. His cuticles even looked good.

She gave herself a mental shake. "Let's go. You take the east side of the garden and I'll take the west and we'll meet in the middle."

"Right."

The garden hadn't been properly tended in many years, as evidenced by the abundance and great variety of weeds. But apparently, the perennials weren't aware of the neglect and had returned as in years past. Tricia couldn't name most of the plants and wasn't sure if some of them were merely weeds—or were they wildflowers? The dirt and remnants of sun-bleached mulch looked like they hadn't seen a spade or trowel in some time. It also reminded Tricia of the potted plants in her apartment and that she hadn't watered them in a couple of days. One of them was particularly thirsty, and if she didn't rectify the situation soon, she'd have to toss the poor thing.

The far end of the garden border was looking just as dry and dusty and Tricia recognized the leaves of a particularly thorny plant and wondered what kind of roses they were. She loved to receive tea roses, but for flowering plants, she admired the old-fashioned ones, which seemed to have a sweeter scent. Tricia stared at the row of bushes, taking in the details, when she noticed David closing in on her location.

"I didn't see anything of note. Did you?"

Tricia shook her head sadly.

"What? Did I miss something?"

Tricia pointed toward the tremendously overgrown rosebush. Its thorny canes reached out in all directions, the ones in front looking as though they wanted to embrace the two.

"I still don't see—"

Tricia crouched down to inspect the ground beneath the bush. David joined her. She pointed. David leaned forward. It took him a few seconds to see what she'd already noticed.

"Okay. There's dirt piled up in the back of this plant."

"Rosebush," she corrected absently.

"Couldn't it be the work of a weasel or something?"

"I can't say I've seen any around, but that doesn't mean there aren't any. But look closer," she encouraged.

Several of the canes around the bottom of the bush were broken—not cut.

"You think someone was messing around under it?" David asked.

"Weasels don't pat the dirt down after they've been digging."

David grimaced. "You don't expect me to dig around the back of this thorn machine to try to find something that may or may not have been buried . . . do you?"

"I'm pretty sure I saw a pair of heavy leather work gloves on the patio behind the mansion. I don't think anyone would mind if we borrowed them—just for a few minutes—to take a look. No one has to know, and we won't be taking them with us when we leave."

"I'll get them," David volunteered, and straightened.

Tricia waited impatiently. She glanced at her watch, thankful they still had plenty of time before the Chamber office needed to open.

David returned with not only the gloves but a diamond-shaped masonry trowel. "I figured this might come in handy," he said, and handed it to Tricia. "You discovered it. You can do the honors."

She accepted the gloves and tool and began to dig around the plant's prickly base. Despite the leather between her skin and the bush, the thorns were able to penetrate the barrier. She winced and ground her teeth, but it didn't stop her from scraping away the dusty soil. She didn't have to dig very far before they heard the dull clunk of metal on metal.

"Aha!" David crowed. "You found something."

"Don't get your hopes up," Tricia warned as she continued to work.

More dirt, more scraping and digging, and in less than a minute Tricia pulled a set of keys from the dirt. She hefted them and noted the FORD insignia on a leather tab.

"Do we know what kind of truck Sanjay drove?" David asked.

"My guess is—wait for it—a Ford," Tricia said, and couldn't help the grin that quirked her lips. She jingled the dusty keys for effect and then handed them to David so he could inspect them as well.

"I suppose we have to turn these over to the cops," he said, sounding less than enthusiastic.

Tricia sighed. "Yes."

"But—" David began. "Just *when* do we have to turn them over?"

"As soon as possible."

"What if we took the long way to the police station?"

"You mean around the village, heading north and through Milford, and just happen to stop the car in front of Sanjay's apartment building?"

"After being buried for days, don't you think they'd need airing out?"

"It's a possibility," Tricia agreed.

"Do you think the wallet will be under there, too?"

"We can look."

But this time David insisted that he do the digging—and accompanied his efforts with sharp intakes of breath, winces, and stifled cries of pain as he worked. Still, it took only about another minute before he came up with a dusty brown wallet. Upon inspection, they saw the wallet had been stripped of its cash, credit cards, and other pieces of identification.

"What if this isn't Sanjay's wallet and keys?" David asked.

"All the more reason for us to test the keys before we hand them over to Chief McDonald . . . wouldn't you say?"

"I would."

Being a gentleman, David helped Tricia to her feet.

"We ought to get going. I mean, we *are* going to open the Chamber office a little late today, aren't we?"

"It looks that way."

"Will I get in trouble with your sister?"

"Not if I'm with you, but we need a plausible excuse," Tricia said.

"How about we take a trip to the big office supply store on the highway? If nothing else, we could buy a case of paper. The Chamber's copier *is* running low," David said.

"A paper chase it is," Tricia said.

David pocketed the keys and wallet and they left the gloves and trowel where they were found on the mansion's stone patio. Then they were off.


**After stopping** for a fast-food cup of mediocre coffee and breakfast sandwiches eaten in the car, Tricia's treat, they arrived at the building where Sanjay Arya had lived. Tricia would've thought he'd lived in a complex, but the apartment was actually the second floor of a home on a side street with an outside entrance. Tricia parked her Lexus at the curb and the two of them left the vehicle and walked up to the older house on the shady side of the street. The home boasted no garage, but lumber stacked along the side of the house told her one might be in the offing. She eyed the stairs that were open to the elements and cringed, thinking about how icy they might be during the winter months.

"What do you think?" David asked.

"It's nice enough."

"I mean, should we actually do this?" he asked, looking around as though to make sure there were no cops in the vicinity. "Is it breaking and entering if you have a key?"

"As you pointed out, we don't even know if they're Sanjay's keys."

"Time to find out, I guess." David pulled the still-dusty keys from his jeans pocket and started up the stairs. Tricia followed. At the top, David inspected the lock and Tricia could see that it said YALE. David chose a corresponding key and it slid neatly into the keyhole. They looked at each other for several long seconds before David turned the key and grasped the handle. The door slid open.

"Well, I guess we now know that the wallet and keys belonged to Sanjay."

"Yes, but did you notice that while they were buried together, his cell phone wasn't with them?"

David frowned. "No, I hadn't noticed." He gestured for Tricia to enter. "Ladies first."

Tricia stepped over the threshold and into the apartment's small kitchen. It looked like a tornado had gone through the place— probably the police looking for evidence. They weren't noted for being neat freaks when searching. Other than the clutter, the place appeared to be spotless. No dust bunnies lurking in corners, no coffee or other stains in the white porcelain sink, and the beige vinyl floor wasn't the least bit tacky beneath their feet.

David wandered past her as Tricia opened the refrigerator, which had little more than a sagging pizza box, a nearly empty two-liter bottle of generic cola, a container of almond milk, and a whole array of condiments, most of which were half-empty. Sanjay wasn't much of a cook—and it looked like he ate most of his meals away from his home base. She peeked into the dishwasher, which housed only coffee mugs and spoons. The garbage bin contained junk mail and paper plates. So, Sanjay wasn't into recycling.

The living room was sparsely furnished with a couch, a chair, and a large drawing table, messy with drawings of what looked like a farmhouse. Sanjay's handiwork?

Tricia found David coming out of Sanjay's bedroom. "Not much to see in there."

"Was the bed made?"

David shook his head. "The mattress is on the floor. I'm guessing it was the cops who put it there."

Tricia nodded. "Any other observations?"

David shrugged. "This wasn't a home. More of a parking space. There's nothing here to give us any hint of his personality."

"Are you sure?"

"I guess."

Tricia frowned and sighed.

"What was I supposed to see that I didn't?" he asked.

Tricia looked over his shoulder and into the bedroom. On the nightstand was what turned out to be a well-thumbed copy of the *Kama Sutra*. She mentioned it.

David shrugged. "So the guy liked sex. Who doesn't?"

Would that statement satisfy some of the locals who'd questioned David's sexual preference?

"Take another look," Tricia suggested. She was beginning to feel a little like Sherlock Holmes schooling Watson.

David gave the room another once-over. "I still don't see anything."

Tricia stepped farther into the room and pointed toward a white tube embellished with a little red rose.

"So. It's hand cream," David said with a shrug.

Tricia stifled a laugh. "It's not hand cream."

David reached down and picked up the tube, reading the label. "Oh." He looked uncomfortable.

"And do you know what that means?" Tricia asked.

"Uh . . . you tell me?"

"That Sanjay was seeing someone who was probably older than him."

David squinted at her. "How much older?"

"Maybe fifteen or twenty years."

"You mean someone your age?"

Tricia's eyes widened and her jaw dropped. "I *don't* need this product."

"I didn't say you did. I was just—" But then he stopped talking.

Tricia shook her head and left the room. David followed. "Do you think the police came to the same conclusion as you?" he asked, looking bewildered.

"Possibly." Another clue to point to Toni Bennett? Tricia glanced around at the apartment's sparse furnishings, the lack of anything decorating the walls, and the indentations in the carpet where chairs and end tables had once stood. And there *had* been pictures or other décor in the rooms, as evidenced by the nail holes that pocked the beige surfaces. Tricia abandoned the living room and entered the bathroom. The medicine cabinet was nearly empty, with just a bottle of ibuprofen, a tube of whitening toothpaste, a toothbrush, and a stick of deodorant. The glass shelves sported faint rings where many other items had once been placed. Until recently, Sanjay had shared his quarters with another living soul.

"Excuse me," came a voice from the kitchen.

Tricia looked up to see an older woman in hot pink capri pants, a wildly floral T-shirt, and white sandals standing in the middle of the kitchen. Her hair was white, cut in a flattering style—not at all like the butcher job Tricia had so recently received—and at just shy of eight in the morning she'd taken the time to put on foundation, eye shadow, and lipstick. Not unlike Tricia.

"Who are you and what are you doing in my apartment?" the woman demanded.

"Your apartment? I thought Sanjay Arya lived here," David said.

"He *did*, but not anymore."

"Then you know he was killed?" Tricia said gently.

"Of course I know. Who do you think let the police in here? If I hadn't, I'm sure they would've kicked the door in—and then I'd be out of pocket to fix it."

"You've dealt with this kind of thing before?" David asked.

"Hell, yes. Everybody who rents has at least one bad apple."

"Was Sanjay a bad apple?" Tricia asked.

The old woman frowned, and for a moment Tricia thought she might cry. "No. He was one of the good guys. He rented from me for the past three years. He was tidy, didn't make a lot of noise—" She paused and her frown deepened as she seemed to think about it for a moment, then continued. "He was probably the best tenant I've ever had—and we're talking twenty years of renters."

"And he didn't live alone . . . until recently," Tricia pushed.

The older woman scrutinized Tricia's face. "He was alone, for the most part, these past couple of months," she asserted.

Which was what Patti Perkins at the *Stoneham Weekly News* had hinted at. And she'd mentioned Sanjay's landlady had spoken to her about it.

"His girlfriend moved out?" David asked.

"Lock, stock, and barrel," the older woman said.

"And her name was?" he pressed.

The woman scowled, growing annoyed. "I don't know who you are. You're trespassing in my home. I don't owe you any explanations. In fact, I've told you far too much already. Unless you want me to call the cops, I think you'd better leave. And just so you know, I've taken down your license plate number."

Which meant Tricia had better get the newfound keys and wallet to Chief McDonald as soon as possible.

"Thank you for your patience," Tricia said sincerely, and the woman stepped aside as they exited the kitchen.

Tricia hurried down the steps and made a beeline for her car.

"Hey," the woman called from the apartment's top step. "How did you get in? Do you have a key?"

Tricia practically jumped into the Lexus with David right behind her. She started the engine, shoved the gear shift into drive, and took off just as the older woman made it to the bottom of the steps. "Hey! Hey!" she hollered.

"Are we in trouble?" David asked.

"Could be," Tricia said as her fingers tightened around the steering wheel.

"Are you worried?"

"Only if Angelica finds out."

"Ha! You're scared of her, too!" David accused.

"I am not."

"Are, too!"

"We'd better get that case of paper before we head back to Stoneham," Tricia said tersely.

"Oh, yeah. I'd forgotten all about that. And then what will you do?"

"Talk to Chief McDonald and hand over the evidence."

"Do you want me to come with you?" David asked.

"No need. The Chamber office needs to be opened. Pixie and Mr. Everett can cover for me if I'm late getting back to my store."

David nodded.

They didn't speak much as Tricia purchased the case of paper nor on the way back to the village. Tricia dropped David off in front of the Chamber office. He was officially late.

"Are you coming in today?" he asked.

"Not unless there's some kind of emergency. I have full confidence in your ability to handle just about anything that comes up."

"Thanks." He rummaged in his pocket for his keys, as well as those belonging to Sanjay—and the wallet. He handed them to Tricia. "Are you upset with me?"

"Why do you ask?"

"I don't know. Ever since that lady chased us off at Sanjay's apartment, you've been pretty tight-lipped."

"I'm sorry. I have a lot on my mind."

"Can we talk later?" he asked almost sheepishly.

"Later," she agreed.

Tricia drove back to the municipal lot where she parked, but she didn't immediately get out of her car. She was angry—not at David. At herself.

What on earth was she doing defying Angelica? Her actions were also sure to annoy Ian McDonald, but she couldn't seem to help herself. And she and David had uncovered two important pieces of evidence.

So why did she feel so guilty?

# TWENTY

**Haven't Got** a Clue wouldn't open for nearly ninety minutes, so Tricia decided to instead head right to the police station and speak to Chief McDonald, prepared for yet another lecture.

Tricia entered the station and a dour-faced Polly did a double take, gawking at Tricia's hair.

"Oh, my, Tricia, what brings you here on this fine day?" she asked, plastering on another fake smile. Her voice had gone rather high and she kept staring at Tricia. The whites of her eyes were so prominent that it rather creeped Tricia out.

"I need to speak with the chief. It's important."

"Well, I'm sure he'll be tickled pink to see you." Polly pressed the intercom button. "Chief, Tricia Miles is here to see you."

"Send her in," came McDonald's disembodied voice.

"Thank you, Polly," Tricia said.

Polly turned a sickening smile on Tricia. "It was my pleasure."

Tricia couldn't help the involuntary shudder that came over her as she stepped over to McDonald's office, rapping on the door before opening it.

McDonald rose from his seat as she entered, his eyes widening as he took in her new hairstyle.

"Uh, hello, Tricia, what's new?" he asked.

"Nothing much," she said, and sat down on one of the seats before his desk.

McDonald sat down again, just staring at her hair. "You look . . . you look nice," he said, and Tricia figured that was about as good a comment as she was going to get.

"What brings you in to see me today?" McDonald asked.

Tricia wished she'd rehearsed possible ways of introducing the subject. "I . . ." she began. "You see . . ." she started again.

McDonald frowned. "What is it?" he asked, not unkindly.

Tricia let out a breath. "On my walk this morning." She paused again. She had better be completely upfront about who was with her when she found the items she was about to turn over. "That is, my associate, David Price over at the Chamber of Commerce, and I took a walk this morning and we got to talking about the Sanjay Arya investigation."

"As one does," McDonald said in a low voice.

"And . . . we wondered about his missing wallet, keys, and phone."

"And?" McDonald prompted.

"We assumed the police had scoured the yard—"

"But you had a look anyway?" McDonald guessed.

"Well, yes."

"And what did you find?"

"In the yard . . . nothing."

He gave a satisfied nod.

"It was the border garden where we found them."

Now she had his attention. "Oh? You can't have found all three items."

"Just two of them. And under a particularly thorny rosebush, so it's no wonder they were missed."

Tricia opened her purse and withdrew the wallet and keys, handing them across the desk to the chief, who examined them, his expression grave. "How do you know they belonged to Arya?"

"We . . . kind of drove to Sanjay's apartment and tested one of the keys. It opened his door. Um . . . the Milford police might be getting in contact with you about that."

"Because?"

"His landlady took down my license plate number and said she was going to call the police."

"Did she now?" he asked, his Irish brogue growing stronger.

Tricia wasn't sure how to take McDonald's quiet acceptance of her story. His predecessor would have probably hit the ceiling in outrage.

"As the murder took place in your jurisdiction, I wanted you to have the items as soon as we ascertained they did indeed belong to Sanjay."

"I assume this is how you found the wallet—empty."

Tricia nodded. "I was wondering if you'd found the phone. I mean, you can ping it for its location, right?"

"We tried. We didn't have any luck."

Tricia nodded. The phone had probably been destroyed right after the murder. She'd have done it with a sledgehammer and *then* dropped it into the ocean as an extra measure.

"Thank you for bringing these items to my attention," McDonald said tersely.

"I know they really don't help your investigation," she said.

"Sadly, no. If only we could have found the phone we might have found out who Arya was meeting and why."

"What if he wasn't there to meet someone? What if his killer just followed him to the mansion and confronted him?"

"About what?"

Tricia didn't have anything to tell him. Secondhand gossip was only that.

"It does prove one thing," she said.

"And what's that?" McDonald asked.

"That whoever killed him hung around and buried Sanjay's property."

"Which makes no sense at all."

"I know. It's kind of like a tease," Tricia said.

"Except, as you pointed out, my team didn't find this."

"To be fair, the disturbed ground wasn't all that visible from the front of the bush."

"You found it."

"I was looking for it."

"And why was that?"

Tricia shrugged. "Just a gut feeling."

McDonald stared at the still-dusty evidence that sat on his blotter. "Anything else?"

"You will cover for me with the Milford police, won't you?" she asked hopefully.

McDonald nodded wearily.

"Thank you."

"What did you find at the apartment?" he asked.

"Evidence that Sanjay's roommate had recently moved out."

"He had a girlfriend," McDonald confirmed.

"And you've spoken to her?"

McDonald nodded.

"You wouldn't want to tell me who she is, would you?"

"No."

She didn't think so.

Tricia stood. "Well, I'd best be on my way. I've got a busy day ahead."

"I'd say you've already had one."

Tricia gave him a wry smile. "Just think what else I might accomplish today."

**Tricia was** about to return to her shop with just under an hour before it was scheduled to open when it occurred to her that it didn't give her time to accomplish much of anything. She hadn't had time to bake anything for the store, so she stopped in at the Coffee Bean to see what delights its owner, Alexa Kozlov, had on offer that day.

"Tricia," Alexa called as the little bell over the door chimed merrily. "It's good to see you."

"You, too." It had been a couple of weeks since Tricia had patronized the little coffee shop. "What have you got in the way of cookies today?"

"Butter cookies with chocolate frosting. So many people love dem," Alexa said. Her Russian accent was charming and only strongly emerged when she was upset about something. That day she was as cool as a cucumber.

"I'll take a dozen and a half," Tricia said. She decided to make small talk as Alexa wrapped up her order. "I don't suppose you ever served Sanjay Arya?"

"That poor man who got kilt last week? Oh, sure. He vas in here for coffee a couple of times a veek when he was working in the village. He liked cherry Danish. If ve didn't have cherry, he'd take cheese—never apple. He didn't like apple anything."

Alexa really knew her customers.

"What did you think about him?"

"A charmer, dat one."

"I never met him. I always worked with his boss, Jim Stark, on a project."

"He liked the ladies," Alexa said in a singsong cadence.

"So I've heard—but not whom."

Alexa scowled. "I don't like to spread gossip."

"I don't, either," Tricia said. No, she just liked to hear it—especially *if* it helped clear up a murder or some other crime. And this wasn't the first time she'd heard Sanjay was a womanizer, which was probably why his former housemate had moved out.

Tricia paid for the cookies and plastered a smile on her face. "It was so nice to see you. I'll be back soon."

"Yes, please," Alexa said.

Tricia left the shop and crossed the street for her own.

So no confirmation from Alexa just who Sanjay had been familiar with . . . but it had been more than one. Had Alexa been speculating about Sanjay's former girlfriend, or was there a third woman who'd been involved with Sanjay—and another possible murder suspect?

Tricia was determined to find out.

Just how that was to be accomplished was a mystery to her.

# TWENTY-ONE

**As always,** the butter cookies were a hit with Pixie and Mr. Everett. So much so that Tricia felt a little jealous, believing that any butter cookies she made would be just as good. But maybe she would step up her game and make something totally different. Sadly, bar cookies were just a little too messy to bake for the people who patronized her store. As it was, more than a few of the cookies she provided ended up dropped and mashed into the rug. Of course, Mr. Everett was a wizard when it came to such clean-ups, and he seemed ever-ready with the carpet sweeper so that a small mess didn't become a stain disaster.

One thing was for sure: Tricia wasn't going to be baking any-thing without hitting the supermarket for supplies. After polling Pixie and Mr. Everett for cookie suggestions, she settled on oatmeal raisin. Now all she had to do was drive to Milford to get the ingredients.

Tricia entered the grocery store, commandeered a cart, and headed for the produce section. She had a hankering for some strawberries and thought about making some shortcake for dinner with Angelica as sort of a peace offering—not that she felt she'd done anything wrong, but Angelica had been so snarky lately Tricia felt the need to try to defuse the situation. Tricia contemplated buying some bananas to possibly make banana bread when she caught sight of a vaguely familiar face across the way, standing in front of the store's community bulletin board. The woman was pinning up a photocopied flyer of what looked like a wedding dress. It took long moments before Tricia remembered where she'd met the woman. It was at Bar None the night she and David had gone on their ill-fated pub crawl.

Tricia pushed her cart to intercept the woman. "Excuse me, aren't you Candace from Bar None?"

"Yes," the woman said warily. "Do I know you?"

"I was a customer a few days ago. I came into the restaurant with a young man who asked you about Sanjay Arya."

Candace studied Tricia's face. "Sorry. I didn't recognize you. Your . . . hair—" She didn't elaborate.

"I wanted to apologize for my friend's rudeness," Tricia said, ignoring the younger woman's comment.

Candace shook her head sadly. "I was just as rude. It was just such a shock." She shook her head and her eyes filled with tears. "I haven't gotten over Sanjay's death." She gave a mirthless laugh. "I'll probably *never* get over his death."

Tricia said nothing, hoping Candace would say more.

She wasn't disappointed.

"You see, we lived together until very recently. I mean—until the end of April."

"You broke up?"

Candace nodded. "It wasn't my idea. I *loved* him. I wanted to marry him."

"And he didn't want to marry you?"

"Sure he did. There was just one little problem," she said tartly.

"And that was?" Tricia asked.

"He was engaged to be married to someone else."

Tricia blinked. "To whom?"

"I have no idea. It was to be an arranged marriage to a woman from India. It was his parents' idea," she said sourly. "I mean, this isn't the Middle Ages. Sanjay was *born* in this country. But he said he didn't have a choice in the matter."

"But if he loved you . . ."

"Oh, he did. But he'd already disappointed his parents by not going to medical school." Candace shook her head and swallowed hard. "They brainwashed him into the whole thing," she said bitterly.

"I take it his parents didn't know about you."

"They most certainly did. He took me to meet them when we decided to live together and that's when they started their whole campaign to marry him off to someone they would approve of."

"Someone they didn't even know?" Tricia asked.

"That was my reaction, too," Candace said sadly. She sighed. "I'm sorry I was rude to your friend. I thought I couldn't be more unhappy when Sanjay and I broke up, but knowing he's gone forever—" Her voice cracked and tears filled her eyes.

"I'm sorry," Tricia said sincerely. She waited until Candace had wiped her nose and dabbed at her eyes with a tissue before speaking again. "Did he have any enemies that you know of?"

Candace shook her head and then frowned. "Some of the guys on the work crew ragged on him. Just the usual racial harassment. Sanjay laughed it off—at least in front of them, but it did bother him."

Why wouldn't it?

"And his boss let them do it?"

"I don't think he knew. Sanjay didn't want Mr. Stark to think he couldn't keep control of the guys on the worksites. Sanjay was good to them. Bought them beers at the bars—sometimes had a case in a cooler in his truck and broke them out at the end of the day."

"Was he a drinker?"

Candace shook her head. "Not really. He'd more likely have a soda—which he also got teased for. They told him he wasn't man enough." She looked thoughtful and a faint smile crossed her lips. "That's where they were a hundred percent wrong."

At least Candace had some good memories of her time with Sanjay. Some might assume that being jilted could be a motive for murder, but Tricia didn't get that vibe. Candace struck her as a woman in mourning. But one of Sanjay's co-workers had told David that Sanjay was a mean drunk. To learn that he seldom drank alcohol was a red flag.

Candace leaned around Tricia, her attention straying.

"Have you heard anything about funeral arrangements?" Tricia asked.

Candace seemed to shake herself and frowned. "Only that Sanjay's sister had claimed his body and had it taken to Boston for cremation. I have no idea where his ashes are to be scattered." She shook her head. "I wouldn't be surprised if it was in the Ganges, although I'm sure that wouldn't be what Sanjay wanted. Then again, Sanjay thought he was invincible."

"Why?"

"Because he thought he'd led a charmed life."

People who live charmed lives aren't murdered with their own hammers.

"I'm so, so sorry for your loss," Tricia said sincerely.

"Thank you," Candace said. Once again she leaned to look around Tricia. This time Tricia glanced over her shoulder.

"Is something wrong?"

"Uh, no. I thought I saw someone I know." Whoever it was, it didn't seem like Candace wanted to run into them. "Uh, I hope you'll come back to Bar None, where I assure you you'll be treated like a welcome guest."

"Thank you. I'll be sure to make a return visit."

Candace nodded and stepped away to continue her shopping.

So, Sanjay had plans that may or may not have included staying in the area. At least, he'd planned to change his life enough to include marriage and perhaps start a family. Would his new bride have wanted to live in such a relatively cold climate? Would she have accepted his career choice? Speculating was a fruitless endeavor. That woman's life had gone through as radical a change as Candace had. Tricia felt sorry for both of them.

Tricia finished her shopping but before she stowed her grocery bags in the back of her car, she took a look at the flyer Candace had put up on the bulletin board. It pictured a vintage wedding dress hanging on a hanger. Had the woman bought the dress in hopes of marrying Sanjay, and now that she'd been dumped and he was dead, decided to get rid of such a sad reminder of what had been? At the bottom of the flyer were tabs with a phone number. She tore one off—just in case.

As she drove back to Stoneham, Tricia couldn't help but ruminate over what Candace had told her. Something just didn't seem right.

Had Sanjay started seeing Toni Bennett during the time he'd been with Candace or just after? And if he ended a relationship because he was supposed to be getting married, why connect with someone else? Had he lied to Candace rather than be man enough just to break it off? Or was he truly betrothed to a woman he'd never met and decided to sow some wild oats before he tied the knot?

Either way, it didn't cast Sanjay in a positive light.

Chief McDonald probably knew the truth. The question was, would he tell her if Tricia asked about the situation?

**Tricia made** the strawberry shortcake, but even the enticement of one of Angelica's favorite desserts couldn't dispel the aura of doom that seemed to permeate the atmosphere in her sister's apartment that evening.

"What is all the talk I've been hearing about you gallivanting around the village—and elsewhere—with David Price?" Angelica asked, stirring the martini mix so violently she was in danger of bruising the vermouth. "Do you realize the ramifications?"

"What ramifications? We're *friends*. I assure you, we *don't* have a physical relationship, if that's what you're inferring. That would be immoral."

"You're damn right it would be. But you know friendships also lead to other things."

"What are you accusing me of?" Tricia asked, her ire flaring.

"I think you're falling in love with him!" Angelica practically hollered.

Tricia glowered at her sister. "I am not. I'm old enough to be his mother."

"That hasn't stopped a lot of May–December romances."

Tricia let out an exasperated breath. May–December romance? Angelica made it sound like Tricia had one foot in the grave—and she was five years younger than her sister!

"You know that David doesn't have any transportation. I've been giving him a lift around the village. I took him to the big office supply store up on the highway this morning to get a case of paper for the Chamber."

"Couldn't you have just gone there by yourself?"

She could have. She didn't.

"There's much more than that little incident," Angelica continued.

"Like what?"

"The two of you were seen in a bar in Milford."

"Yes. Where David had something to eat because he'd run out of food. In case you've forgotten, there are no grocery stores here in Stoneham and David doesn't have transportation to the nearest one. Do you expect him to starve?"

"You were seen walking around the village in the early morning on multiple occasions."

"Is there a law against that? And you know I always walk around the village every morning. That David decided to join me a couple of times doesn't make it a habit." Tricia scrutinized her sister's face. "Why are you so upset, anyway?"

"I'm *not* upset!" Angelica cried, clearly upset.

"I don't understand what's going on. You're the one who hired David. You were very excited about him coming to work for the Chamber, but it seems like you took an instant dislike to him the minute you met him in person. Is there a reason?"

Angelica pouted for long seconds. "He . . . he wasn't what I expected."

"And what did you expect?"

"For one thing, not for *you* to fall for him."

"I haven't fallen for him," Tricia said defensively. "We're friends. Or at least I'd like to think so. We have common interests. It's natural that we'd talk about them. What's really behind all this animosity?"

Angelica didn't answer, but Tricia had an inkling.

"You're jealous!"

"I am not!" Angelica cried.

"Since David arrived, I haven't been paying as much attention to you, that's why you're angry."

"I'm *not* angry," Angelica said in a tone that belied that statement.

"Then what's going on?"

Angelica pouted and slumped against the counter. "Well, maybe I *am* just a little jealous. But just a teensy bit." Her lip trembled. "Now that Ginny's starting work again, Sofia is going back to daycare. They've got a nanny for little Will . . ."

"How does that affect you?" Tricia asked. For all she knew, Angelica was probably paying for both situations. And with all her business ventures, Angelica didn't have the time to devote to the little ones as a babysitter.

"It doesn't affect me," Angelica cried, and then she literally *did* cry, bursting into tears.

Tricia was instantly on her feet, rounded the island, and was at her sister's side in a moment, embracing her. "Come into the living room and sit down and tell me what's going on."

Angelica shuffled along, sniffing as she went, and Tricia snagged the box of tissues off the end of the counter, bringing it along. Angelica plunked onto the couch and Tricia handed her the box, settling in beside her sister.

"Now, what's going on?" Tricia asked again, her voice gentle.

"Oh, it's just that . . . nobody needs me."

As though to refute that statement, Sarge appeared, rested his front paws on his mistress's knees, and whimpered, eager to bring some comfort to his weepy human mama.

"Sweet boy," Angelica said, and picked up the dog. Sarge tentatively licked the tears from her cheeks.

Tricia reached over to pet the dog's head. "Apparently Sarge begs to differ."

"Yes, but he's a dog," Angelica said, and pressed a balled-up tissue to her runny nose.

"Are you feeling left out of Antonio's and Ginny's lives?" Tricia asked.

"Sort of," Angelica admitted. "I suppose I was spoiled these past few months while Ginny's been on maternity leave, seeing my grandbabies nearly every day and now that's at an end. Now Mrs. Bridges has the baby *all* to herself all day. Before that, I spent months seeing to *all* the details of their house rebuild. They needed me. Even you needed me. But now you've got your little boy toy—"

"Angelica!"

"Well, it's true, isn't it?"

"No, it isn't. He's a friend. Are you trying to tell me I shouldn't seek out friendship? That I should be alone when I'm not at work or with you?"

"No! It's just . . . oh, hell, I don't know what I'm saying. I'm just . . . in a bad place right now."

Tricia stared at her sister's bloodshot eyes and the droop of her mouth. A wave of compassion flowed over her.

"Ange, I'm not abandoning you. Neither are Antonio or Ginny. I'm sure if you want to go see the baby any time of the day, no one's going to stop you. And Sofia is getting to the age where the best thing in the world is going to be a sleepover with her nonna who spoils her rotten."

"Royally, not rotten," Angelica corrected her sister.

Tricia placed an arm around her sister's shoulder. "Have it your way."

"I do . . . *most* of the time." Angelica sniffed and rested her head on Tricia's shoulder. "Our martinis will be room temperature by now."

"If that's the biggest problem we have, then we have *no* problems," Tricia said flatly.

Angelica offered a weak laugh. She blew her nose and straightened, letting out a breath. "I'm sorry, Tricia. Can we start happy hour all over again?"

"Of course."

"I promise I won't yell or accuse you of anything."

"You don't have to promise me anything. But we can talk about what's eating you and then maybe we can figure out a way to make it better."

Angelica's frown deepened. "You're too nice to me."

"You've been pretty nice to me, too."

Angelica sighed once more. "I have, haven't I?"

Tricia glowered at her sister—and then they both laughed.

Tricia stood. "Let's drink our warm martinis and have something to eat, shall we? And then we can have that strawberry shortcake. I've been hankering for it all day."

Angelica grabbed a couple of fresh tissues and rose.

"Life is short. We'll eat the dessert first."

# TWENTY-TWO

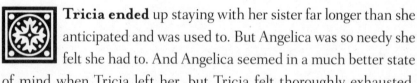**Tricia ended** up staying with her sister far longer than she anticipated and was used to. But Angelica was so needy she felt she had to. And Angelica seemed in a much better state of mind when Tricia left her, but Tricia felt thoroughly exhausted. That's why she decided to go to bed early and had just settled in with a good book—Agatha Christie's *Cat Among the Pigeons*—when the ringtone on her phone sounded.

Thinking Angelica might have had another emotional crisis, she picked up the phone and winced.

"Hey, Tricia, it's Becca."

Like Tricia hadn't read the name on her cell phone's screen. Tricia closed her eyes and wished she'd just let voice mail take a message. She sighed. "What can I do for you?"

"Nothing, just calling to see how things are with you."

Which was bull. "I'm fine. And you?"

"Peachy keen." Something in Becca's tone was off.

"Are you sure?" Tricia asked.

"Well, now that you mention it," Becca said, but then paused.

Oh, dear. Was Tricia going to have to play psychologist for a second time that evening?

"It's just that . . ." Another long pause followed, and Tricia tried not to lose her patience. "I don't have a lot of friends around here but I consider *you* to be one of them."

Tricia didn't reply in kind. They *weren't* friends. They were wary acquaintances at best—or at least that's the way Tricia felt. Still, Tricia wasn't beyond reaching out to a troubled soul.

"You don't sound fine. Can I help in any way?"

"Don't be silly. I'm perfectly . . ." But then Tricia heard what sounded like a sob.

"Becca?"

"I . . . I've lost someone dear. It was sudden—nothing anyone could have expected. I guess besides grief, I'm sensing my own mortality."

Becca hadn't sounded as upset when Tricia had first met her the previous fall after the death of her ex-husband and Tricia's lover, Marshall/Eugene.

"Is there something you want to tell me?" Tricia asked.

"This person was someone I'd been . . ." Becca took a breath, as though she wondered how she could categorize the relationship. "Uh, intimate with."

"Was it anyone I knew?"

"I don't think so. I mean, not personally."

The only person Tricia knew who'd died recently was—

Tricia frowned. "Why didn't you tell me you had a relationship with Sanjay?"

"It wasn't a relationship. We got together a few times. I realize it was a terrible breach of protocol for him to sleep with his client, but it was as much my fault as his. But one does get lonely, especially after relocating."

Yes, one certainly did.

"And?" Tricia prompted.

"And . . . when someone is kind to you, you tend to gravitate toward them."

That was true.

"Do you know anything about Sanjay's death that could help the police solve the case?"

Becca sighed. "We talked about my project, but when it came to pillow talk . . . well, there wasn't a whole lot of it, if you get my drift. But I did like him. We had some fascinating conversations. And he was—" She seemed to struggle with a descriptor. "Exotic—at least to me."

"Because he wasn't your privileged white guy."

"No, he was a pretty privileged brown guy and a damn fine lover. I miss him. I miss the conversations we might have had, as well as the sex."

This was more information than Tricia really wanted to know. "Why are you telling me this?"

"I guess because I need to grieve . . . if only a little bit. I mean, I knew there was no future in a relationship with him, but, as I said, I really did like him. He was sweet. And he made me smile. It's been a long time since a man made me smile."

Was that an allusion to her ex-husband? Had Eugene—known to Tricia as Marshall—actually been the love of Becca's life?

"Do the police know?"

"Oh, yeah," Becca said, sounding more than a little embarrassed. "They seem to know everything about me and everybody I've ever known."

She *had* been a suspect in Marshall's death, if only peripherally.

"I don't suppose they mentioned where they were in the investigation."

Becca sniffed. "Of course not. Why would we mere mortals need to know?"

"I suppose they figure it will all come out eventually."

"Meanwhile, those of us who cared about Sanjay are left in the dark about what happened to him and why. And what if they *never* figure out who killed him?"

It happened all too often.

"And now that Sanjay's gone, Jim Stark's secretary tells me my project could be put off for months—maybe even a year."

At least someone at Stark Construction was making and taking phone calls.

"Will you wait for him?"

"Are you kidding? I want this first tennis club up and running ASAP. I've already put out a call to every contractor I could find in southern New Hampshire."

Becca had done no such thing. Her people had done the groundwork. She just paid the bills.

"Did you know Sanjay was with Toni Bennett, too?"

Becca hesitated before answering. "Maybe."

"Becca!" Tricia chided her.

"Okay, yes," she answered testily. "But she was only in it for the sex, too."

"That's what Sanjay told you?"

"Of course."

"And it didn't bother you?" All Tricia could think about was sexually transmitted diseases that could be traded back and forth by those who let their animal natures control them.

"I'm not a fool," Becca said, as though reading Tricia's mind. "I took precautions, or at least I insisted that Sanjay take them."

Tricia didn't consider herself a prude, but if she'd found one of her lovers had been with other women, she'd have ended the relationship. If the idea of monogamy was old-fashioned, then she was stuck with that label. But she didn't judge Becca on that account. She'd lived much larger than Tricia ever had. Someone who'd met and been befriended by rock stars, politicians, and every other kind of celebrity would have a broad perspective. But it just went to prove that small town or large city, big names or everyday people, the forces of nature held great sway.

"According to Sanjay, he wasn't the only Stark Construction worker Toni was sleeping with."

Tricia's eyes widened. "Would you care to drop a name?"

"He never said."

"I'm sorry for your loss," Tricia said sincerely.

"Thank you," Becca said, all traces of grief now erased from her tone.

What Tricia had really wanted to ask was: *What do you expect me to do about it?* Instead, she asked, "What do you know about Sanjay's death?"

"Only what I've heard on the news and what you told me. We might not have loved each other, but I did feel a connection to the man. He had a bright future. I want to see whoever killed him in an orange jumpsuit with shackles on his wrists and feet."

"And what if it was a woman who killed him?"

"Do you honestly think a woman could kill in such a brutal fashion?" Becca asked.

"You're darn right. Especially if she thought Sanjay was stepping out on her."

"Sanjay was nothing more than a boy toy—at least to others."

Had Becca been channeling Angelica by using that description?

"You keep saying that"—in one way or another, Tricia thought. "And if that's so, then why are you so upset?" she asked.

"I'm not a monster. I *do* have feelings, you know."

"I didn't mean—"

"Why are you being so monstrous to me?" Becca accused.

"I'm not. I—"

"I'm sorry I even called you now. And I thought we were friends," Becca said, sounding bitter. And with that, the connection was broken.

Tricia closed her eyes and let out a long breath before she very gently placed her phone back on the nightstand. She felt like flinging it across the room, but her annoyance was with Becca, not the phone. And now Tricia was sure she'd never drift off to sleep.

She read the same page three times before it began to make sense, and by then Tricia was too tired to care. Placing a bookmark between the pages, she closed the book, set it aside, and turned off the light, wondering, as she sank into slumber, why she let Becca annoy her as much as she did.

Maybe they truly *were* friends.

**Tricia's ringtone** broke the quiet once more. She awoke feeling groggy, and after her conversation with Becca, she wished she'd turned off the phone for the rest of the night. But then she reached for it and glanced at the caller ID and saw it was Angelica calling. What did *she* want at this time of night? Tricia stabbed the call-accept button to find out.

"Trish? I just got a call from Antonio. The mansion's on fire!"

Tricia's sleep-heavy eyes blinked open and she sat bolt upright in bed. "What?"

"I've got to get there. Will you come with me?"

"Yes! Yes! Let me throw on some clothes and I'll meet you on the sidewalk outside the Cookery." Tricia didn't even wait for her sister's reply and stabbed the end-call icon and leapt out of bed, tossing on the clothes she'd dumped into the hamper just hours before. She grabbed her purse and keys and hurtled down the stairs, with Miss Marple following in her wake, no doubt wondering what the trouble was. Tricia had no time to explain and slammed and locked the door behind her. Angelica was already on the sidewalk.

"Hurry! Hurry!" she called.

They didn't run, but they could have won prizes for speed walking to the municipal parking lot. Tricia unlocked her car and they jumped in. She started the engine and they were off in seconds, heading for the mansion.

"What all did Antonio say?" Tricia asked.

"Just that he'd gotten a call that the mansion was ablaze. Since they live outside of the village, we should get there before he does."

It took little more than a minute before Tricia pulled her car to a halt behind the fire and rescue trucks. There was no sign of fire, just smoke curling from the back of the house into the dark sky.

The sisters exited the car and hurried to stand before the mansion, which was lit up with lights coming from a police car and the fire engine. The air reeked with the acrid odor of charred wood, but the firefighters, decked out in their heavy gear, were ambling around the yard and no one seemed to be in any kind of hurry.

"Looks like the fire's out already," Tricia said. "Let's ask."

"No!" Angelica said sharply. "We need to wait for Antonio to arrive. He's the one with the NR street cred."

Tricia eyed her sister. "Street cred?"

"Oh! You know what I mean. For all they know, we're just innocent rubberneckers. They won't talk to us."

"I see what you mean."

And so they waited. For a Long. Five. Minutes.

By the time Antonio's car arrived, the firefighters had disconnected the hoses from the nearest hydrant and were winding them up and replacing them on the trucks.

"That's got to be a good sign," Tricia said. "Maybe it was only a small fire."

Antonio hurriedly joined them. "What do you know?" he asked, somewhat breathless.

"Nothing. But as you can see, they've apparently already put out the fire," Tricia said.

"Wait here," Antonio said, and went off in search of a higher authority.

"The front of the building looks fine," Tricia told her sister, trying to sound cheerful.

"But what about the back? And what could have caused it?"

Tricia had been thinking about the possibility of arson since the moment she'd received Angelica's call. She suspected her sister felt the same way. She glanced at Angelica. The harsh, bright light highlighted every crease in her face, and her brow was furrowed with worry.

"What are you thinking?" Tricia asked.

"That this is going to set the project back even further. Ginny's team isn't going to be able to move in by the end of July."

"You can afford to billet them somewhere else for a couple of weeks," Tricia said reasonably.

"It's not the money. Screw the money. But it could have a devastating toll on their morale. I want my people to be happy in their work. Unhappy employees do lousy work."

Tricia grabbed her sister's shoulder and pulled her closer. "You'll make sure they're well taken care of in their temporary digs."

They watched as Antonio spoke to the fire chief, nodding every so often. Finally, he looked in their direction, but his expression didn't betray what he'd just learned. The fire chief clapped him on the shoulder and Antonio started across the short-cropped grass to join them once again.

He let out a weary breath before speaking. "It looks like arson," he confirmed.

"I knew it," Tricia muttered.

"But . . . thanks to the lady across the street." The women looked and saw the woman Tricia and David had spoken to days before. "She took her dog out to pee and smelled the smoke. She called the fire department and they were here in minutes."

"How's the damage?"

"We can go look if you like, but the chief said it was confined to the kitchen."

"Oh, no!" Angelica wailed. It was her favorite part of the house.

"He said the damage was minimal because they got here so soon."

"Thank goodness for that," Tricia said.

"You may go look, if you wish."

"I wish," Angelica said tersely.

"Will it look funny? I mean—"

"Do not worry. I have your cover story planned, Mama."

"Shhh!" Angelica warned.

Antonio shook his head but a wry smile covered his lips. "Come."

The sisters followed him around the building, which was still lit up like daylight, and they picked their way through the debris that had already been taken from the building. The original windows were broken, and the double doors that led to the back garden were held open by the vintage urns that had once boasted flowers, but now held nothing but dirt and weeds.

They peered through the windows. The floor was scorched and the subway tile was covered in soot, but the room appeared to be intact. Perhaps the original cabinetry could be restored. Tricia was no expert in that regard.

Tears filled Angelica's eyes.

"Hey," Tricia soothed. "It's not so bad."

"It can be repaired," Antonio assured her. "And no one was hurt."

"Thank goodness," Tricia agreed.

Angelica wiped a hand across her eyes and nodded. "Who would do such a thing?"

"Off the top of my head . . . the person who killed Sanjay Arya," Tricia said.

"But why?"

Tricia shrugged. "Maybe he or she thought there might still be some incriminating evidence in the building."

"The police were very thorough," Angelica deadpanned.

"Well, they missed Sanjay's wallet and keys," Tricia muttered.

"What wallet and keys?" Angelica asked.

"Didn't you hear? They were found buried in the garden."

"No, I didn't hear that. How did *you* hear about it?"

Tricia shrugged. "I'm interested in such things. People tell me that kind of stuff."

Angelica didn't look convinced.

"We'll have to get Jim Stark out here first thing in the morning to assess the damage," Angelica said, turning back to gaze at the mess. "And we've got to get this place buttoned up so no one else can vandalize it."

"The chief has already asked the police to call the emergency enclosure people. It may take them a few hours to get here, but it will be boarded up before morning."

Angelica nodded, still looking dispirited.

"It could have been much worse," Tricia said.

"Yes. We will not look a gift horse in the mouth," Antonio said.

The sisters turned on him with questioning stares.

"Did I say something wrong?"

Antonio spoke beautiful English, but sometimes he got his clichés confused. "That's not exactly the correct analogy, but I get the drift," Tricia said.

"Why don't you go home and get some sleep?" Antonio said.

"You're the one who should go home," Angelica said.

But Antonio shook his head. "Little Will does not yet sleep through the night—which means none of us sleeps through the night, either."

"But won't Ginny need you?" Angelica asked.

"She told me to do what I must. She wants to move her office into the mansion as soon as possible. I will call her as soon as I send you two on your way," he said pointedly.

"I'd be glad to wait with you," Angelica said.

Antonio shook his head. "It's best you go before people ask questions about you two being here at all."

"Come on," Tricia coaxed. "I'll take you home and make you some cocoa. You'll feel better. I will, too."

Angelica nodded and Antonio gave his mother a quick peck on the cheek. Tricia clasped her sister's arm and practically dragged her from the site. Angelica slogged along to the car, looking absolutely desolate.

The sisters didn't talk on their way back to the municipal parking lot, but Tricia's mind was awhirl. Would the killer have returned to try to eliminate evidence? Wouldn't it have been easier just to take whatever it was they were after and sneak off into the night? Could it have been just some kid who wanted to wreak havoc?

Those were questions she was sure would keep her from having a good night's sleep.

# TWENTY-THREE

**When she** stepped outside Haven't Got a Clue the next morning for her usual walk, Tricia wasn't surprised to find that David was once again waiting for her.

"Penny for your thoughts," she said by way of a greeting.

"I heard about the fire at the mansion last night," he said grimly.

Tricia let out a breath and kept walking north. "The grapevine is certainly up to date. You heard it in person or via the media?" she asked.

"The Nashua TV station, although there wasn't any video. I'm assuming you've already checked it out."

"Now why would I do that?" Tricia asked.

"Because not much happens in this village without you knowing about it," he said soberly.

Tricia saw no point in denying it. "Yes, I was there last night, and it was unofficially deemed arson. A full investigation will be made, but it was pretty obvious even to someone like me."

They paused at the corner. Since there was no traffic, they crossed Main Street against the light.

"Any suspects?" David asked.

"No. But . . ." She paused to look both ways before crossing the side road and heading north once again. "I thought I'd walk past the mansion again this morning. The woman we spoke to the other day was the one who called it in. She took her dog out for a potty break last night and smelled the smoke."

"Do you think she saw anything of interest?"

"I wasn't going to knock on her door and harass her about it in the dead of night, but if she happens to be outside watering her flowers again . . ." She let the sentence trail off.

"Sounds like a plan," David said, grinning.

"Just so you know, people are beginning to talk about us," Tricia said.

"What about us? What do you mean?"

"Well, that we're apparently gallivanting around the village."

"We're going from place to place seeking out amusement and entertainment?" David asked, giving a dictionary description for the word and sounding doubtful.

"That's the scoop."

David looked all around them. At this hour of the morning, there was very little in the way of foot or vehicular traffic. "Who's saying this?"

"My sister has it on good authority—not that she'd share *who* told her."

"Small towns are known for being gossip mills," David told her.

"That they are," Tricia agreed. "But it's just one of the very few downsides. I lived in Manhattan for more than fifteen years. They were good years, but there came a time when it all became too much. Too many people, too much noise."

"Too much crime?" David asked. "I mean, this place has had a plethora of murders. The highest in the state—worse than New Hampshire's biggest cities."

"Passions run hot here," was all Tricia had to offer as an explanation.

"Maybe there's something in the water," David suggested in jest.

"Could be," Tricia agreed.

They turned onto Maple Avenue and strode straight toward the Morrison Mansion, pausing to stand before it. The yard had been badly trampled the night before—not that it hadn't been virtually destroyed by construction vehicles in the weeks before.

"I did some research on the guy who built this house," David said.

"Was he a robber baron?"

"Not far from it. It's said he was a tyrant who made his workers toil six days of the week, and if they gave him any lip, he'd fire them on the spot. There was always someone who'd take their places. He didn't like the fact that they all wanted the sabbath off. He considered them a bunch of malingerers."

"I'm glad I never worked for him," Tricia said.

"Pity the people who did. At least the Stoneham Historical Society didn't try to paint a rosy picture of the man. I wonder if he'd been a kinder person if his home wouldn't have fallen into . . . well, not ruin, but it's apparently been badly abused since his fortunes faded," David commented.

"You've really made yourself at home here in Stoneham, learning its history and all in such a short time," Tricia observed.

"I like it here. It's got a lot of charm, some interesting history, and except for the exceptional amount of murders that seem to happen here, the people seem pretty friendly."

As though to prove him right, they heard a voice call from across the street.

"Hello!"

Tricia and David turned to see the elderly woman they'd spoken to five days before. They crossed the street to speak with her.

"I've seen you walking through the village for years," the woman said to Tricia. "There aren't many who are as diligent," the woman commented.

"It's my favorite way of exercising."

"You're Tricia, and you're David," the woman remembered.

"Yes, but we don't know your name," Tricia said.

"Elise McKenzie." She scrutinized Tricia's face. "You're also the woman who keeps finding dead bodies around the village."

Tricia blinked, startled.

"I thought I recognized you the other day. I've seen your picture in the *Stoneham Weekly News*. You own that mystery bookstore."

"Yes, I do."

"We heard you called nine one one about the fire across the street last night," David said. "We wondered if you saw anything of note."

"No, but once again my door camera did. Of course, the resolution wasn't good enough to identify the person, but it did pick up someone skulking around the building just before I came out with my little dog." They could hear muffled yapping from inside the house.

"And that's when you smelled smoke?"

"When I was a little girl, our house caught fire. It couldn't be saved. It's an odor you never forget," she said sadly. "So as soon as I caught a whiff of burning wood, I called nine one one. I figured better safe than sorry."

"I'm sure the building's owner is extremely grateful you did."

Elise shrugged. "Probably not. When I heard that Nigela Ricita Associates had bought the building, I had hoped they'd do right by it by restoring it as much as possible, but it looks like it's just going to be a spit-and-polish kind of renovation."

"I know they're doing what they can to save architectural elements by covering them up rather than removing them," Tricia said.

"Big deal," the older woman said.

"I spoke to Ms. Ricita's associate about the garden versus the parking lot," Tricia said.

Elise brightened. "Are they going to restore it?"

"No, but she was going to inquire about a smaller footprint for the lot. Unfortunately, it seems that they need the parking for the workers."

Elise scowled. "There are pictures of the gardens at the Stoneham Historical Society. You might want to bring them to Ms. Ricita's attention."

"I'll do that. Perhaps they could at least restore a part of the garden."

"Part is better than nothing, I suppose," Elise said.

The dog's barking continued.

"It's time I feed my little dog."

"What's his name?" Tricia asked.

"Benny. Benny Goodboy."

Tricia smiled. "And is he?"

Elise beamed. "The best."

"We'd better get going, too," David said. "Work awaits."

"It was so nice speaking with you, Elise. I'll try to find out more about the Morrison Mansion garden for you."

"Thank you. Have a good day."

"You, too."

Tricia and David retraced their steps, heading toward Main Street.

"Did you really talk to someone at NR Associates about the garden?" he asked.

"Of course. Did you think I was lying just to curry favor with Ms. McKenzie?"

"Well, no . . . but why would Ms. Ricita care about a garden?"

"She cares about a lot of things. In fact, I think it's actually breaking her heart not to be doing a full restoration as Elise would like to see. I also think she'd love to *live* in the mansion, but it's just not practical."

"Who cares about practicality when you've got her kind of money?" David asked.

"Cash flow. A lot of it is tied up in her various businesses."

David shrugged. "She probably already lives in a mansion. I heard she splits her time between New Hampshire and Manhattan."

"Not really. And she actually has quite a modest home."

"You've been there?" David asked, sounding surprised.

"Once or twice," Tricia said, which was bending the truth more than a little.

"What's it like?"

"Her home?"

"What are we talking about?" David asked.

"She lives in an apartment."

"Where?"

"I've been asked not to say."

"Sounds fishy to me."

"I assure you, she's very much on the up-and-up—and she values her privacy."

They made it to Main Street and paused at the intersection. "Are you going to start your day at the Chamber?" David asked.

Tricia shook her head. "I'm going to keep walking for a while. I have some thinking to do and strolling around the village usually helps me clarify my thoughts. That is, of course, unless you need my help on some specific problem. Why?"

David shrugged. "I like your company."

She wished he wouldn't say things like that, but part of her didn't mind at all.

**Much as** she tried, Tricia couldn't seem to make sense of the muddle of information about Sanjay's death that was floating around her brain. Two women—lovers and possibly rivals—could have had a motive for murder. Then there was Toni Bennett's gun-owning, jealous husband who might have had a motive, but the killer had used a hammer, not a firearm, to kill Sanjay. And Stark needed Sanjay. Killing the man responsible for keeping every project Stark Construction undertook on track would be madness. And what about Candace with no last name? Was she the apologetic sweet thing Tricia had met in the grocery store or was she an angry, jilted woman who'd been thrown over for a mail-order bride?

As Tricia approached the Morrison Mansion for the second time that morning, she noticed a dark-skinned woman of perhaps thirty dressed in a white dress and with long, shining black hair cascading down her back, standing in front of the building. It didn't take a leap in logic to guess who she might be.

"Excuse me," Tricia said as she approached the woman. "But are you Sanjay Arya's sister?"

The stunningly beautiful woman turned to face her. "Yes. And you are?"

"Tricia Miles. I'm one of the bookstore owners here in the village," she said, extending her hand.

"Radha Arya," the woman said, accepting Tricia's offered hand. They shook on it. "Did you know my brother?"

"Uh . . . no," Tricia admitted. "But I was here when his body was found. I'm so sorry for your loss."

The woman turned back to gaze at the mansion. "Thank you," she said sadly.

"I'm rather surprised to see you here," Tricia said. "I understood you claimed his body days ago."

"Yes, and now I'm back in Stoneham to clear out his apartment, although it doesn't look as though he accumulated much during his stay. But the woman who owns the house is eager to get a cleaning crew in and rent the place as soon as possible."

Tricia could understand that from a business point of view, but it seemed she was pushing the victim's family pretty hard, considering their recent loss.

"I was so upset last week that I didn't have the time or emotional strength to come here, to the place where my brother died. I wonder still if I do."

"I can well understand your conflicted feelings," Tricia said. "My—" She paused. Technically, Christopher Benson was her ex at the time of his death, but she plowed on anyway. "—husband was murdered. Even though I saw his killer sentenced, it brought me no peace. Nothing could."

Radha nodded and went back to staring at the mansion's stone front.

"As I mentioned, I didn't personally know Sanjay, but during the past few days I've met a number of people who did."

"And the consensus of opinion is?" Radha asked.

"That he had a quick smile and was a congenial kind of guy."

Radha nodded. "He was the happier of my parents' two children, that's for sure," she said bitterly.

"Would it be presumptuous of me to ask why?" Tricia said.

"The charmer gets his way far more than the hardworking sibling."

Was the relationship between the Arya children strained by gender inequality? Probably. Or was it that she was the younger sibling who was treated differently? In Tricia's family, Angelica could do no wrong, and in their mother's eyes, Tricia could do nothing right.

"Is it true that your parents wanted him to be a doctor?"

"Yes, but they eventually gave up on that idea because it was obvious Sanjay was never going that route. I mean, he showed at a very early age where his interests lay when he used to binge-watch *This Old House* reruns. He'd save his allowance to buy tools and would build and fix broken things around the house, although if you ask me, sometimes I think he broke them just to see how they worked." She sighed. "My parents tried to push him into going to college to be an architect, even threatening to disown him, but instead he became an apprentice to study residential carpentry."

"That must have been hard for your parents. I understand you came from a very traditional family," Tricia said.

Radha glanced at her askance. "In what way?"

Tricia shrugged. "Your names, for one. And the fact that Sanjay was going to go into an arranged marriage."

Radha actually did a double take. "What? You've got the first part right, but you are *way* off on the second," she said.

"But . . . I was told he had to break up with his girlfriend because he was marrying someone from India."

"Well, that was a big fat lie. Or whoever told you that was terribly misinformed. Yes, our parents are pretty traditional, but they're not reactionary. And who told you that, anyway?" Radha said, placing her hands on her hips and looking more than a little perturbed.

"Sanjay's ex-girlfriend Candace."

Radha's eyes widened. "He had a girlfriend?"

"That's news to you?" Tricia asked.

"Yeah. He never mentioned being with anyone."

That was odd. Candace had distinctly said she'd met Sanjay's parents. Why wouldn't the elder Aryas mention Sanjay's live-in lover to his sister?

"Apparently, they'd been living together for some time. She said she'd met your parents, who disapproved of their relationship."

"Who is this Candace person?" Radha asked, her voice hardening.

"A server at one of the restaurants in Milford. Would you like to meet her?"

"Not really. I mean, what's the point? You said she was an ex-girlfriend. Did they part amicably?"

Was she thinking Candace might be a suspect in her brother's death?

Again Tricia shrugged. "She seemed sad, but she didn't appear angry about it to me. More resigned."

"I would've been pissed as hell. But then I don't suppose she knows the truth. Yet. Will you tell her?"

"It's not my place," Tricia said. "What will you do now?"

Radha sighed. "Try to be a good daughter. Unlike my brother, *I* went to medical school. I did *everything* they wanted me to do. *I* didn't break their hearts. But . . . I'm not a son, either," she lamented.

"I'm sorry."

"What have you got to be sorry for?" Radha asked.

"I suspect you and I have a lot in common."

Radha raised an eyebrow but didn't comment. She shook her head and went back to looking at the building. "Shouldn't someone be working here?"

"They closed down the renovation after what happened to Sanjay," Tricia reported.

"That can't be good for the person who owns the building—*or* the construction company."

"No. And what's more, there was a fire here last night."

Radha's mouth opened in shock.

"They suspect arson," Tricia said, trying to keep her voice neutral.

"Did it have anything to do with my brother's death?"

"That's one theory."

Radha shook her head sadly.

"Did Sanjay talk much about his job and his position in the company?"

Radha shook her head. "It wasn't a happy topic at family gatherings."

"So, you knew nothing about his work?"

"Not really. Just that he seemed to love it. Like I said, he was always good at tinkering with broken things. Fixing broken toys, lamps, and household appliances. That *was* appreciated, but not as a choice of career." Radha sighed, pulled out her phone, and looked at the time. "I really should be going. I want to clear out that apartment, go home, and never visit this place again."

"What'll happen to Sanjay's things?"

"Most of them can go to charity. From what I saw, he didn't have much of a personal nature. The police took his computer. I suppose they'll eventually give it back to us—not that we have a call for it. They never found his phone—or at least if they did, they didn't tell us."

"I know his wallet was found empty. Do you know if anyone tried to use his credit cards?"

"Not as far as I know. I suppose I'd better make it my business to find out."

"I'm sure if they had, the police would have told you."

"They know that kind of stuff?" Radha asked.

Tricia nodded. "You might want to speak to Chief McDonald of the Stoneham PD about it. He might be able to give you a copy of Sanjay's credit report. It could save you a lot of time shutting down all his accounts."

"Thanks for the tip. And thanks for bringing me up to date on my brother's life. The police certainly haven't been as forthcoming."

"I'm glad I could be of some help," Tricia said sincerely.

Radha nodded, gave the mansion one last look, and began to walk away. Tricia watched as she got into a silver Mercedes, started the car, and steered toward Main Street.

Tricia began walking in the same direction, retracing her earlier steps. So, Sanjay had lied to Candace about his so-called arranged marriage. But why? Just as an excuse to dump her? But they still resided in the same vicinity. He had to know that eventually she'd find out that he'd conned her into leaving him. Or had he planned on one day just telling her the whole affair had been called off?

If Candace found out about Sanjay's big lie, would she have been angry enough to kill him? She seemed broken up about his death, but she could just be a good actress. Tricia had been taken in by a glib tongue on more than one occasion.

Those thoughts that had been muddling Tricia's mind seemed to be whirling a lot faster after her conversation with Radha. With no resolution in sight, she headed back for Haven't Got a Clue and her workday.

It would be a long one.

# TWENTY-FOUR

**Tricia was** relieved to get back to her store. She'd been through enough during the past fourteen hours and craved routine. *No more drama today,* she vowed, but that wasn't what fate had in store for her.

No sooner had Pixie and Mr. Everett arrived for the day, with the coffee made, and the three of them ready to sit down in the reader's nook for their start-of-day ritual, when Tricia got a text from Angelica.

*I need you.*

Sighing heavily, Tricia felt like collapsing into a boneless heap on the upholstered chair, but instead, she answered. *What for?*

*I'll be right over.*

Tricia stared at her sister's text. She hadn't even had time to mention the fire to her friends and employees, although the way news traveled in Booktown, she wouldn't have been surprised if they'd both seen it on the news as David had.

"Looks like Angelica's having a bad day," she said, standing and pocketing her phone. "She's coming over for a chitchat."

"Is there anything we can do to help?" Mr. Everett asked.

"I'll let you know," Tricia said.

Angelica was true to her words and arrived only seconds later. Her eyes were bloodshot and puffy, no doubt from crying. Still, she greeted Pixie and Mr. Everett without bursting into tears but signaled that she wanted to speak privately and headed for the stairs leading to Tricia's apartment.

Miss Marple followed the sisters, probably hoping for an additional kitty snack. She was to be disappointed.

Upon arriving at Tricia's kitchen, Angelica slumped onto one of the kitchen island's stools.

"Do you want some coffee—or do you need a stiff drink?" Tricia asked.

"I want the latter, but I'll take the first," Angelica said wearily.

Tricia pulled the canister of coffee from one of the cabinets and got started. "You've been crying your eyes out over the mansion, haven't you?"

"Is it that obvious?"

"I'd say from about twenty feet."

"I need to go over there in daylight to assess the damage for myself."

"Does Antonio know you want to do that?"

She shook her head. "He'd only try to talk me out of it."

With good cause.

"I don't think it's a good idea."

"Why not? It's *my* building."

"It's an NR Associates building."

"Yes, *mine*," Angelica asserted. She softened her voice. "Will you come with me?"

"Back to the mansion?"

"Well, I would think you'd be interested in seeing what's left of my beautiful kitchen."

Tricia decided not to tell her sister that she'd already visited the mansion twice that day and it was barely past ten in the morning.

"Of course I will."

"We can walk if you'd like."

Tricia had already done two circuits around the village and was in no mood for a third. "I think we can take the car. Shall I drive us?"

"Yes, please. But after we finish our coffee. I feel the need for fortification. Have you got any cookies?"

"*Yow!*" Miss Marple agreed from her spot by the empty bowl by the fridge.

"Sorry. I should freeze a few every time I make a batch—just for emergency purposes."

"I would consider this an emergency."

Tricia wasn't sure she agreed, but she kept that opinion to herself.

They drank their coffees before heading for the municipal parking lot to pick up Tricia's car and then drove to the mansion.

Tricia parked the car on the empty driveway and as she got out, she noticed Elise McKenzie was back out working on her flower beds.

"Back again?" she called, and laughed. "Why don't you just move in?"

Tricia smiled, waved, and turned her back on the woman.

"What did she mean by that?" Angelica asked.

"Nothing," Tricia said, and ushered Angelica toward the back of the house.

As promised, the emergency-enclosure people had arrived sometime after the sisters had left the evening before and all the windows and doors had been boarded up.

"There, you see—nothing to see," Tricia said. "Maybe we ought to—"

"I've got a key to the front door. We'll go in that way," Angelica said authoritatively, opened the fanny pack she wore around her middle, removed a set of keys, and did an abrupt about-face.

A reluctant Tricia followed. "Where did you get the keys?"

"I had another set made after Antonio loaned them to me the other day."

"Does he know about them?"

"Of course," she said, but then muttered, "not."

Tricia sighed and shook her head.

The once-beautiful oak door had been marred with a succession of locks that had been changed over the years. The current dead bolt took a bit of effort, but Angelica soon had it open.

The mansion's interior reeked of smoke, and Tricia swallowed down her revulsion. Angelica again reached into her fanny pack and extracted a couple of surgical masks. "I never travel without them," she told Tricia, and handed her one. It wasn't as efficient as Tricia would have liked, but she appreciated the thought behind it.

Angelica next pulled out her phone and activated its flashlight. Tricia did the same and they picked their way through the house, stepping over soggy cardboard and other detritus until they reached the kitchen. Angelica shook her head at the destruction, which appeared to be more from water damage than the fire itself. She played the light around the room and her brow furrowed. Tricia could imagine her mouth quirking into a frown behind the mask.

"What's wrong?" Tricia asked.

"I'm not sure," she said. She stood there for long moments, moving the light back and forth before she turned and began to retrace her steps. Tricia followed her to the front of the mansion where there were still some windows letting in daylight. The firefighters hadn't smashed them all.

Angelica stopped in the middle of what had once been a parlor, the lines on her forehead growing deeper.

"What's wrong?" Tricia asked.

Angelica pointed toward the ceiling. "Where are my plaster medallions?" she cried, frustration evident in her tone.

Tricia looked up at the latticework of metal that would hold a suspended ceiling. She'd been told that vintage pieces like crystal chandeliers had been removed and preserved before the renovation had begun, but there was a gaping hole in the original ceiling's plaster where the decorative ornament had previously resided.

"Is it something they would have taken down to prevent it from being destroyed?" Tricia asked.

"No! Leaving it up there is what would prevent it from being destroyed." Angelica's breaths were coming out in short pants, sort of like a bull who was snorting before attacking a matador. "I wonder what else is missing." She took off, for what might have once been a grand dining room where the suspended ceiling had already been completed, providing fluorescent lighting, as well as soundproofing for a future conference room.

Angelica grabbed an aluminum ladder that leaned against one of the walls and struggled to move it to the center of the room, viciously kicking pieces of wood and other debris out of her way.

"Ange! What are you doing?" Tricia cried.

"I'm going to check to make sure that the magnificent medallion that was in this room is still on the original ceiling." She yanked the ladder open and began to climb. Tricia rushed forward to steady it, afraid that Angelica might fall due to her ill temper.

Angelica held on to the ladder with one hand and grabbed one of the acoustical tiles with the other, ripping it from its place in the metalwork and peering into the darkness above.

"Well?" Tricia asked.

"I can't tell." Angelica withdrew her phone from her pocket and again switched on its flashlight, pointing it into the gap in the new ceiling. "Arrrgh!" she growled. "It's missing, too!"

The phone tumbled from her hand and Tricia barely caught it before it would have hit the floor. The ladder shuddered and Tricia had to grab it with her free hand to steady it.

By the time Angelica reached the floor, her face was beet red and she was seething. "I told them, I *told* them I wanted everything preserved!"

"You told them? Or was it Antonio who told them?"

"I told Antonio to tell them—and I know he did. It's in the contract we signed that nothing—and I mean *nothing*—of historical value was to be removed from the mansion. Just covered up so that in the future it could all be restored."

"I don't get it," Tricia said. "I've seen those home restoration shows where they put some kind of silicone goop over plasterwork so they can replicate it. Why remove the original?"

"Those molds don't last forever. And if you've got the original ornament, you can repeatedly make molds and sell them," Angelica said tersely.

"Is there a market for that kind of thing?"

"Of course there is!" Angelica practically shouted. She bowed her head, fighting tears. "I'm sorry, Trish. I've had a bad feeling about this project from the get-go. I knew I was cutting corners, not giving this old house the love and attention it needed, but we were on a short timeline. I needed to get my people in a new office space, and at the time this seemed the best option."

She let out a deep breath and straightened before she took out her phone and tapped the gallery icon. Separated into a photo album all its own was the Morrison Mansion. Angelica had apparently taken shots of all the rooms in the state she'd first found them, documenting all the home's architectural treasures. She left the big ballroom and entered the entryway, comparing what was there to the pictures on her phone. That she kept shaking her head made Tricia's heart sink even lower.

"What are you going to do about this?"

"Ream somebody a new a—"

"Angelica!" Tricia protested.

"*Somebody* is going to pay for this. And I'm starting with the head man himself. Jim Stark."

She tapped the contacts list on her phone and stabbed one of the entries. The line rang and rang—no answering machine or voice mail picked up.

Angelica ground her teeth together and growled, stabbing the end-call icon after what had amounted to more than a dozen rings. "That man hasn't answered my calls for a week now. I don't know why I expected anyone to pick up now." She let out a harsh breath. "Let's get out of here."

Angelica led the way back to the main entrance and locked the door behind them. Ripping off her mask, she stalked toward Tricia's Lexus, wrenched open the passenger side door, and got in.

"Where to?" Tricia asked.

"Tulip Avenue. That's where Jim Stark lives."

"Do you plan on hunting him down?"

"If that's what it takes," Angelica said with determination.

But there was no sign of anyone at the house. Angelica called up the Chamber's contact list on her phone and called the Antiques Emporium but was told Toni Bennett had left town on a business trip.

"Very convenient," Angelica said sourly.

"What's next?" Tricia asked.

Angelica sighed. "I guess I'll just have to wait for Jim to show his face. And then . . ."

"What?" Tricia asked.

Angelica's resolve seemed to dissolve. "I don't know. But mark my words, it won't be pretty."

**The first** in a succession of Granite State tour buses arrived in the village just before noon. While they were welcomed by all the merchants along Main Street, it was sometimes inconvenient because there was no warning, despite the fact the Stoneham Chamber of Commerce had a good relationship with the company. The excuses varied from "an unexpected change of plans" to just plain "we forgot to mention it." That didn't help if one hadn't scheduled enough help to run registers and restock shelves. And it was hard to get a handle on inventory if an onslaught of tourists bought out your stock on a Monday, leaving you with bare shelves for days to come.

Haven't Got a Clue was so busy that Tricia had to cancel her standing lunch date with Angelica. It was just as well, as Angelica ended up back at Booked for Lunch helping out in the kitchen and serving their influx of customers. She bitterly complained, as she wanted nothing more than to track down Jim Stark, but Tricia suspected she missed helping out at the little café. It was probably good for her to get a little hands-on experience every once in a while.

It was nearly closing time when the last of the buses drove off, leaving diesel fumes in its wake.

"That was a day," Pixie said, collapsing into one of the comfortable chairs in the reader's nook.

"I'm sorry you two didn't have much of a lunch hour," Tricia apologized. They'd each ducked out to grab a sandwich from the Eat Lunch food truck, and even then there'd been hardly any selection. Such was the price of success.

"I'd best get to my dusting and vacuuming," Mr. Everett said, but Tricia waved a hand to encourage him to join Pixie in the nook.

"We can do that in the morning."

They all had a pretty good idea of what books were languishing in the storage area in the store's basement, but Tricia asked the question anyway.

"Not as much as you'd think," Pixie said. "There's still those boxes of books I got over the weekend that need to be inventoried so we can get them on the shelves."

Tricia nodded. She wasn't about to ask her staff to put in overtime to do the job, as they both looked exhausted. It would be up to her to complete that task. She considered canceling dinner with Angelica, too, afraid that after a couple of martinis she might just pour herself into bed soon afterward. She had too much to accomplish that evening to do that. But as she'd missed lunch, she needed sustenance, although she was pretty sure Angelica would be just as tuckered out as she felt.

"Why don't you guys take off," Tricia said. "We'll figure out what needs to be done in the morning."

"I can come in an hour early," Mr. Everett volunteered.

"Me, too," Pixie echoed him.

"I'll have a look downstairs and figure out what needs to be done. Why don't you text me in the morning when I have a better idea and I'll let you know."

"Sounds like a plan," Pixie said.

Tricia watched as her employees hung up their aprons and gathered their things before leaving for the day. She waved them good-bye and pulled out her phone, giving Angelica a call.

"I'm pooped!" she announced to her sister.

"Same here. I didn't have the energy to cook and I don't want to get dressed up to go out," Angelica declared. "How about we meet over at Booked for Lunch? There must be something we can scrounge for sandwiches and I might be able to rustle up a couple of bowls of soup. What do you say?"

"It sounds like heaven. Be there in ten minutes."

Tricia took the time to give her cat a snack and do a quick tidy around the register before she crossed the street to join her sister. She studied Angelica's face. "You look as tired as I feel."

"We didn't shut down the kitchen until after four—the customers just kept streaming in. Tommy already put in a call for the wholesaler to resupply. We should be good to go by lunchtime tomorrow."

"And what's on offer tonight?"

"We have sliced cheese. Cheddar, provolone, and American. That's it. It's grilled cheese or nothing."

"I'll take cheddar. And the soup?"

"Tomato. What else?"

It wasn't going to be homemade, but Tricia wasn't about to complain, either.

"Anything new on the fire investigation?"

"I haven't heard a peep from the police or the fire department. And, of course, I still haven't been able to get in touch with Jim Stark," Angelica said as she rummaged through the shelves, looking for the soup.

"You personally, or NR Associates?"

"Both. Antonio has his people calling them on the hour."

"Wouldn't that be thought of as harassment?"

"They're a business. They're in business to *do* business. Avoiding your clients isn't a good business practice." She found an enormous can of tomato soup, frowned at it, and replaced it on the shelf.

"How about we just have something to drink with our sandwiches? I'll split a milkshake with you."

"What flavor?"

"Vanilla. I think that's the only ice cream we have left."

"Fine with me."

Angelica opened the walk-in fridge and took out a large, and nearly empty, plastic container with several packages of cheese. It was nearly empty, too. "If you make the sandwiches, I'll make the milkshake."

"That seems a fair division of labor," Tricia said.

Angelica pulled out a skillet, butter, and a loaf of bread and left Tricia to woman the stove while she collected the ice cream and milk for the shake. One side of the sandwiches was nicely browned when she returned with a frosty glass for Tricia.

"Anything happen to you since we spoke this morning?" Angelica asked.

"Besides making more sales today than all of last week? Not much."

Angelica nodded and sipped her shake, leaving her with a vanilla mustache. Tricia wasn't about to mention it.

Tricia turned off the burner and, spatula in hand, lifted the corner of one of the sandwiches, deciding it was toasted to perfection. Placing each golden slab onto a plate, she sliced them into triangles, handed one serving to Angelica, and they exited the kitchen to take seats at the lunch counter.

"So, uh, what do you and David do when you're on a date?" Angelica asked, her tone neutral.

Tricia turned to face her sister, frowning. "We are not dating!"

"Well, you seem to get together almost every evening."

"No, we don't. But when we are together, we talk. It turns out I'm starved for conversation," Tricia said, separating her sandwich halves and getting a nice cheese pull.

"What are you talking about? You speak to me every day. Same for interacting with your employees and customers."

"It's not the same thing," Tricia insisted, and took a sip of her milkshake. Too much vanilla syrup. She preferred just ice cream and milk for her shake.

"Are you having some kind of craving for the scent of testosterone or something?" Angelica asked, apparently perfectly serious.

Tricia shuddered. "Oh, don't be vulgar."

"I'm truly interested. When you're not talking about Sanjay Arya's murder, what *do* the two of you talk about?"

Tricia wasn't going to admit that it was the excuse she used to convince herself that Sanjay's death was the basis of her friendship with David. She wasn't about to confess she might actually have feelings for the young man. She certainly hadn't let him know that she'd been suffering in silence—just like she had back in middle school with unrequited infatuation (she couldn't call what she was currently experiencing love)—and could do it again.

"I don't know. Things." But, if she was honest, *mostly* about Sanjay's murder. She didn't want to think—or talk—about it, at least with Angelica. Instead, she chattered on about the work she would need to complete that evening in order to be ready for the next day of potential sales. It didn't take long for Angelica to become bored with that subject.

"Have you heard from Becca lately?"

Tricia rolled her eyes and related her last conversation with the former tennis star.

"If you look on the bright side, she might not bug you anymore."

"I don't especially enjoy her company, but I don't want to be enemies with her, either. I'm sure things will smooth over. Becca hasn't got many—*or any*—friends in the area, and she did say she considers me a friend. Friends fall in and out."

"I'd say right now you're definitely out," Angelica said, and polished off the last of her shake. She set her glass on the counter and rubbed her eyes. "I'm so tired I can't think straight."

"Did you get back to sleep after the fire last night?"

"No. And I've been so busy today that I didn't have time for a nap."

"Then you should go right home and go to bed."

"I can't. I have so much to do."

"Like what?"

But then Angelica couldn't seem to come up with anything that couldn't be put off for another day.

"I can clean up here and lock up," Tricia offered.

"I couldn't ask you to do that."

"You didn't. I volunteered."

"You're an angel."

"No, I'm a sister. And, if I say so myself, a pretty good one."

Angelica managed a weak smile. "Yes, you are." They just stared at each other for long seconds before Angelica got up from her stool. "What else are you going to do this evening? Seeing David?"

"No, I have some work to do on the computer. Today's customers practically emptied our shelves. I need to finish inventorying the new stock and get it ready to shelve in the morning. Pixie and Mr. Everett said they'd come in early to help."

"What dears."

"How's your stock holding up?"

"Pretty well, but June is coming in early, too, and we're going to load up the shelves and hanging displays, as well."

"Isn't it great to have such a problem?" Tricia asked.

"The best," Angelica agreed.

Tricia walked her sister to the door, said good night, and locked it behind her. They hadn't made much of a mess, and Tricia had the counter and kitchen looking neat and tidy in less than fifteen minutes. She locked up and headed back to Haven't Got a Clue. She did have computer work to do, but it wasn't all about the inventory.

# TWENTY-FIVE

**Tricia stayed** up far longer than she intended to, determined to find out all she could about the architectural salvage business. Antiques—and salvage—were rife in New England. People had been buying and trading them for generations. In the immediate area, there were at least four businesses that dealt with vintage and antique items for sale, and goodness only knew how many more between Stoneham and Nashua, not to mention the rest of the state. And, for lower-end items, there was always Craigslist and Facebook Marketplace. And who said whoever was pillaging Angelica's mansion had to sell locally?

Tricia's head was spinning by the time she shut down her computer and went to bed, not that she slept well. She kept dreaming of a building with holes in the walls, ceilings, and floors, and the oppressive feeling that danger was nearby, and awoke late feeling tired and a little depressed. But that didn't keep her from her morning walk. David didn't join her—probably because she started off half an hour earlier than usual. And she abandoned her usual route once again to divert to Maple Avenue and what she was beginning to think of as Nigela's mansion.

She walked slowly past the building. Thankfully, none of the neighbors—especially Elise McKenzie—was out, so it allowed her to stop and once again admire the facade. She'd begun to look at it the same way Angelica did, not in its present form, but as it *should* be— restored to its former glory. What a pity that wasn't going to happen, but at least it had a good roof and a steward who would take care of it in the interim. Although Angelica wasn't going to bring it back to its former self, she'd caught the restorative bug and had passed it on to Tricia and now Tricia ached to see the old building as it once was. Her imagination had taken over and she found herself daydreaming about how unique an experience it would be to be the lady of such a manor.

Tricia was reminded of her discussion with Elise concerning the gardens. She'd meant to ask if Angelica had done any research into them and put it on her list of things to do. Suddenly, she wanted to see what they would have looked like in their heyday. If the Stoneham Historical Society had any pictures, perhaps she could find them online. Vintage shots would be black and white, of course, but there were websites that could colorize old photos. It might be fun to try that.

After a glance at her watch, Tricia decided she'd better get back to her shop. Its opening time was just an hour away and once again she hadn't done any baking for her employees and customers. That meant another trip to the Coffee Bean to stock up on treats. She really must make time to do more baking. She had, after all, restocked her baking supplies just days before. Perhaps she'd ask David what his favorite cookie was and bake it for him. If he was having trouble stretching his food budget, it might be a welcome treat. And it was the neighborly thing to do. That or bake him a couple of loaves of banana bread. She'd think about it.

Before she made it back to Main Street, the ringtone on her phone sounded. She looked and saw it was Ginny.

"What's up?"

"I'm afraid I'm going to have to cancel our first lunch now that I'm back at work."

"What happened?"

"I'm just so backed up, and now we're going to have to find somewhere to work until the renovations are finished at the Morrison Mansion. Can I have a rain check?"

"Only if you promise you won't cancel next week."

"I pinky swear," Ginny said, and laughed, but Tricia also remembered how many times their standing lunch dates had been canceled during the previous year.

"Okay."

"I've spoken to Angelica. She'll be expecting you at Booked for Lunch at your usual time."

"You sure think of everything," Tricia said wistfully.

"That's just part of my job. I'll see you on Sunday for sure," Ginny said, and ended the call.

At least Alexa at the Coffee Bean seemed to have anticipated Tricia's arrival and had a fresh batch of Mr. Everett's favorite thumbprint cookies—with raspberry jam—available. Tricia arrived back at her home in time to take a quick shower. One good thing about her new hairstyle: it took very little time to maintain. She toweled off the back and ran a comb through the front fringe as she waved the blow dryer in front of it for less than a minute and she was good to go. Maybe she should reconsider covering her head with a bag after all.

Tricia made it back to the shop with a milk glass cake plate to display the cookies just as Pixie and Mr. Everett arrived. "Good morning," she called.

"Hi!"

"Hello, Ms. Miles," Mr. Everett said.

Pixie inspected the beverage station, saw that the coffee hadn't been started, and went to fill the carafes as Mr. Everett set out the creamer, sugar, and napkins. Ten minutes later, the three of them were seated in the reader's nook, sipping mugs of joe and nibbling on the thumbprints.

"I feel like I'm lollygagging here when I should be working on the inventory," Mr. Everett commented, looking guilty.

"No need. I finished it last night. The boxes are sitting in the back of the shop. All we need to do is restock the shelves. We shouldn't be inundated this morning. There's plenty of time," Tricia assured him.

"Did you stay up late doing it?" Pixie asked.

"It didn't take all that long," she said, but she wasn't going to reveal what had kept her up. That said, Tricia kept thinking about what she and Angelica had discovered the afternoon before and decided to pick her assistant manager's brain.

"Pixie, you regularly shop at the Antiques Emporium, don't you?" Tricia asked.

"Oh, sure. There's three vendors who regularly deal in vintage clothing, among other things. I've found some pretty spiffy outfits there over the past few years," she said, and took a sip from her mug.

"Do you know if anyone there carries salvaged architectural pieces?"

"Oh, sure. You see all kinds of that stuff there. Things like rosettes—you know, those little square pieces of wood that look like a bull's-eye that go on the trim and window casings of old houses."

Tricia thought she knew what Pixie was talking about.

"And you'll always find chunky wooden corbels that are peeling

God only knows how many layers of lead paint. That's shabby chic gone crazy, if you ask me. Sometimes," she continued, "there's stained glass—not the religious kind—and even just plain old windows and doors. It's not *my* kind of décor," she amended.

Tricia knew Pixie's taste in furnishings leaned toward mid-century modern, even if she preferred to dress circa World War II.

"Do you know who sells those architectural pieces?" Tricia asked innocently.

"Not offhand, but I could look. I mean, they have each vendor's name posted in the booths. And I presume after your recent run-in with Ms. Bennett that you don't want to darken the Emporium's doors."

"It would be awkward," Tricia agreed.

Pixie shrugged. "Sure. I can have a look for you. Anyone's name in particular you're looking to find?"

"No," she said.

"That's okay. Me and Mr. E can go there after lunch for a quick look-see." She turned to her co-worker. "That is if you'd like to go, Mr. E. They have the old neon sign from your grocery store hanging in the back of the building all lit up and looking pretty snazzy."

"Really?" he asked, his eyes brightening. "Yes, I think I'd like to see it once again—for old times' sake," he added.

"It wasn't lit the last time I was in there." Which had been some time ago. "Would you mind taking a picture so I can see it, too?" Tricia asked.

"Sure thing."

"If you need more time for lunch—feel free to take it," Tricia encouraged. She wanted that information, and if it meant she'd miss her own lunch once again, then that would be okay. Although how she was going to explain that to Angelica . . .

A customer entered the store, and the three of them got up from their seats to begin the real workday, with Pixie restocking shelves while Mr. Everett attacked the shelves with his lamb's wool duster. Luckily, a steady trickle of mystery readers entered the shop and before Tricia knew it, it was time for Pixie and Mr. Everett to leave for their midday meal.

Tricia watched as her employees headed out the door. She decided she ought to warn Angelica that she might be late meeting her for lunch and sent a quick text, finishing up as a customer walked into the store. The said customer spent nearly a hundred dollars, and Tricia was feeling pretty good about the day and wondering if they'd have enough stock to last the week. And then David walked into the store, and she brightened even more, part of her wondering why he had that effect on her.

"Thanks for shopping at Haven't Got a Clue," Tricia said, handed the woman her purchases, and smiled as she left the store.

"Another successful sale?" David asked as the echo of the bell over the door faded. He was carrying a small brown paper bag, which he set on the counter.

"You got it. What can I do for you? Need another Christie whodunnit?"

"I could probably use one. But I came in to bring you lunch."

"Lunch?" Tricia asked, surprised.

"Yeah." David opened the bag and withdrew a plastic bag containing a sandwich made with slabs of Italian bread and cut in half on the bias—no doubt the Patisserie's day-old bread from the day before.

Tricia bit her tongue so as not to remind him that she usually had lunch with Angelica. "What kind is it?"

"PBJ."

*Peanut butter and jelly? Oh, gosh, he's so young.*

"When was the last time you had one?" David asked.

Tricia thought back. "Probably thirty years ago."

"Then it should bring back pleasant memories. And this is *not* your average PBJ—it's made with *raspberry* jelly."

"That's better than grape?"

"Of course," he said in a tone that made her feel like she might have been missing out on something fantastic for the better part of her life. "Do you know how hard it is to *find* raspberry jelly? Stores usually only sell preserves, which are filled with seeds. They get stuck in my teeth."

That was true.

"If raspberry jelly is so hard to find, where did you get it?"

"I brought a jar from home. I'm going to have to ask my mom to send me a care package. Either that or go home for a weekend and get some myself."

For some reason, the thought of him leaving—even for a couple of days—caused Tricia to swallow down a pang of disappointment. Just why, she wasn't sure.

Tricia knew accepting the sandwich would spoil her lunch with Angelica, but she didn't want to hurt David's feelings, either. "It was very thoughtful of you," she said as he withdrew a couple of paper napkins from the bag and set them on the counter to use as makeshift plates. "I thought your generation didn't buy paper napkins."

"We don't, not when paper towel works just as well—although, I like cloth napkins best myself. My grandmother always *insisted* on cloth napkins. But when you find the paper kind in the cupboard and don't have to pay for them . . ." He let the sentence trail off and withdrew one of the sandwiches from the plastic bags and set it on his napkin. Tricia did the same.

"Are you getting bored of eating out?" she asked.

"My stipend only stretches so far," he said. And he'd made her a sandwich, sharing what he had with her. Of course, he'd spent cash on his estate-sale purchases days before, but Tricia wasn't going to mention that. So, was it kindness or loneliness that had brought him there that day?

"For nearly his whole childhood, my brother ate only PBJs and corn," David said conversationally.

"That's it?" What kind of parents allowed that? "Did he suffer from malnutrition?"

"It wasn't a good diet, but he's six four now, so it didn't stunt his growth, either. He just didn't like food, which was good for me because I got to have doubles on anything he didn't want—especially dessert."

Tricia bit into her triangle of sandwich and chewed. It was surprisingly good—the salty peanut butter with the sweet raspberry jelly. The bread wasn't at all stale, either, which was surprising. Tricia wasn't a fan of the soft white sandwich bread that her grandmother used to call "bunny bread." This sandwich was *good*.

They stood there, looking at each other, chewing their bites of sandwiches, and smiling.

It felt good to smile.

"So, what's been going on?" David asked between bites.

Tricia swallowed. "My sister and I may have figured out why Sanjay was killed."

David's eyes bugged. "Get out!"

Tricia nodded. "We just happened to be at the mansion yesterday afternoon and Angelica noticed that some of the architectural features were missing. When the building was purchased, Nigela Ricita specifically asked that they not be disturbed so that the building might be returned to its former glory at some point in the future."

"And now they're missing?"

Tricia nodded.

"And you think Sanjay found out and was killed for it?"

"It's a possibility."

David frowned. "It seems like such a petty thing."

"Selling vintage materials can be quite lucrative."

"But is it worth being killed for?"

"You'd be surprised how little it takes sometimes," Tricia remarked.

It was a sobering thought, and David's expression conveyed his discomfort.

"So, who's the killer?"

"I have no idea."

"But you'll find out, right?" he asked, an inquisitive sparkle lighting his eyes.

"Well, not me or Angelica specifically, but if we find anything to corroborate our suspicions, we'll of course share them with Chief McDonald."

David nodded. "So, what's next in your unofficial investigation?"

"I've got Pixie and Mr. Everett going on a spy mission for me."

He gave Tricia a sharp glance. "How? Where?"

"After lunch, they're going to check out Toni Bennett's Antiques Emporium looking for anything that might have been pilfered from a construction site and relay the names of the vendors."

"You don't think whoever took the items is going to blatantly sell the stuff right here in Stoneham, do you?"

"Not specifically, but it's a starting point."

David didn't look convinced. Oh, he of little faith.

"Why didn't you just go to the Antiques Emporium yourself? Are you afraid Ms. Bennett might throw you out?"

"Exactly. Pixie's a regular customer, so it wouldn't look suspicious for her to be there."

"Yeah, she told me she gets vintage clothes there. If Ms. Bennett wouldn't toss me out, too, I might go and have another look." David glanced at his watch. "I need to run an errand, so I'll have to leave in a couple of minutes—probably before they come back. Could we talk about it this evening after you have dinner with your sister?"

"We could," Tricia said.

"Great. I could come by this evening, say eight o'clock?"

Tricia hesitated before answering. She wasn't going to invite him into her home. They could sit in the reader's nook, with the blinds open for all to see that there was no hanky-panky going on.

"That would be great," she heard herself saying.

"All right." David gathered up the sandwich bags and napkins, tossing them into the paper sack and squashing it all together before looking around for a wastebasket.

"I'll take that," Tricia said, and tossed it into the trash, feeling like she was hiding the evidence from the world and feeling just a little guilty about it. They were friends. Friends talked. Friends ate lunch together. Friends spent time with each other.

She was old enough to be his mother.

She was his friend.

She sighed. "See you later."

# TWENTY-SIX

 **Pixie and** Mr. Everett returned from their extended lunch break in great spirits. Pixie sported an Antiques Emporium brown paper bag with string handles, as well as an ear-to-ear grin.

"You look mighty happy. What did you get?" Tricia asked.

Pixie set the bag on the counter and withdrew the tissue-wrapped contents, pulling back the paper to reveal a sexy black satin slip embellished with lace. She held it up for Tricia to admire. Ever the gentleman, Mr. Everett averted his gaze. "Isn't it gorgeous? And it's just my size," Pixie said, and giggled. "Fred is going to *love* it!"

Tricia wasn't interested in where or how Pixie intended to wear the garment, and was more focused on whether her spies had been successful with their information gathering, but didn't say so. Yet.

"How was the Everett's grocery sign?"

"Oh, let me show you," Pixie said, and withdrew her phone from her purse, punched the gallery icon, and tapped one of the images. She tapped it again until it filled the screen and passed the phone to Tricia.

The neon sign was a vibrant turquoise, which she hadn't expected, and Pixie had staged it so Mr. Everett stood before it, beaming. "Wow. That's fantastic. Was that the sign's original color?" Tricia asked.

Mr. Everett shook his head. "When I had it commissioned, it was a true blue. I preferred that color. It was more dignified as befitting my store," he said. Yes, Mr. Everett was dignified. He wasn't the kind to go for excessive flash. Had Toni Bennett had the neon replaced? That would've cost a pretty penny and she didn't seem the type somehow.

"Is it for sale?"

The old man nodded. "And for far more than I originally paid for it," he said rather wistfully.

Tricia studied Mr. Everett's face. She could tell the failure of his grocery store was still a heavy burden on his soul.

Pixie began to rewrap her purchase and Tricia had to rein in her impatience and not demand to know who, if anyone, at the Emporium was selling architectural salvage. Pixie placed the slip into the bag and was about to step away from the counter when she seemed to remember why she and Mr. Everett had been sent on their clandestine mission.

"Oh, and I took a couple of other pictures," she said, grabbing her phone once again and scrolling to find them. She handed the phone over to Tricia. Each booth at the Emporium bore a stylized plaque with the vendor's name and a number underneath. Pixie had taken shots of three of the nameplates. They were: Janine Janson, number 16; Elma Fisher, number 27; and Michael Foster, number 45. Tricia frowned. Now, where had she heard that last name before?

She thought about it for long seconds before it came to her. Only it wasn't *Michael* Foster she recalled, it was *Mike* Foster.

He worked for Jim Stark. And, at least temporarily, he'd taken Sanjay Arya's job.

"Did you take pictures of the items these vendors were selling?" Tricia asked.

"Shoot. I guess I should have. Sorry," Pixie apologized.

"Do you remember what each of them was selling?"

Pixie looked thoughtful. "One of them had a couple of stained glass windows. They weren't very pretty, kinda boring colors, and a couple of the little panes were cracked. And the price they wanted! Scandalous. I think that was Janine Janson's booth."

"And the other two booths?" Tricia asked.

Pixie chewed her lower lip. "Elma Fisher's booth had an antique slipper tub. It had been reconditioned, so it was in great shape, but the price on that was more than I make in a month—and you pay me really well," she added.

"And the last one. Michael Foster's booth?" Tricia inquired, mentally crossing her fingers it would be plaster medallions.

"He had a lot of spindles. You know—like from an old staircase. I seen lots of videos where people make them into candleholders." Again she looked thoughtful. "I bet he could charge more for that if he took the time to convert them. I wonder why he didn't?"

Probably not worth his time, Tricia thought.

"Was it worth us going to the Emporium?" Pixie asked.

Tricia nodded.

Pixie asked no more questions—she didn't like to gossip, even if she did listen to it—and she came around the counter to stow her purse and the paper bag under it, ready to get back to work.

It was Tricia's turn to look thoughtful. She wasn't sure whom she wanted to share this information with first—Angelica or David. And who else should she talk to about Mike Foster? Chief McDonald? Maybe not yet. After all, she had no proof that Foster was stealing from the Stark Construction worksites or that he'd killed Sanjay Arya to hide his crime.

And she wasn't sure how she could get that proof, either.

**Tricia was** nearly twenty minutes late to meet Angelica for lunch, not that she was hungry after her quite satisfying PBJ. Angelica had already ordered her entrée, and Tricia went for a bowl of vegetable beef soup.

"And what have you got to tell me?" Angelica asked, taking a bite from her half egg salad sandwich. She'd gone for the soup-and-sandwich combo yet again.

Tricia leaned in closer and whispered, "Last night, I told you I had computer work to do." Angelica nodded. "I thought I might look into the market for architectural salvage." Angelica's eyes widened. "As we thought. A member of Jim Stark's work crew has a booth at the Antiques Emporium and is selling salvaged pieces. His name is Mike Foster."

"How do you know this?"

"Pixie and Mr. Everett did a little snooping over their lunch hour."

"And?" Angelica prompted, giving her sister all her attention.

"Pixie texted me pictures of the vendor names." Tricia withdrew her phone from her purse and pulled up the photos.

Angelica frowned. "I don't suppose they found my medallions or cove molding."

"No, but it proves that Foster is selling *some* kind of salvage. He might have an Etsy shop or sell stuff on eBay. We ought to check that out."

"Do they list the sellers by name?"

"I don't think so. I think you'd need to know the business name."

"And I don't suppose you do."

Tricia shook her head. "They only list the booth owners' names at the Emporium."

"I wonder if he's got a DBA." Doing-business-as registrations were filed with the county.

Angelica shook her head and dipped her spoon back into her soup just as Molly the server showed up with Tricia's bowl.

"Thanks," Tricia said as Molly also deposited two little cellophane bags of oyster crackers on the table and departed.

"Why only soup today?" Angelica asked.

"Uh . . ." Tricia wasn't sure she wanted to tell Angelica about the PBJ. But then why shouldn't she? "David came by the shop and surprised me with a sandwich."

Angelica frowned. "What could be better than something from Booked for Lunch?"

"I won't say better, but interesting."

Angelica raised an eyebrow.

"Peanut butter and jelly."

Angelica's brow rose even higher.

"Admittedly not haute cuisine, but surprisingly good," Tricia remarked. "When was the last time you had a PBJ?"

Angelica actually pouted. "Last week."

"What?"

Angelica shrugged. "Sofia offered me a bite. It's all she wants for lunch. That and hot dogs."

"Uh-oh. Better watch that girl. David said as a child his brother ate *only* PBJs and corn."

"Thanks to *my* influence, Sofia has been exposed to a variety of nutritious *and* delicious foods."

Angelica *was* a fantastic cook.

"So, tell me more about the guy who's stealing my medallions," Angelica said, getting back to the matter at hand. "What's his job?"

"A carpenter. He's selling a bunch of stair spindles at the Emporium. Have any gone missing at the mansion?"

"Not so far. Do you think he's really our guy?"

"He's not *my* guy, but I suspect he *is* having an affair with Toni. He's certainly got the opportunity to pillage job sites, although I'm not sure how we'd prove it unless we could catch him in the act or get him on video."

"I don't like the idea of confronting this guy," Angelica said.

"Nor do I," Tricia agreed.

"Is it time to talk to Chief McDonald about this?"

"Not yet."

"Then what do you propose we do?"

"We need to do some more digging."

"We, or you and David?" Angelica asked with just a tinge of reproach in her tone.

"Probably me. *Alone.*"

"And put yourself at risk? Oh, no you don't."

"I'm not going to put myself at risk."

"That's what you always say." Angelica reached across the table and tapped Tricia's arm. The one she'd badly broken when she fell into the high school's empty pool after confronting a killer. There'd been very few times when Tricia had actually been injured when pursuing a criminal. She wasn't going to let Angelica's concern scare her away from poking into Sanjay's death . . . but she also had no intention of taking any chances, either. When the time was right, she would take all her facts and suspicions to Chief McDonald.

And she hoped that time would be sooner rather than later.

# TWENTY-SEVEN

 **Always punctual,** Tricia found David standing behind the door at Haven't Got a Clue at precisely eight o'clock that evening.

"You're so dependable," she praised him. "You always arrive when you say you will."

"It's not nice to keep people waiting. I always make sure I'm on time or even early. It's just the polite thing to do."

He must be very disappointed when visiting doctors' offices.

"Come in," Tricia said with a sweep of her hand. For some reason, she felt a little odd, maybe even shy. But then they were only going to have another little chat. "Have a seat," she said, and gestured toward the reader's nook.

He looked at her. "Oh."

"Oh?" she asked.

"I thought . . ." He shrugged. "When you invited me over I thought

I was going to get to see your apartment. I kinda wanted to see how you'd decorated it."

"Oh." It was getting to be a much-repeated word. In fact, David had invited himself. "Sure." Tricia locked the door. "Right this way."

She led David through the store to the door at the back marked PRIVATE, and then up the stairs. Upon reaching the apartment, she stood back and let him take in her home.

"Nice. And you said Jim Stark's people renovated it for you?"

Tricia nodded. "They did a great job, which is why it's so strange the way the man has seemed to disappear since Sanjay's death."

"Has he?"

"He's not answering calls from NR Associates, at least he hadn't done so the last I heard, which was a couple of hours ago."

"Wow."

David gestured toward the French doors. "Is there a balcony or something back here?"

"Yes," Tricia said. She stepped forward and opened the doors, letting in the warm evening air. She led him outside.

"This is nice. The perfect place to watch the sun come up with a cup of tea. Do you do it often?"

"I'm not a big tea drinker, but I have come out with my first cup of coffee to admire the day."

"Do you put up lights for Christmas?"

"It never occurred to me to do that. I mean, who'd see them?" A churchyard lay just beyond the alley.

"Do you get much traffic in the alley?"

She shook her head. "No."

"Can I see the rest of the place?"

"Of course," Tricia said, and stepped back inside the apartment.

David followed. He gestured toward the bay window. "Can I—?"

"Oh, sure." She led him past the lighted cabinet that held her collection of vintage mysteries and other treasures, through the living room to the window that overlooked Main Street. He gazed out over the quiet village.

"You've got a really nice place," he said.

"It serves me well," Tricia said.

David turned to look around the open-concept living and dining areas and the kitchen beyond. "So, your bedroom is upstairs?"

Tricia felt her cheeks grow warm. "It's a suite. Bedroom, bathroom, walk-in closets, and a reading nook. I *had* to have a reading nook."

"I wouldn't expect less from a bookseller."

Tricia figured she'd better snap into hostess mode. "Would you like something to drink?"

"What have you got?"

"Just about everything hard, and several soft drinks."

"I wouldn't mind a beer if you've got one."

"I've got a couple of bottles of Bashful Moose ale."

"It's good stuff. I'll have that, thanks."

David stood at the kitchen island and watched as Tricia retrieved the beer from the fridge, cracked the cap, and poured it into a pilsner glass. She poured herself a glass of chardonnay. She handed him the beer. "Shall we sit?" She gestured toward the living room, where David took a seat on the couch and Tricia slid onto one of the side chairs.

"So, anything new in our Sanjay Arya investigation?" David asked, getting straight down to business.

"Kind of," Tricia said. She told him what Pixie had discovered at the Antiques Emporium.

"Does it really make sense for someone to kill another person over something so trivial? We're talking antiques, not antiquities."

"Except it's difficult to quietly sell antiquities on the open market. American antiques—not so much."

David nodded and gazed into his beer, looking thoughtful. "Shall we talk about the other suspects in Sanjay Arya's murder case?" he asked as he stretched his legs out before him.

Tricia fought to suppress a smile. "Why don't you give me your list and we'll compare notes."

"Okay, great." He took a swig from his glass as though to fortify himself before speaking. "First, there's Candace the waitress."

"Server," Tricia corrected. "They like to be called servers these days."

"Whatever. She had a major reason to be pissed at Sanjay. Dumping her and lying to her about being forced into an arranged marriage had to be enough to trigger rage for anyone."

"That's true," Tricia agreed. "So, she may have had a motive, but did she have the opportunity? She could very well have a concrete alibi."

"Which we have no way of discovering."

"Not unless she's confronted—and I don't see how to do that without causing all kinds of trouble. Chief McDonald no doubt knows and he isn't going to tell us a thing. Who's your second suspect?"

"Jim Stark, of course. Sanjay was messing around with his wife. She might have thought her husband was fine with her extramarital activities, but you didn't get that impression."

"Nobody wants to be cheated on," Tricia confirmed.

"Stark could have easily lured Sanjay to the building site, they could have argued—"

"Or not," Tricia pointed out.

"—and then—*blam!*—he hit Sanjay in the head repeatedly with his own hammer. I assume most of the blows were to the back of his head, meaning his attacker struck before Sanjay could react."

"It's possible," Tricia agreed.

"And what about Toni Bennett herself?" David asked.

"And your theory?" Tricia wanted to know.

"She could have been over Sanjay and wanted to end the affair. But what if he didn't want to?"

"She was *that* good in bed?" Tricia asked.

"Or he thought he might get something else from her. Perhaps blackmail her by telling her husband about their relationship."

"Which may or may not have been an issue," Tricia said.

"Should we confront Mrs. Stark about her relationship with Sanjay Arya?" David asked.

"There's no point since the police have undoubtedly already done so."

"Yeah, but we don't know what was going on between them or how intense their liaison was."

"I think we can guess," Tricia said.

David's frown was almost a pout. "So, you're just going to give up on that aspect of the case?"

"I didn't say that, but I see no point in annoying Toni Bennett just because we can."

"But what if she's the killer?" David insisted.

"What's her motive?" Tricia countered.

"That Sanjay saw other women, of course."

"Not necessarily. They might have just been friends with benefits."

Tricia had had that kind of relationship with Marshall Cambridge, not that she would admit it to David. She'd liked Marshall, felt comfortable with him, and had quite a bit in common with him, but she'd never loved him. Had Toni Bennett felt the same way about Sanjay Arya?

"Okay, so Toni had no motive to kill her lover, but her husband certainly did."

"Might have," Tricia said. "It's said Jim Stark is the jealous type— or at least he was in the past. Would he be angry to find his wife had taken a lover? Probably. And what if he had a medical problem he wasn't willing to address that made him unable to satisfy his wife?"

"Oh, come on. Pharmacology to the rescue," David insisted.

"Not necessarily," she said again. "The first step in solving a problem is for someone to *admit* they have one. Some men are too embarrassed to ask their doctor for that kind of . . . intervention. And if Stark didn't want to admit it to his doctor—he might not be willing to admit it to his wife, either. In that case, he could have just turned a blind eye to his wife's philandering."

"You just said Stark was the jealous type," David protested. "Jealousy is a powerful motivator."

And how would he know that?

David sipped his beer, which was slowly disappearing. "And then there's your good friend Becca Chandler."

Tricia eyed him. She hadn't told David about her conversations with Becca. "What about her?"

"They say she was seen making goo-goo eyes with Sanjay at a fancy restaurant in Litchfield. It's located right next door to a suites hotel."

Goo-goo eyes? Where was this kid coming up with such descriptors? Still, what David said sounded plausible. And Tricia bet Becca didn't pay for a hotel tryst. She wouldn't want to leave a paper trail. "Where did you find this out?"

David shrugged. "People come into the Chamber office and talk."

"People?"

"A person," he clarified.

"And that person is?"

He shook his head. "I'm punctual, *and* I don't tell tales."

Well, that was good to know. And it was probably also fair. She hadn't shared with him everything she knew about some of the people who might be connected to Sanjay's death, either.

"So, where does that leave us?" David asked.

"Puzzled?" Tricia suggested.

"Frustrated," David corrected.

"May I remind you that every year half of all murders reported in the US go unsolved," Tricia said.

"Wow—that many?"

Tricia nodded. "Most investigations take months, even years before a suspect is indicted. It's been a little over a week since Sanjay was killed. In investigative terms, that's like the blink of an eye."

"Does it usually take you months to put the pieces together on crimes here in Stoneham?"

"Well, no. But the police have to present the district attorney with an ironclad case, and that *does* take a long time."

"So the wheels of justice turn slowly," David commented.

"Yes, even when they aren't mired in mud," Tricia retorted.

David finished his beer, looking pensive. "What's our next move?"

"I'd like to track down Jim Stark. Right now, he seems as elusive as a slippery fish."

"I don't get that."

"What?"

"That he's pulled a disappearing act. From what I gather, he'd been as dependable as Old Faithful."

There he went again deploying yet another old saw.

Tricia considered David's last statement. Yes, in the past Jim Stark had been as dependable as the sunrise. Why he'd gone to ground was baffling. What did he have to hide? Could it just be embarrassment, guilt, or something else? Unless someone could track him down and make him talk, it was anyone's guess.

David set his glass down on the coffee table.

"Would you like another?" Tricia asked.

"No, thanks." The sun had already dipped behind the building across the street. As though to reinforce that fact, David said, "I should probably go home."

"It's nice that you feel comfortable enough to call that apartment home."

David frowned. "I didn't say that. It seems to have come with a lot of baggage." His gaze met Tricia's, as though to dare her to reveal all she knew about the last two men who'd lived within those walls.

She didn't comment.

"Thanks for showing me your place and for your hospitality."

Tricia smiled and led the way down the steps and back into her shop. She opened the door and David stepped out onto the sidewalk. "Will you be coming into the Chamber office tomorrow morning?"

"I don't know. I don't think there's anything pressing I need to deal with."

David nodded. He looked disappointed. "Okay, well . . . keep in touch about everything Sanjay."

"I will."

David just stared at her and for a moment she thought he might lunge forward and kiss her.

Or was she just imagining that?

"Good night," he said.

"Good night."

Tricia watched him head south down the sidewalk and then cross the street to the building that housed his temporary abode. She closed and locked the door and set the security system for the night before returning upstairs to her apartment.

The door to the balcony was still open, and Tricia moved to close it when a voice called her name.

"Tricia?"

It was Angelica.

Tricia stepped out into the evening air once more. "Ange?"

"Don't you Ange me," Angelica said rather unkindly.

Angelica's balcony was only feet away from Tricia's and she stood next to the rail. Her expression was just as surly as her voice had been. "What on earth were you doing entertaining David Price in your apartment?" she demanded.

"I wasn't entertaining him. He came over for a drink and we talked. And how did you know he was even here?"

"I took Sarge out for a comfort call and saw the two of you on the balcony. Are you planning on decorating it for Christmas after all?"

Tricia felt her cheeks grow hot with embarrassment. But then, nothing she and David had discussed that evening could be called romantic in nature. Why should she feel guilty?

"Do you always eavesdrop on conversations?"

"We discussed this more than once and you promised me—"

Tricia fumed and Angelica continued.

"You cannot continue to fraternize with the help."

"I fraternize with Mr. Everett on a regular basis—and so do you."

"It's not the same thing and you know it," Angelica grated.

"For once and for all, I'm not interested in David Price. I am not dating him, and I wish you'd stop intimating that I am or want to."

"There's been enough scandal surrounding the Chamber. We can't afford the perception that any kind of hanky-panky is going on. You see that, don't you?" Angelica demanded.

Tricia pursed her lips and didn't answer.

"From now on, I think I had better be the one he comes to for questions on Chamber business. Don't you agree?"

*You are not my mother!* Tricia felt like screaming, but instead she bit her tongue.

"Are you going to answer me?" Angelica challenged her.

"No, I'm going inside and going to bed. And don't call me. I don't want to talk to you anymore tonight."

"Tricia. Tricia!"

Angelica hollered, but Tricia slammed the door and then leaned against it, as though to keep her sister out. She swallowed several times, and then the tears began to fall.

Funny, she wasn't exactly sure why she was crying.

# TWENTY-EIGHT

**For the** first time in a long time, Tricia cried herself to sleep. Not so much over David, but over Angelica's tyranni-cal orders concerning him. And yet, Angelica wasn't wrong. Tricia was being stupid, obstinate, and not making good decisions about herself and for the Chamber. When she'd done her little inves-tigations into crime in the past, she'd only ever involved Angelica, who was, at best, usually a reluctant participant. Both of them had been injured at one time or another during the process—and more than once. She didn't want that to happen to David. Good grief, she'd never wanted it to happen to her or Angelica, and yet despite her good intentions . . .

Still, Tricia was angry with her sister. And when her phone pinged and she saw it was a text from Angelica, she tried not to look at it. Curiosity got the better of her, however.

*See you at lunch?*

Tricia waited a full minute before she sent a terse message back.

*Yes.*

With that decided, she got ready for the day, deciding to forgo her usual walk and head down to the basement and her treadmill once more. Afterward, she showered, dressed, and was in her shop getting the beverage station ready for the day's customers.

Pixie arrived just before ten. "Morning," she called brightly.

"Good morning to you, too."

That day, Pixie was dressed in a peach silk blouse with a black pencil skirt that tended to make her derriere stick out. It was so tight that she had to shuffle when she walked, but at least she'd ditched the high heels for more sensible pumps. Soon she was clad in her hunter green Haven't Got a Clue apron and ready for work. But first—coffee!

The women sat in the reader's nook and reviewed their aims for the day, discussing the pros and cons of a Fourth of July sale. It was worth the trouble, they decided, and Tricia would choose the titles for a special display on a bookshelf near the front as she knew of at least five or six mysteries that dealt with the holiday and that they had multiple copies in stock. With the shop talk concluded, they turned the conversation around to more personal topics.

"Do you have plans for the weekend?" Tricia asked.

"Just the usual. My stint working over at Booked for Beauty tomorrow and thrifting on Sunday. David Price is coming with me again."

"Oh? The other day you didn't seem too keen on the idea. Did you reach out to him?"

Pixie shook her head. "He caught me as I walked past the Chamber office on my way here." She shrugged. "If nothing else, he's good to have around to carry the heavy stuff."

"I thought he was broke," Tricia said, remembering David's comments that accompanied the PBJs.

"Aren't we all?" Pixie asked, and laughed. "Seriously, he doesn't have a lot to do to occupy himself, and having a second pair of eyes is a big help to me. And anyway, it's the thrill of the hunt that attracts us."

Tricia nodded, but she didn't want to leave it there.

"It sounded like David spent an awful lot of money at the sales last weekend."

Pixie shook her head. "Not really. I told you, at the end of the day, the estate sale people practically beg you to haul stuff away so they don't have to pack it up."

"So, what did he spend?"

"About ten bucks."

Tricia was taken aback. "Oh."

"Yeah, the kid's been paying off his student loans. Quite the responsible young man, eh?" she said, and laughed. "He figures he might have them all paid off in no time once he has a real job."

No wonder David hadn't been eager to pick up a check. Tricia wondered why he'd confided his financial situation to Pixie but not to her. Was he embarrassed?

The discussion was cut short as their first customers of the day arrived. Soon, Tricia was too busy to think about Sanjay Arya's murder or to be annoyed with Angelica. The cash register rang up the sales and once again Tricia was grateful Pixie would be back on the trail to replenish their stock within two days.

She was just as busy when Pixie took her lunch hour and all too soon it was time to face Angelica, something she'd tried to put out of her mind, but found herself dreading nonetheless.

As usual, Booked for Lunch was packed, but being the owner meant there was always a booth for Angelica. Tricia sat down opposite her sister, who was flipping through her e-mails and barely looked up.

"Business has been brisk at the Cookery," Angelica said.

"And at Haven't Got a Clue," Tricia agreed.

"Just so you know, Antonio has reported the theft of the mansion's architectural details to both the police and our insurance company."

"How can you prove Mike Foster did the deed?"

"That's not up to us. *We* don't get involved with law enforcement," she said pointedly.

"And how hard is the Stoneham Police Department going to look into the theft or where the items disappeared to?" Tricia asked.

"According to Antonio, the chief said they'd do their best."

"And you don't think that's going to be good enough?"

"Of course not. They don't have a stake in it. And as the chief pointed out, the ceilings are going to be covered. He really doesn't understand why we're so upset."

Why *she* was so upset, but then Angelica hadn't spoken to the chief—Antonio had.

Molly the server showed up, poured coffee, and recited the specials. Tricia had no appetite, so she went for just a bowl of chicken noodle soup. Angelica did likewise. Good. If Tricia had to feel lousy about the situation between them, she was at least satisfied to know that Angelica was feeling just as bad. It wasn't charitable, but it was reasonable.

They filled the rest of the time with small talk, avoiding any conversation about David and the Chamber. How long were they going to have to ignore the proverbial elephant in the room? Sooner or later, Tricia was going to have to go into the Chamber office to complete her work and she would have to face David, wondering just what Angelica had said to him. Or she could just phone him.

That was probably her best option because she couldn't just cut him out of her life. And he still had weeks to go before he would leave Stoneham to go back to school and his regular life.

Regular life. Tricia hadn't felt like she'd experienced that since before her move to Booktown. Being divorced wasn't much of a life, but moving to New Hampshire had been the adventure of a lifetime.

Angelica was the first to say she needed to get back to work. "So, I'll see you tonight at my place?" she asked.

"At the usual time," Tricia agreed, thankful the lure of a couple of martinis would be her reward. "I'm just going to finish my coffee and then I'll be on my way, too."

Angelica nodded, got up from the table, spoke to Molly on her way out, and left the café.

Tricia's phone pinged. She retrieved it from her purse and looked at the message—from David.

*Word has it Jim Stark has been seen. We might catch him tonight at his work trailer.*

*Whose word?* Tricia asked.

*Sworn to secrecy,* he answered.

No. She couldn't meet him. Not after the dressing-down Angelica had given her.

*Sorry, no. And don't you go, either. It might not be safe.*

*Worrywart.*

*Spoiled brat,* she countered.

*Love U 2.*

Tricia stared at the message, her stomach doing a flip-flop.

She was glad she'd had only soup for lunch.

**Happy hour** with Angelica wasn't as awkward as Tricia had anticipated, and Angelica had obviously tried to soothe Tricia's ruffled feathers by making shrimp scampi, although a little heavy on the garlic. Was it a calculated move so that Tricia wouldn't feel comfortable kissing anyone?

She didn't ask.

Tricia returned home and waited until it was full dark before she left her apartment to pick up her car and drive across the village. She saw no one walking a dog or out for a moonlit stroll when she parked her car on the side of the road where the shabby, time-worn construction trailer sat, away from the village and prying eyes. As she approached the building, she saw the lights were on and the shades were down, and she could see the shadow of someone standing in the middle of it. She climbed the weathered wooden steps and rapped on the pitted aluminum door. "Jim Stark, are you in there? It's Tricia Miles."

"What do you want?" came the muffled voice from within.

"Can we talk?"

Tricia heard the sound of approaching footsteps and she took a step back as the door before her was wrenched open. Stark stood silhouetted in the frame. "Haven't you caused enough damage?"

"Me?"

"Poking into everyone's business when no one asked you to do so."

"I thought I might come to ask if you needed anything. To remind you that we're friends."

In the dim light, Tricia saw Stark's face twist into a sneer. "You're not my friend. You're a customer, nothing more."

Tricia exhaled a sigh. He was probably right. But he sure hadn't given her that impression during the times he'd worked on her store and her home. She'd provided him and his team with endless cups of coffee, dozens of doughnuts, and paid him handsomely for his expertise. They'd shared hours of conversations that went above and beyond the scope of the work his company had performed. Sadly, she'd mistaken those intimacies as proof of friendship. It left her feeling bereft and more than just a little used.

Of course, his wife, Toni, hadn't said what problem had forced her to seek a lover, but Tricia suspected a man's man such as Jim Stark would never admit to anyone, least of all a customer, his failure to perform in the bedroom.

"Aren't you going to ask me one of your incredibly intrusive questions?" Stark demanded, walking back into the trailer. Tricia followed.

"I don't see the point, given your present state of mind. You'd hardly be willing to answer them."

Stark retreated to his desk and glanced down at the pile of architectural drawings that littered its surface. He heaved a sigh and looked defeated, sinking into the ratty office chair that looked like it should have been replaced half a decade before. It was then Tricia noticed his pallor. "I guess it really doesn't matter."

"I was just going to comment that it had to be devastating for you to know that Sanjay had initiated a relationship with Toni."

"He didn't initiate it," Stark muttered sadly, his head sinking lower. "This isn't the first time Toni has stepped out on me."

Tricia hadn't thought so, either.

"I wish . . ." Stark began again, but then he merely shook his head wearily. "The thing is . . . I was close to that boy." He laughed. "He was a man, but he had that boyish—impish—smile. That one could charm the socks off a snake."

Tricia wasn't sure about that analogy, but she said nothing.

"What will you do without a right-hand man?" she asked.

"Mike Foster is my chief carpenter. He's stepped up to take on Sanjay's tasks until I can find someone to take his place. But Mike's let me know he wants to be a hands-on carpenter, not figuring out how many nails and board feet of lumber a job needs."

"I imagine it'll be hard to find someone with that kind of experience."

"You have no idea. I trained Sanjay—it took five years before I could trust him with every aspect of the business. The only thing I couldn't trust him with was my wife."

Tricia studied the dispirited man before her.

"How does Sanjay's death affect the projects you're working on?"

"It sets every one of them back from weeks to months. The fire at the Morrison Mansion and the postponement of the tennis club just made it worse."

So he'd at least inspected the damage to the mansion. Still, as far as Tricia knew, NR Associates hadn't been given an updated timeline on when the work would be completed, and Tricia had to bite her tongue to keep from asking.

"Have you spoken to Antonio Barbero recently?"

"No, but he's left enough messages."

"Then you know about the architectural details that are missing from the Morrison Mansion."

Stark said nothing.

"Did you know that your new right-hand man has a booth at the Antiques Emporium and that he sells a lot of architectural salvage?"

Stark's expression darkened. "What's that got to do with anything?"

Tricia didn't answer. She had a more important question to ask.

"Is it true the company is in terrible financial trouble and about to go under?"

Stark's head snapped up, and he glared at her, his eyes blazing. "No, it is not true!"

"But you *are* having some financial trouble. Enough to sell off some of your most important equipment."

"I haven't sold one piece," he said menacingly.

"I've heard about an excavator that's in the process of being sold."

Stark's eyes widened until the whites seemed to dwarf his irises. So, there was some truth—at least when it came to that particular piece of equipment.

"I have not sold one piece of my equipment," Stark reiterated.

"Are you *missing* any equipment?" Tricia asked.

Stark looked away. Aha. Had someone spirited away said excavator? Had it just disappeared? Surely there were serial numbers—like the VIN numbers on motor vehicles—that could trace such equipment. Tricia wasn't sure. Since Stark wasn't going to talk to her about it, she wondered if Ian McDonald might.

"I see no point in this conversation," Stark said. "I think it's time you left me in peace."

Tricia let out a breath and turned for the door. She reached for the handle but pivoted. "Do you have an alibi for the night Sanjay died?"

The old saying "If looks could kill" would have perfectly described Stark's expression. "Get out!"

"Good night, Jim." Tricia opened the door.

"Wait!" he called.

Tricia turned to face him and Stark squinted at her, as though really seeing her for the first time. "What did you do to your hair?"

"Striking, isn't it?" Tricia said neutrally, her head held high.

"It looks like hell."

She shrugged. "I'm getting used to it."

"I suppose it'll grow back. In the meantime, you ought to consider wearing a bag over your head. Perhaps a plastic one?"

Tricia ignored the comment—and the malice behind it. He was trying to unnerve her. He wasn't about to succeed.

"Good night," she said again, and closed the door.

As she walked to her car, Tricia realized she was going to have to find a new contractor the next time she needed work on her building.

# TWENTY-NINE

**Tricia didn't** take the direct route home and instead circled around the village and wasn't surprised when she saw lights inside the Antiques Emporium. They'd been closed for business for hours, but like her husband, Toni Bennett seemed to be burning the not-quite-midnight oil.

Tricia wondered if it was wise to rile Stark's wife with the questions she had in mind. Then again, she had nothing to lose, since Toni bore no goodwill toward her.

Tricia parked outside the Emporium, marched up to the door, and rang the bell. Nothing happened. Except for the bright office lights, the place was illuminated with just safety lights in the ceiling, and the Everett's grocery sign somewhere in the back was dark as well. Tricia rang the bell three more times, counting to ten between rings before Toni finally appeared from out of her office. She did not look pleased. She marched toward the door, unlocked it, and flung it open.

"What do *you* want?"

"I wondered if you'd be willing to talk about your relationship with Sanjay Arya."

Toni's eyes widened, her cheeks beginning to glow, and her lips pursing. For a moment, Tricia wondered if the woman might lunge forward and hit her. And truthfully, she would probably deserve it. Toni owed her no explanations and Tricia wondered why she was feeling so reckless.

"Nothing about my life is any of your business," Toni said, her glare scorching.

"That's true. But I'm not the only person in the village who knows you had a relationship with Sanjay."

"Lousy gossips," Toni muttered.

"The police undoubtedly know, too," Tricia added.

"I've already spoken to them," Toni said bitterly.

"And what about Jim?" Tricia persisted.

"What about him?"

"I'm sure the police suspect him because of your affair." Tricia looked around and saw a man walking a dog approaching from the south. "Can we finish this discussion inside?"

"I have nothing to discuss with you."

She was about to close the door when Tricia inserted her foot between it and the jamb and was actually surprised when Toni didn't crash the door into it. Instead, she turned, leaving Tricia to follow her inside the shop. She closed the door and faced Toni, who stood with her arms crossed, practically seething.

"Not that it's any of your business, but my relationship with Sanjay was purely sexual. I love my husband. I would never betray him by having an emotional love affair."

"Then he was aware of your tryst?" Tricia asked, even though she knew the answer to the question.

"Not until after Sanjay's death," Toni remarked.

"Am I to assume that Sanjay wasn't your first?"

The blush on Toni's face deepened. "No," she answered tersely.

"Surely you knew Sanjay was seeing other women as well," Tricia said.

"Of course. But he broke up with his little girlfriend not too long ago," Toni said, confirming what Tricia already knew.

"Did he mention he was going to have an arranged marriage?"

Toni laughed. "Bull! He told his little chippy that lie to dump her. He had plans and they didn't include a *waitress*." She said the word with contempt. Was that how Toni viewed anyone she felt was beneath her privileged status?

"And what were Sanjay's plans?"

"Not to get tied down. He was a builder, but he didn't want the little house with a white picket fence and a passel of snot-nosed kids."

"And that's what Candace wanted?"

"Isn't that every young, *common* girl's dream life? Well, it wasn't Sanjay's."

And it obviously hadn't been Toni's dream life, either. She sounded so smug, so contemptuous. A quote from Shakespeare came back to Tricia: *The lady doth protest too much, methinks.*

"And what about you?"

"Me? You mean do I miss Sanjay? Of course."

"But there are more where he came from. Like Mike Foster," Tricia suggested.

"Shut up, bitch," Toni grated.

"Toni," Tricia chided her.

"For your information, Mike is one of my vendors. That's it."

Tricia didn't believe her, but she decided to change tacks. "So, what is your alibi for the night Sanjay was killed?"

"Ironclad," Toni said. "I was in Nashua, sitting at my husband's bedside while he was treated for a kidney stone at St. Joseph Hospital. It's been verified by Chief McDonald, so you see, neither of us is responsible for Sanjay's death. Now, why don't you crawl back under the rock you came out from and leave me and my husband alone."

Passing a kidney stone was no easy matter. Stark had looked rather sickly when Tricia had spoken to him not long before. No wonder he'd been in such a bad mood. And now she'd not only made an enemy of him but of his wife, too.

Both of them were Chamber members. What if they filed a complaint against her? The way she was alienating people these days, Tricia wondered if she might lose her position within the organization. And, in all honesty, a part of her didn't care. But it would be an embarrassment to Angelica. She supposed she'd done enough of that already in the past couple of weeks, at least to hear Angelica say so.

"I'm sorry. I didn't know."

"Yeah, well, now you do. And I think it's about time you left my shop. And please don't come back. Ever. Again."

And with that, Toni shoved Tricia toward the door.

Tricia left and was sure if Toni could have slammed the door, she would have. Without a backward glance, she got in her car and drove to the municipal parking lot.

Her list of suspects had gone down by two. That left Mike Foster, who *might* be guilty of grand theft excavator and endless counts of theft of architectural elements from dozens of homes and other institutions, not to mention murder. She'd never met the man. Perhaps it was time she tracked him down. And Candace, too. But that could happen another day. She was tired and ready to turn in for the night. Whether she would be able to sleep after her unsettling conversations with Stark and his wife was another matter.

\*    \*    \*

**As predicted,** Tricia didn't sleep well. And when she did awake, she felt an overwhelming sense of regret that made her feel as gloomy as the gray sky. While she had found the answers to many of her questions surrounding Sanjay Arya's death, she wasn't proud of the way she'd done it. Whatever relationship she might have had with Jim Stark was effectively destroyed. She'd never been friends with Toni, but the latter had at least been civil to Tricia. It was doubtful she'd remain that way.

Angelica would be livid if they lodged complaints against Tricia with the Chamber.

If she was honest, Tricia had never truly wanted the job as its co-president. Angelica overshadowed her, in taking command and making most of the decisions for the organization. Tricia seemed to be co-president in name only. And now Angelica was angry at her for the friendship she'd struck up with the intern *Angelica* had hired.

Tricia tried not to think of that as she got ready for the day. As it looked like rain, she again utilized her treadmill to get her exercise in for the day. By the time she finished and returned to her apartment, the heavens had opened and the rain came down in sheets.

Despite the inclement weather, Mr. Everett breezed in just before opening with a sodden umbrella and a cheery hello before he went to the back of the store to grab his apron. Tricia poured coffee for them both and they took their usual places in the reader's nook.

"That's some weather," Mr. Everett commented. "Seems more like November than the end of June."

"I'm afraid it'll put a damper on today's sales," Tricia said quietly, staring down at the contents of her mug. She took a sip, and when she looked up she saw Mr. Everett eyeing her with concern.

"You seem down today, Ms. Miles. Is there anything I can do for you?"

Tricia shook her head and offered him a wan smile. "No, but thank you for asking."

Mr. Everett looked like he wanted to say something more and Tricia knew he probably wouldn't share his thoughts unless she invited him to do so. The problem was, they had seldom spoken of their personal lives—as Mr. Everett was a very private person and she never wanted him to feel she was prying.

He cleared his throat before speaking. "Ms. Miles. I wanted to thank you again for helping make Grace's and my first date day at the inn last week such a success. They made it memorable."

She shrugged. "I made a discreet suggestion. It was the management who stepped up to make it special for you."

He nodded. "I'm so lucky to have Grace in my life," Mr. Everett said fondly. "When I lost my Alice, I thought I would be alone for the rest of my days. Of course, you know all this as it was you who helped bring Grace and me together."

"You flatter me. I just helped Grace when she was in a difficult situation."

"We've never forgotten the debt we owe you."

"You owe me nothing," Tricia said.

Mr. Everett looked into his coffee cup for long seconds, chewing at his lip as he seemed to contemplate exactly what he wanted to say. "I just wanted to remind you that it isn't every day that love arrives on our doorsteps." He looked up at her, his blue eyes reinforcing the sincerity of his words. "And that we ought to be open to it because we never know if it will come again or be snatched from us in a heartbeat."

Was he talking about her ex-husband, Christopher, or her ex-lover Marshall?

A sudden chill passed through Tricia.

Or could he be talking about David Price?

"Sometimes," he began, and paused, as though trying to make sure he best conveyed his thoughts, "it's best to trust our hearts over what others may think and say," he advised.

Was he giving her permission to at least examine her feelings for the young man? Something she'd been afraid to do in detail.

"You're very astute, Mr. Everett. Thank you for sharing your wisdom."

He nodded and was about to get up when she stopped him.

As long as they were having a heartfelt conversation, there was another point she wanted clarified. "Mr. Everett, I have a rather delicate question to ask you."

Mr. Everett's eyebrows rose, his crystal blue eyes widening.

"It concerns Nigela Ricita."

He nodded. "Ah. I was wondering if you'd ever ask."

"That's the thing. I don't want to ask but need to know if . . ."

"If I'm aware that the elusive Ms. Ricita is your sister?"

It was Tricia's turn to cast wide eyes on him.

"Uh, yes," he said, with the barest hint of a chuckle.

He held a clenched fist to his lips as though to stifle a smile. "It is a rather bad anagram of her name, but I suppose it was the closest she could come up with."

"And?" Tricia prompted.

"An excellent one for your own name."

Tricia nodded. "How long have you known?"

Mr. Everett looked thoughtful. "Let's see . . . It was before Antonio and Ginny tied the knot."

"That long?" Tricia asked, surprised.

"I have been reading mysteries for a very long time," he told her kindly.

"And do you always puzzle them out?"

He shrugged. "Not always. I like to be surprised."

"And Grace?"

"She figured it out as well."

"And how about the rest of the village?" Tricia asked, dreading the answer.

"As my mother used to say, 'They know what side of their bread is buttered.'"

Tricia was afraid of that. But then if no one wanted to blow the whistle on Angelica, so much the better for everyone.

"Thank you for sharing that with me," she said.

Mr. Everett glanced at his watch. "We'd best get to work. Those shelves aren't going to dust themselves, and I want everything to be just so for our customers."

Tricia had never heard Mr. Everett speak as many words on any occasion before. She hated for this momentous occasion to end, but, as always, he was practical.

As she waited on their first customer, Tricia's mind couldn't seem to let go of Mr. Everett's words. While he had given her his blessing to live her life the way she wanted, she wasn't quite ready to do the same for herself.

# THIRTY

**Saturdays were** usually the busiest day of the week for most of the shops along Stoneham's main drag, but that day the steady rain seemed to have chased the tourists away. It had been so quiet that Mr. Everett went down to the basement office to sort through what they had in their inventory and choose tomes to restock the shelves while Tricia stayed in the shop to handle any customers who might arrive.

But it wasn't a customer who crossed the threshold but Chief McDonald. He wasn't in uniform and Tricia silently prayed that it was not an official visit.

"What can I do for you today, Ian?" Tricia asked. "If you're feeling a little homesick, I can recommend a few mysteries set in Ireland."

"That's an enticing offer, but I came to speak to you about the Sanjay Arya investigation."

Tricia cringed. So much for prayers being answered. Had the

Starks gone straight to McDonald to complain about what they had no doubt deemed her harassment?

"Would you like a weak cup of tea or a coffee?" she offered.

"No, thank you." He gestured to the reader's nook.

Tricia's limbs felt heavy as she trudged from behind the sales counter over to the nook and took a seat. McDonald followed. She didn't dare look at him.

"You look like a dog waiting to be hit by a cruel master," McDonald commented.

Tricia didn't comment just in case he was there on some other mission. As though sensing her reluctance, McDonald took the conversational initiative.

"As I'm sure you know, Antonio Barbero came to my office with a theory about a possible motive for Arya's murder concerning one Michael Foster."

Tricia nodded.

"I take it you have not met the man."

"No."

McDonald nodded. "I wanted to let you know that while there may be some evidence Mr. Foster could be guilty of a crime—and perhaps more than one—we can safely rule him out as a suspect in the Arya murder."

Tricia's interest had definitely been piqued. "Oh?"

"Arya was struck from behind by a left-handed assailant."

"And Foster is a lefty?" Tricia surmised.

McDonald nodded. "However, he recently suffered a workplace injury—to his left shoulder. His rotator cuff."

Tricia frowned. No doubt he'd suffered it while chiseling out the medallions and other plaster details at the Morrison Mansion. She didn't voice the opinion. "But his boss told me he'd stepped in to take Sanjay's place—at least temporarily—on the job sites."

"He's supervising the workers, not lifting steel beams and concrete slabs," McDonald informed her.

With such an injury, he couldn't have bludgeoned Sanjay to death.

Tricia waited for McDonald to berate her for speaking with the Starks, but instead, he brought up another subject. "I'm sure you've already met Candace Mitchell."

So that was her last name.

"Yes. We've met. Twice, as a matter of fact."

"She's also left-handed," McDonald said.

That's right. David noticed it when they first ran into her at Bar None in Milford. "Did you know she's been trying to sell a wedding dress?"

"Yes, as well as other wedding accoutrements. She'd apparently been collecting such items in hopes of a wedding between herself and Mr. Arya."

"Yes, I heard he wasn't interested in matrimony—at least to Candace. And that he'd told her he was going into an arranged marriage, which his sister said was patently untrue."

"Oh, so you've met her, too," McDonald remarked.

"I get around," Tricia said demurely. "So, Candace is your prime suspect because hell hath no fury like a woman scorned?" Tricia asked.

"Something like that."

"What will you do now? Put her under surveillance?"

"I don't think that's a discussion we need to have. What I would like you to do is keep your distance from Ms. Mitchell. Let me—and my team—investigate this crime."

"And without my assistance?" Tricia asked.

McDonald nodded.

Well, at least he'd asked politely. And, at that point, Candace was the only viable suspect Tricia could think of. And she had no doubt about McDonald's sincerity.

"I think I can do that," she assured him.

"Thank you. The last thing I want is for you—or anyone else—to get hurt."

Tricia saluted the police chief. "Yes, sir."

"I mean it."

"So do I," Tricia said solemnly. And this time, she truly did.

**Tricia was** glad they'd had so many good sales days earlier in the week, because the shop was so quiet that Saturday that she could count on one hand the number of customers who'd crossed the store's threshold. It was so quiet that she and Mr. Everett had retreated to the reader's nook and were happily visiting old friends in their favorite vintage titles when the door to the shop opened and the little bell rang.

Tricia looked up from her copy of Agatha Christie's *Crooked House* to see Clarice from Booked for Beauty enter. It had been a week since Tricia had received that fiasco of a haircut and had almost forgotten Angelica had mentioned Clarice would eventually show up with an apology. Here she was, but instead of looking contrite, her expression was more akin to defiance.

"Hello, Clarice," Tricia said, her tone level.

"Ms. Miles." Her voice was cold, too. "I suppose you know why I'm here."

"I was told you might pay me a visit."

"I'm only here because I was told if I didn't apologize to you that I would lose my job. I've worked with Randy Ellison for over twenty years. Twenty years of loyalty and he pulls this crap on me."

"I did *not* speak with Randy about what happened last Saturday."

"No, your sister did."

"Angelica *owns* Booked for Beauty. It's reasonable for her to—"

"Bully her staff?"

"Did she speak to you?"

"No. She had her underling do it."

"Randy *is* your boss, not Angelica. Did he bully you into coming here?"

"Well, no. But he let me know that if I didn't apologize to the owner's *sister* . . ."

"So, am I to assume you're *not* here to apologize?"

"You're damn right." Clarice stood taller, her chin jutting forward. "I quit."

Tricia nodded. "That's too bad. I understand you're very good at your job and have been considered an asset to the business."

It was obvious Clarice hadn't expected to hear that sentiment.

"Just answer me one question," Tricia said. "Why did you butcher my hair? Was it just out of spite?"

"I . . . I . . . I don't know," Clarice said. "You bugged me and . . . I . . ."

"Lost your temper?"

"It's not like I physically *hurt* you. It *will* grow back."

"You just wanted to shame me. You hoped others would do the same, too."

"Maybe," Clarice said churlishly.

Again, Tricia nodded. "You got the first part right, but not the second. People were startled, but they weren't unkind."

"I suppose you think I'm supposed to learn some great lesson from that. How altruism beats all or some crap like that."

"I don't expect anything of you," Tricia said blandly.

"And that's what you're getting."

And with that, Clarice turned and left the shop.

Tricia stood staring after the woman for long seconds. It was Mr. Everett who broke the quiet.

"That woman holds a lot of anger."

"I'm afraid she does."

"Just think how much happier she'd be if she just let that go."

Tricia turned a kindly eye on her friend. "Wouldn't we all."

# THIRTY-ONE

**Tricia arrived** at Angelica's apartment at precisely 6:05 that evening, happy to be done with the long, dreary day at Haven't Got a Clue. The weather was supposed to clear after midnight, and the forecast was for warm breezes and sunny skies the next day. That was the good news.

"I heard from Randy at Booked for Beauty," Angelica said before Tricia even had a chance to toss Sarge a couple of dog biscuits.

"And?"

"Clarice quit. Just up and quit on him." Angelica shook her head sadly.

"And Randy's reaction was?"

"Shock. They'd been friends for years."

"Did he yell at her?"

"Apparently not. He'd given her a timeline to apologize to you and it was up this morning. When he pressed her on it, she apparently caused a scene at the shop, packed up her scissors, and left the building."

Tricia noticed that Angelica hadn't prepared for their evening rendezvous. Angelica reached into one of her cupboards and retrieved the bottles of gin and vermouth.

"Clarice came to see me this afternoon," Tricia said.

Angelica paused before reaching for the shot glasses. "Really?" And then it was her turn to say, "And?"

"I didn't receive an apology."

Angelica frowned. "Was she terrible to you?"

"Not really. But I think I disappointed her by not getting upset."

"Ah, the perfect reaction to a bully," Angelica said.

"But after she left, I felt sorry for her."

"It was her own stubbornness that made her quit her job." Angelica shrugged and proceeded to measure gin into the Hawthorne shaker. "Well, it's probably for the best. I don't want someone so filled with spite working in one of my businesses and treating my customers with such disrespect. But I do feel sad for Randy. He was quite upset. I don't think he realized just who Clarice was or what she was capable of."

Tricia nodded. She was tired of that subject and went on to tell Angelica about her conversation with Ian McDonald instead.

"So, that's it?" Angelica asked as she stirred the glass pitcher before pouring their drinks. "Sanjay was killed by his ex-girlfriend?"

"She's the prime suspect," Tricia confirmed.

"And her motive was because she was jilted?"

"Dumped," Tricia said succinctly. "Sanjay never asked her to marry him. From what I gather, she was a live-in cook and bottle washer, or at least washed his tighty-whities."

"I never lived with a man before I married him," Angelica said. "It might have saved on lawyers if I had—but I never wanted to be in the position Candace was in."

Tricia *had* lived with Christopher before they were married. They'd ended up divorced anyway, but it wasn't at her instigation.

"I hope this means you're going to drop your little investigation," Angelica said, and retrieved the chilled glasses with their garnishes from the fridge, setting them on a tray.

Tricia picked up a cracker from the plate in front of her. Angelica had spread red pepper jam on each one. "Dropped. I'm done. I think they're going to arrest her anytime now."

"Good," Angelica said, and picked up the tray, indicating Tricia should bring the plate of crackers into the living room, where they settled in their usual places.

"I hope you're going to call your little friend off the killer trail."

Tricia sighed. "Are you talking about David?"

"You know I am."

"I'll let him know."

"Why don't you text him right now?" Angelica suggested.

"Fine," Tricia said, and pulled out her phone.

*Good news*, she texted. *The Stoneham police are closing in on Candace Mitchell in the Sanjay Arya murder.*

She waited long seconds, and when no reply came, she picked up her glass.

Angelica was ready with a toast. "To the Stoneham police force. May they solve all crimes as quickly as this one."

Tricia raised her glass but she really didn't feel like celebrating. Yes, Candace was the most likely suspect, but Tricia hadn't gotten the sense that the younger woman had a killing instinct. She hadn't even sounded particularly angry when speaking about the failure of her relationship with Sanjay . . . more like sad. Where did sad people work up the passion to murder?

Tricia's phone pinged. It was David.

*R U sure*

Tricia couldn't help herself. When she wrote a text it was in full sentences with punctuation. She didn't think she could ever send one without them.

*I'm sure. Have a great rest of your weekend.*

*U 2*

No, she wasn't an Irish band. She sighed and set her phone on the coffee table.

"So, now we can go back to our normal lives."

"When have we had a normal life since moving to Stoneham?"

"There's always a first time!"

They drank their drinks, had a lovely dinner of spaghetti with homemade meatballs and garlic bread, and bid each other good night.

For some reason, Tricia felt rather deflated. She knew just because the investigation into Sanjay's death was essentially over, it wouldn't stop Angelica from hounding her about David. She'd keep her distance, just as she promised.

Tricia was about to head for her bedroom and personal reading nook when her ringtone sounded. She glanced at the screen and saw it was Becca. Now, why would she be calling?

"I thought you were angry with me," Tricia said without preamble.

"You're the only one I can talk to about Sanjay," Becca said, sounding contrite.

Nice. Tricia wasn't a friend, she was a sounding board. But she supposed she could at least offer the woman that service.

"I couldn't go to his funeral service. I mean, it's not that I'm ashamed of what we had, but it would've disrupted the proceedings and I didn't want that for his family. The press—" she said unnecessarily. Although for someone who was worried about being hounded by the paparazzi, there'd been a distinct lack of interest from newspeople and photographers since Becca had moved to the area. Tricia supposed that might change after the first of the hoped-for franchised tennis clubs opened.

"So, you lied to me," Tricia said.

"Lied?"

"You said what you and Sanjay had was purely—"

"I did say that," Becca said, cutting her off. "And I guess you're right. I lied."

"And what was it Sanjay thought you had?"

Tricia heard Becca sigh. "That we were friends."

"With benefits?"

"Well, it worked for *you*," Becca said sarcastically.

It had, so Tricia wasn't in a position to judge.

"But we did talk," Becca said. "And more important for me, we laughed." Her voice broke on that last word. "You have no idea how long it's been since I laughed."

Tricia could well imagine it. She wasn't entirely unhappy with her life in general, but she hadn't felt truly loved in a very long time. And she hadn't had much to laugh about, either. David was a lot younger than her, but she enjoyed his company in a completely different way than she'd enjoyed being with Marshall—and even her late husband.

"What did you think about your age difference?" Tricia asked, extremely interested in the answer.

"What's ten years?" Becca said rather flippantly.

Ten years was one thing. Twenty . . . that was quite another.

"Did you know that they think Candace Mitchell might have killed Sanjay?"

"That little mouse of a thing?" Becca asked.

"Why do you say that?"

"I don't know. He said she didn't have much going for her. She didn't have a plan for her life. She was just coasting until she found someone like him. But according to Sanjay, he wasn't all that interested in her because of her lack of ambition."

If Sanjay liked ambition, no wonder he was attracted to women like Becca and Toni Bennett.

"They met at that bar. He was busy working long hours at Stark Construction and she just kind of moved in on him," Becca continued. "She said she needed a place to stay and could she please just crash on his couch for a few days. The days turned into weeks, and then months. They didn't have much in common, but she was okay doing the dishes and laundry." That was quite different from what Candace had implied.

"And then Sanjay started seeing you?" And Toni.

"Yeah. I guess he liked what he saw. He started thinking very hard about what he wanted out of life, and it wasn't to settle down with a waitress."

"And what did he want out of life?"

"Of all things, a farmhouse. He wanted to single-handedly build one."

Those were the plans Tricia had seen on her and David's visit to Sanjay's apartment. How sad that he'd never have the opportunity to build his dream house.

Tricia heard a noise and realized Becca had just blown her nose. Were her eyes filled with tears, too? Tricia felt more than a little sorry for Becca—and especially for Sanjay.

"Are you okay?" she asked Becca.

"I will be," Becca said, but there was a sadness in her voice Tricia had never heard before. "Do you think maybe we could do lunch again soon?"

Tricia closed her eyes and winced . . . but only just a little. "Sure," she said brightly. "When?"

"I'll text you."

"You do that."

"Talk to you soon."

Before Tricia could say good-bye, the connection was broken.

She was about to set her phone down when it pinged. A text from David.

*Guess who I scored a date with?*

Tricia's stomach did a flip-flop. She stared at the words in the little blue dialog balloon and it took her long seconds before she fumbled to answer. *Who?*

*Candace Mitchell. We're meeting in the gazebo in the village square.*

*When?*

*Any minute now.*

Holy crap!

*That's not a good idea,* Tricia texted back.

She waited. And waited. And waited.

After pacing her living room for five minutes and receiving no reply, Tricia knew she had to do something. And that something was to go to the gazebo and find out what was going on. But should she go alone?

She stabbed her phone's contacts icon, not even needing to scroll through the list because Angelica's name popped up first. She answered on the second ring.

"What's up?"

"I need you to come with me to the village gazebo. Right now."

"What?"

"Put a leash on Sarge and I'll meet you downstairs in one minute."

"But, Tricia—?"

Tricia didn't wait for her sister's reply. She pocketed her phone, grabbed a jacket and her keys, and trundled down the stairs to her shop with Miss Marple following in her wake. "You stay here. I'll be back soon," she promised the cat before she fled out the door. Angelica wasn't quite so speedy, and Tricia waited anxiously, peering through the big display window until she saw her sister make her way through the Cookery with Sarge tucked under her arm, his leash dangling.

"What's going on?" Angelica demanded as she set Sarge down on the sidewalk before locking her door.

"David's in trouble."

Angelica did an abrupt about-face, her eyes widening in what seemed like anger. "Well, for heaven's sake—call the police!"

"I can't because I'm just not sure."

"Of what?"

"We'll talk as we walk," Tricia said, and grabbed her sister's arm, pulling her forward.

Tricia quickly filled Angelica in on the texts David had sent as they power walked up Main Street. They slowed their steps as they approached the gazebo, which was lit up so that they could plainly see David standing in the middle of the structure, awaiting Candace. Angelica picked up her dog, tucking him under her arm once more.

Tricia was about to call out to David when a woman stepped out of the shadows. "David?"

David pivoted. "That's me!"

Tricia still couldn't see who the woman was. Could it be Candace? She wasn't sure. She tugged on Angelica's sleeve and gestured that they should circle to the back side of the gazebo where there was more cover, and also so they could be closer to the action and listen to the players speaking. They only had to hope that Sarge wouldn't bark and give their position away.

Tricia and Angelica crouched among the lilac bushes, straining to listen.

"Glad you could make it," David said.

"I just wanted to get you off my back. What's this burning need you have to know about my relationship with Sanjay?"

"I worry that they might never find his killer."

"So? What's it to you?"

"I'm an interested citizen," David said with a shrug.

"I checked up on you. You're here as a summer intern at the Chamber of Commerce. You've only been in Stoneham for a couple of weeks."

"That's true. But it doesn't mean I can't be civic-minded."

"Or just plain nosy," she said snidely.

"That, too," David conceded.

"So, what do you want to know?" Candace asked as she settled her bottom on the edge of the gazebo's stone railing.

"Why does he have to know anything?" came another voice from the shadows.

Candace's head jerked to her left.

"Who's that?" Angelica whispered.

"Shhh!" Tricia admonished.

A man walked into the wan light that illuminated the ground around the gazebo. Why hadn't the Board of Selectmen gone for better lighting when the structure had been rebuilt several years earlier?

"What are you doing here, Ted?" Candace asked, sounding annoyed.

Ted? Who was Ted? And then Tricia remembered: the bartender at Bar None—Candace's co-worker.

"Just making sure you're safe."

"You followed me?" she asked, her voice rising. She stood, ramrod straight.

"I'm looking out for you."

"More like you're stalking me," she said angrily. "I don't need a bodyguard. I thought I made that clear to you."

"You did. I'm not a bodyguard. I'm your friend."

"I'm not even sure about that," Candace muttered just loud enough for Tricia to hear.

"Who is that guy?" Angelica whispered.

Tricia squinted at the man. "The bartender at Bar None in Milford."

"What's he doing here?" Angelica asked.

"Shhh!"

"Who is this guy?" David asked, sounding confused.

"A co-worker," Candace practically growled. She turned toward Ted. "You can leave now. I can handle junior, here."

"Hey!" David protested.

"No, I think *you're* the one who should leave. You're always getting yourself into dangerous situations. You need someone to take care of you," Ted told Candace.

"Excuse me?" she retorted. "I've been taking care of myself since I left home at eighteen."

"Oh, yeah, and look at how successful you've become. A *waitress*."

He said it with the same contempt Becca had voiced not an hour before.

"So says the *bartender* at the same joint where I work—that your *uncle* owns. And you're at least five years older than me, Ted, so don't go casting aspersions before you take a look in your own mirror."

"Shut up, bitch," Ted growled.

"Yeah, but I'm not your bitch, so just leave—and leave *me* alone."

"You can't talk to me like that," he grated.

"I just did," Candace asserted.

It was then that Tricia caught sight of the heavy piece of chain Ted held in his left hand.

Left hand? So, Ted was also a member of the southpaw brigade.

"Holy crap!" she gasped.

Suddenly, he charged at Candace and Sarge lunged forward, growling.

"Get 'em, boy," Angelica said, and let go of the dog's leash.

The little white dog bounded across the grassy distance and leapt into the air, his teeth gleaming as they attached to Ted's right arm.

"Yah!" he shouted, trying to shake Sarge off.

Candace hopped down from the gazebo and shoved Ted, knocking him over. He swung the chain at her as he toppled and it wrapped around her arm, yanking her down with him.

Ted screamed—a sound that turned Tricia's stomach—as Sarge hung on, snarling at his prey.

"Do something, do something!" Candace screamed to no one as David dashed forward.

Angelica was on her phone, presumably calling 911, while Tricia hovered over Ted and David helped Candace to her feet.

"Get this damn dog off me!" Ted hollered, violently swinging his arm, but Sarge's jaws were locked tight, his once-pristine white fur now covered with Ted's blood.

"What do we do?" David hollered when Ted suddenly screamed and rolled onto his side, his light-colored jacket covered with blood.

Tricia wasn't sure what to do, but Ted had ceased trying to dislodge Sarge.

Angelica was suddenly at Tricia's side. "Sarge, sit!"

Immediately, the well-trained dog let go of Ted's arm and sat down, looking at his mistress for his next command.

Ted rocked on the dewy grass, the stain on his jacket growing larger.

Angelica had her phone out and activated its flashlight. The beam flashed against the blade of a wicked-looking unsheathed knife Ted must have had concealed, but which was now embedded at the top of his left thigh.

"Good lord!" Candace cried, taking in the sight.

"Yank it out, yank it out!" Ted hollered, but Tricia wasn't about to do it since doing so might cause more damage.

"Lie still!" she ordered, which was a futile command but was all she could come up with.

The focused beam of light disappeared as Angelica was on her phone once more, this time asking the 911 dispatcher to send an ambulance.

While Ted continued to writhe in pain, the significance of Ted's new injury occurred to Tricia.

David and Candace moved to stand by Tricia. "Wow, we caught him."

"We didn't catch him. Sarge did," Tricia said.

"Yeah, but now we know who killed Sanjay," David said.

"We have no proof," Tricia said, despite her suspicions.

"There's one way to find out."

David moved to hover over Ted. "Hey, Ted, did you kill Sanjay Arya?"

"Yeah, and I would've killed you, too, if it wasn't for that damned dog."

David straightened and flashed a smile at Tricia. "See, I told you so."

# THIRTY-TWO

 **Chief McDonald** gave Tricia a sour look. "I thought you weren't going to carry on investigating Sanjay Arya's death."

"Well, I didn't. I mean, when David texted me that he was meeting Candace, I had to do *something*."

"You should have called nine one one."

"We did. It just took a few minutes," Tricia said in her own defense.

"Isn't it the coolest thing?" David asked, popping up behind McDonald.

McDonald turned. "No, young man, it isn't," the chief said sternly.

David took a step back.

The ambulance crew had already taken Ted off to the hospital—with a couple of cops tagging along to make sure he didn't cause any more mayhem. He left the air blue with foul language and threats of revenge against everyone in attendance. Tricia had heard the same kind of talk from other felons. She wasn't intimidated by the likes of Ted whoever he was.

"Did you ever suspect Ted?" Tricia asked McDonald.

"No. But then, the possessive way he acted toward Ms. Mitchell, I'm sure it would have come to light sooner rather than later."

Candace stood to the side of the gathering, looking subdued. But at least she didn't have the threat of arrest hanging over her head anymore. When asked, she seemed genuinely shocked that Ted had killed Sanjay because of her. Tricia suspected it would be a long time before she would get over it.

"I have a lot of paperwork to take care of. I'll expect the three of you to come into the station tomorrow to make official statements."

"I'll be there," David said eagerly.

"Fine," Angelica said. "Can I go home now? This damp air is making my hair frizz."

"Yes, you may leave."

"Tricia?" Angelica said, her tone clipped.

"I'll be along soon."

Angelica gave her a look of disapproval but reined in her dog. "Come along, Sarge. There's a bubble bath just waiting for you." They started off for Main Street, with a jaunty Sarge leading the way.

"I'll see you tomorrow, Tricia," McDonald said, and moved to speak with Candace.

That left Tricia and David standing alone by the gazebo.

"Well?" David asked, sounding jubilant.

"Well?" Tricia repeated.

"We did it."

"*We* didn't do it. And if things had worked out differently, *you* might have been the one carted off to the hospital—or the morgue— with a stab wound. I have no doubt Ted would have attacked you. He seemed fixated on Candace. We'll probably know more when all is revealed at the trial—next year."

"That long?"

"Things don't happen as quickly in real life as they do on television dramas."

David nodded. "So, where do we go from here?"

"Well, as far as I know, you're going thrifting with Pixie tomorrow, and I'm going to be working at my store."

"But now that the Arya case is solved, we can start working on something else?"

"Like what?"

"I don't know," he said, moving closer so that their faces were only inches apart. "We'll figure it out."

Tricia shook her head. "I have a store to run and a volunteer job at the Chamber. You've got a real job there. I think it's best if we both stick to what we need to be doing."

"You're just saying that because Angelica is jealous of our friendship."

"You figured that out?"

"It wouldn't have taken a genius."

Tricia looked at him, with his silly man bun and the little gold scarab that was pinned to his shirt, and felt a pang of regret.

"I value your friendship," she said.

"I think we could become more than friends."

Oh, dear. He'd said it out loud.

Tricia shook her head sadly. "I wish things were different."

His expression darkened. "Is that all you have to say?"

"I'm afraid so."

David took a step back and his gaze dipped to take in his shoes. "I'm sorry you feel that way."

Tricia could spout a hundred reasons why it could never work out between them, but instead, she chose to remain silent. She didn't want to argue.

David cleared his throat. "Uh, can I at least walk you back to your store?"

"Yes, thank you."

And so they started off across the grass toward Main Street. Tricia's toes were wet by the time they hit the sidewalk. A minute later, they were standing in front of her door.

"Will I see you on Monday at the Chamber?" David asked.

"I don't know, but I'll be coming in a couple of times a week just to keep my desk clear."

He nodded, his gaze once again fixed on his shoes. "Well, I guess I'll see you around then."

"I guess," Tricia agreed.

He waited until she unlocked the door and entered her store before he started off without a backward glance.

Tricia waited to see that he'd made it back to his apartment building before she turned and started through her darkened shop toward the stairs that led to her apartment, where she decided she'd pour herself a glass of wine and have a damn good cry.

# THIRTY-THREE

**July slipped** into August and Tricia found she spent less and less time at the Chamber office, leaving Angelica to take up the slack—which she seemed more than happy to do. But she couldn't help sharing little stories about their summer intern. Like how David had hand-colored old photographs of the Morrison Mansion's gardens, which had inspired Angelica to see about restoring them, which would no doubt please Elise McKenzie, with whom she'd shared her plans.

Work on the mansion did continue once Jim Stark found someone to help manage the on-site work—and without Mike Foster, who'd been arrested on multiple counts of theft of salvaged items from a score of Stark Construction sites. And, it was he who was trying to sell off Stark's excavator—just as Tricia had predicted. Still, Ginny and her marketing team weren't going to be moving into the mansion's new offices until nearly October, making do with a sublet suite in a professional building in Milford.

Tricia and Angelica interviewed seven women to fill the full-time opening at the Chamber of Commerce for an administrative assistant. All of them were extremely competent and, in a nod against ageism, over the age of fifty. (Not that they asked for such information.) The sisters chose one Fay Sutter, giving her a week to work with David to learn the job. He'd done an excellent job of writing up the Chamber's standard operating procedures. Fay came with a knowledge of accounting, which meant that additional responsibility would more than fill the forty hours a week she'd be working.

The four of them went to lunch at the Brookview Inn on David's last day and it was all Tricia could do to keep a smile on her face and a tremor out of her voice as they spoke of plans for the Chamber, and David shared some of his future plans with Fay, who seemed as charmed by the young man as most of the Chamber membership—and Pixie and Mr. Everett—had been.

They said their good-byes and Angelica drove David and Fay back to the Chamber, while Tricia drove herself back to the municipal parking lot. The walk to her store never seemed so long.

"Tough lunch?" Pixie asked once Tricia had arrived back at Haven't Got a Clue.

"Yes," Tricia admitted.

"Yeah, I'm going to miss David, too. He's been a good little thrifting buddy."

Little? David had to be at least four inches taller than Pixie—when she wasn't wearing spikes.

Tricia looked at the clock. It was nearly two hours until quitting time, but there were no customers in the store, and since the street hadn't been filled with tourists, she just didn't have the heart to go back to work that day.

"Why don't we close shop for today?"

"It's awfully early," Pixie said.

"Go home and have a wonderful evening with Fred. Do you have any plans?"

"Homemade pizza—and it won't be me making it," Pixie said with a grin.

Tricia smiled. "Grab your purse and go before I change my mind."

"Yes, sir, boss lady," Pixie said, already taking off her apron. She turned the sign on the door from OPEN to CLOSED. "See you Monday," she called as she headed out the door. Seconds after it closed, it reopened—but it wasn't Pixie who entered the store once more.

"David. What are you doing here?"

"It was a great lunch, but there were two too many people sitting at the table."

*Oh, please,* Tricia thought. *Don't start on that,* she mentally implored.

"I wanted you to know that I've had a change of plans," David said.

"Oh?"

"I decided I might as well finish my graduate degree online and get right into the job market while the getting's good."

"You've already found a job?" Tricia asked, her throat suddenly feeling tight.

He nodded. "An opening came up in one of my favorite places on earth—the perfect job as a children's librarian. It's a new position. They've never had one before, so I'd get to build the program from the ground up."

"It . . . it sounds like a wonderful opportunity," Tricia said, trying to sound supportive.

"It is. And it's not something most people my age have the opportunity to do."

"I envy you starting a new life," Tricia said.

"Really? But you did the same thing seven years ago."

Yeah, when David was just eighteen—a mere child. The thought made her feel really, *really* old.

"Do you have any regrets?" David asked.

Tricia hesitated before answering. She sure did . . . but not when it came to her store. And especially not when it came to reestablishing a relationship with Angelica and all the people who came into her life to make a family that had little to nothing to do with bloodlines.

"Everyone has regrets—at least if they're honest with themselves. But most of mine are minor."

"Maybe I'm too young," David said, and laughed.

*Too young for me*, Tricia told herself.

"I can't believe tomorrow night I'll be sleeping in my new apartment," David said, sounding almost joyful.

"Was staying here in Stoneham really so bad?"

"Oh, no. The apartment was great. It just wasn't mine, you know?"

Tricia nodded. It *had* come with a lot of baggage—and, luckily, none of the bad luck that had entangled its two former tenants had been visited upon David, for which she was thankful.

"And you'll be starting your new job on Monday?" she asked.

"The best job in the world."

Of course. He was going to work in his field of study. He'd been marking time over the summer in a job that was beneath his abilities. It brought back memories of Tricia's first meaningful position and how she'd looked forward to going to work every day, years before life had handed her lemons and she'd felt jaded.

"Well, I wish you all the luck in the world," Tricia said sincerely.

"Thanks. Hey, can I ask a favor?"

"Anything."

"Could you give me a lift to Milford? I want to show you something."

Tricia couldn't think what he could possibly show her that would be new or unique.

"Sure. I'd already decided to close shop early. Let's go," she said, grabbed her purse, locked her store, and they walked to the municipal parking lot.

"My dad's just bought a new Jeep and he's giving me the old one as a sort of pre-graduation present. I'm going to take possession of it over the weekend."

Not a new one? Well, Tricia didn't know his parents' financial circumstances. Maybe that was the best they could do for their son.

Tricia pressed her key fob to unlock the Lexus's doors and they got in.

"My folks have been very generous. My mom has been collecting stuff all summer and they're going to move it all down to my new place and help me set it up over the weekend."

"It's too bad I won't get an opportunity to meet them," she said, keeping her eyes on the road.

"I think you'd like them."

Yeah, she was probably just a couple of years younger than them. They probably had a lot in common.

"How do they feel about your change of plans?" Tricia said as she steered her car out of the lot.

"They're all for it. I mean, they'd already resigned themselves to the fact that I probably wouldn't find my dream job in our hometown. And it's not so far that I can't hop in the Jeep and visit them anytime I want."

"You're a good son."

David laughed. "Oh, yeah. I've got a virtual halo and wings."

They passed the last of the commercial section of Main Street, heading out of the village.

"What was it you wanted to show me?" Tricia asked.

"It's a surprise." He gave her directions. "Take a left. Go right." Another left, and finally . . .

Tricia braked, stopping the car outside the house where Sanjay Arya had lived. She almost didn't recognize the place because beside the home now stood a two-car garage where the big pile of lumber had stood two months before, and the stairs to the apartment had been enclosed.

"Pull right up in the driveway," David instructed.

Tricia did as she was asked. She turned off the engine and turned her head to face her passenger. "Why did you want to come here?"

"It's my new home," David said, grinning.

Tricia's brow furrowed. "What?"

"I rented the upstairs apartment."

"But?" Tricia asked, confused.

"You never asked me *where* I found the perfect job."

No, she hadn't. She'd assumed he found employment in a bigger city with a sprawling library system, a place like Boston, New York, or Philadelphia.

"So, you'll be working in Milford?"

"No, the Stoneham Public Library."

"I know you spent a lot of time hanging around it, but . . ."

He grinned. "I convinced them that they need me. That reference letter you wrote for me sure didn't hurt, either."

Tricia found herself swallowing—a lot—and tears threatened.

"I'm . . . I'm pleased you'll be staying in the area," she somehow managed.

"It wasn't only the job that was the draw, you know."

"Oh?"

"It was you, too."

"Me?"

"Yeah. I couldn't bear the thought of leaving you behind."

"Don't be silly," Tricia said, looking away, even though she wanted to hear more.

David touched her chin with his index finger, directing her attention his way. "As of today, you're no longer my boss. That means there shouldn't be an issue when it comes to dating me."

"Dating you? But I'm old enough to be your—your older sister."

David laughed. "That's true. But I'm serious."

Tricia felt an amalgam of emotions: glee, trepidation, and denial. Her voice cracked as she asked, "But what would people say?"

"That either I'm the luckiest guy on the planet, or you're the luckiest woman. And who cares what anyone thinks? That is . . . if you don't find me repulsive."

Tricia's eyes filled with tears. "Not at all."

"Then what do you say?"

"I guess we could try it . . . see where things go."

David grinned. "Great." And with that, he lunged forward and planted a sturdy kiss on her lips. Startled, Tricia laughed.

David drew back. "Was it that bad?"

"Oh, no."

He tried again, this time taking it slow. It was much better the second time. Still, perhaps a little practice couldn't hurt.

Finally, he pulled back and smiled, then reached into his pocket to retrieve a set of keys. "Come on."

They trundled up the steps to the apartment and he unlocked the door, holding it open for Tricia to precede him.

Once inside she took a look around. Except for the lack of furniture and personal items, it hadn't changed.

"Well, what do you think?" David asked.

Tricia turned to face him and reached for his hand.

"Welcome home."

# TRICIA'S COOKIE RECIPES

## SUGAR COOKIES

**INGREDIENTS**

**THE COOKIES**

1 cup butter, softened

1 cup granulated sugar

1 large egg

1½ teaspoons vanilla extract (or any flavor you choose)

2½ cups all-purpose flour

¾ teaspoon baking powder

¾ teaspoon salt

**SUGAR COOKIE FROSTING**

*3 cups confectioners' sugar, sifted*

*3 to 4 tablespoons milk*

*2 tablespoons light corn syrup*

*½ teaspoon vanilla extract (or any flavor you choose)*

*Food coloring (optional)*

*Sanding sugar and/or sprinkles for decorating (optional)*

In a large bowl, combine the butter and sugar and beat with an electric mixer until fluffy. Add the egg and extract and beat until completely combined. In a separate, medium-sized bowl, whisk together the flour, baking powder, and salt. Slowly stir the dry ingredients into the wet until the dough is smooth and completely combined. Wrap in plastic wrap or waxed paper and transfer the dough to the refrigerator. Chill for at least 2 hours.

Preheat the oven to 350°F (180°C, Gas Mark 4) and line a baking sheet with parchment paper. Dust a clean surface with confectioners' sugar. Roll out half of the dough (⅛ inch for a crisper cookie or ¼ inch for thicker, softer cookies). Add additional confectioners' sugar as needed so the dough doesn't stick.

Cut out shapes with cookie cutters and transfer them to the prepared baking sheets, spacing at least 1 inch apart. If not frosting the cookies, decorate them with sanding sugar before baking. Bake for 8 to 10 minutes or until the edges begin to turn golden brown. Cool the cookies completely before frosting them.

## SUGAR COOKIE FROSTING

Combine the confectioners' sugar, 2 tablespoons of milk, corn syrup, and extract in a medium-sized bowl and stir until combined. If the frosting is too thick, add more milk. If coloring the frosting, divide into bowls and color as desired. Frost the cookies and add the sanding sugar or sprinkles. Allow the frosting to harden before eating, stacking, or storing the cookies.

*Yield: approximately 3 dozen cookies (number will vary depending on your cutter size)*

# New Hampshire Maple Syrup Cookies

### INGREDIENTS
½ cup shortening
1 cup packed brown sugar
1 egg
½ cup maple syrup
½ teaspoon vanilla extract
1½ cups all-purpose flour
2 teaspoons baking powder
½ teaspoon salt
1 cup flaked coconut
½ cup chopped walnuts or pecans (optional)

Preheat the oven to 375°F (190°C, Gas Mark 5). In a mixing bowl, cream the shortening and brown sugar until fluffy. Beat in the egg, syrup, and vanilla until well mixed. Combine the flour, baking powder, and salt; add to the creamed mixture. Stir in the coconut and nuts (if using). Drop by teaspoonfuls onto greased baking sheets. Bake for 12 to 15 minutes or until lightly browned.

*Yield: 3 dozen cookies*

# GLUTEN-FREE PEANUT BUTTER COOKIES

### INGREDIENTS
*2 large eggs, room temperature, beaten*
*2 cups granulated sugar*
*1 cup creamy or chunky peanut butter*

Preheat the oven to 350°F (180°C, Gas Mark 4). In a large bowl, combine all the ingredients until the mixture forms a dough. Roll about a tablespoon each of the dough into balls. Place on a parchment-lined baking sheet and flatten with a fork in a crisscross fashion. Bake until crisp, 12 to 15 minutes. Remove to a wire rack to cool.

*Yield: 4 dozen cookies*

# Oatmeal Raisin Cookies

**INGREDIENTS**
¾ cup shortening
1 cup brown sugar, packed
½ cup granulated sugar
¼ cup milk
1 egg
1 teaspoon vanilla extract
1 cup all-purpose flour
1 teaspoon cinnamon
½ teaspoon baking soda
¼ teaspoon salt
3 cups rolled oats
1 cup chopped walnuts
1 cup raisins

Preheat the oven to 350°F (180°C, Gas Mark 4). Grease cookie sheets (or use parchment paper). Combine the shortening, sugars, milk, egg, and vanilla; beat until light and fluffy. Combine the flour, cinnamon, baking soda, and salt. Stir in the oats, walnuts, and raisins. Drop by teaspoonfuls onto the cookie sheets. Bake for 12 to 15 minutes.

*Yield: 3 dozen cookies*